the
simplest
words

ALSO BY ALEX MILLER

ALEX MILLER

the
simplest
words

a storyteller's journey

Selected and arranged by Stephanie Miller

ALLEN&UNWIN
SYDNEY•MELBOURNE•AUCKLAND•LONDON

First published in 2015

Copyright © Alex Miller 2015

  This project has been assisted by the Australian
Government through the Australia Council,
its arts funding and advisory board.

Australian Government

Allen & Unwin
83 Alexander Street
Crows Nest NSW 2065
Australia
Phone: (61 2) 8425 0100
Email: info@allenandunwin.com
Web: www.allenandunwin.com

Cataloguing-in-Publication details are available
from the National Library of Australia
www.trove.nla.gov.au

ISBN 978 1 74331 357 2

Internal design by Lisa White
Set in 12/16 pt Minion Pro by Bookhouse, Sydney
Printed and bound in Australia by Griffin Press

For
Ross, Erin, Amelie and Adrienne
Kate and Mato

And I always thought: the very simplest words
Must be enough.

Bertolt Brecht

Contents

Introduction

'The goal of storytelling,' Alex Miller has said, 'is finally to account for one's own story. It is through the poetics of my fiction that I have sought my personal truth.' *The Simplest Words*, a collection of stories, excerpts, memoir, commentary and poetry, is Alex Miller's first collection of occasional writings. His eleventh novel, *Coal Creek*, was published to wide critical acclaim in 2013. Alex is twice winner of Australia's premier literary prize, the Miles Franklin Literary Award, first in 1993 for *The Ancestor Game* and again in 2003 for *Journey to the Stone Country*. He is an overall winner of the Commonwealth Writers' Prize, in 1993, for *The Ancestor Game*. His fifth novel, *Conditions of Faith*, won the Christina Stead Prize for Fiction in the 2001 New South Wales Premier's Awards. In 2011 he won this award for the second time with his novel *Lovesong*. In 2007 *Landscape of Farewell* was published to wide critical acclaim and in 2008 won the Chinese Annual Foreign Novels 21st Century Award for Best Novel and the Manning Clark Medal for an outstanding contribution to Australian cultural life. Following the publication of *Autumn Laing* he was awarded the prestigious Melbourne Prize for Literature in 2012. His latest novel, *Coal Creek*, won the 2014 Victorian Premier's Literary Award. Alex is a Fellow of the Australian Academy of the Humanities and a recipient of the Centenary Medal for an outstanding contribution to Australian cultural life. Alex is published internationally and his works have been widely translated.

Robert Dixon's 2014 monograph *Alex Miller: The Ruin of Time* describes Alex's novels as 'immediately accessible . . . works of high literary seriousness—substantial, technically masterly and assured, intricately interconnected and of great imaginative, intellectual and ethical weight'.

Stephanie Miller
Castlemaine 2015

In the Blood

My father and grandfather told stories every day of their lives, and my mother and grandmother had babies and offered a gentle resistance to the persistent story making of their men. But for my father a day without story was soup without salt, and he loved his salt lavishly. At nine years of age, when my young brother fell ill and I told him stories *to save his life*, I became my family's storyteller.

As we gathered around the fire last thing in the evening, my father drew on his pipe and looked at me. 'Have you got a story for us then, Alex?'

My mother touched his arm. 'It's already past their bedtime, Manny.'

My father looked into the fire and drew on his pipe. 'Och, well, just a wee one then, boy.'

So I began my story, never knowing where it would take me or how it would end, nor how long it would be in the telling, my sisters and brother staring into the fire with my father, my mother pretending not to listen. 'An old man was walking down a road one day when he came across a sack that had been thrown aside into the hedge . . .' Who was *not* listening now?

When I was thirty-eight, I published a story and became a story writer as well as a storyteller. I telephoned my father to let him know.

'You could always tell a story, lad,' he said, neither his Glasgow accent nor his attitudes softened by the years. He was not impressed. Writing was not for him an advance on telling. For my father it was the company of the telling that cherished the spirit of story. But I'd slipped over onto the page and it was too late. I kept at it. And when I was fifty-two I published my first novel. I'm seventy-one now and still at it, closing on a draft of my ninth novel, *Lovesong*, and dreaming of Sophocles producing his masterpiece *Oedipus at Colonus* when he was eighty-nine—and loving it. It's in the blood.

2008

Ross and the Green Elfin

My two sisters and I waited in the front room of our flat, crouched together by the dying embers of the coal fire, I in my pyjamas and the girls in their nightdresses. We were silent and fearful and we gazed into the embers of the fire. I have no memory of my mother crying out, but only that my father alone acted as the midwife of the occasion. It seemed to have come upon us suddenly. I had hardly known my mother to be expecting another child. I had thought we three were our entire family. My father came out of our parents' bedroom and he stood over us and we looked up at him in great anxiety and perplexity. His sleeves were rolled above his elbows, his collarless shirt open at his neck, his bare chest gleaming with beads of sweat. As he stood looking down at us I saw a gentleness in his gaze that was mysterious and distant. I had never seen such a look in my father's eyes before. He was like a stranger. Another man. A new man whose existence I had only dreamed of. I gazed with faint horror at the livid and disfiguring scars of his wound. He smiled and invited us softly, 'Come and meet your wee brother.'

In the half-light of my parents' bedroom my mother lay with the tiny baby in her arms, cradling it to her breast. Our father instructed us and in turn we each leaned over and kissed our new brother on his forehead. The magical translucence of his skin, so tender the lightest blow would surely dissolve him. Was he as yet quite with us, I wondered in astonishment, or was he the advance of himself, a promise of what the world might be, of what we humans might be before we are born, an image of unsettling perfection, his smell of that long-forgotten world from which he had come to us and from which we ourselves had come so long ago it was a distant and foreign country to us now and we had forgotten the language. Precious beyond reckoning by the ordinary values of our days, here was my brother. A gift I had not expected to receive.

I looked my questions into my mother's beautiful dark eyes, and she smiled and looked down at him, her new son. After we had left the bedroom my father mixed a bucket of wet dross and built the smoking hummock behind the coals in the grate, then he sat in his armchair and lit his straight-stemmed pipe and filled the room with the sweet perfume of his tobacco. We three children waited for him, sitting silently on the hearthrug watching him. He said at last, 'Your mother and I are calling him after my brother, your uncle Ross.' We had never met our uncle Ross. He lived in Glasgow. We lived in South London.

Alex's father, 1955

Two years later, when my brother fell ill and we thought he would die, I stayed with him in his darkened room and told him stories of the Green Elfin, a little being who struggled to meet the terrible challenges of existence. My precious brother recovered, and I was known thereafter in my family as the storyteller. It is where it began for me, this business of writing fiction. It has become my sacred country.

2008

In My Mother's Kitchen

South London, July 1944. My mother handed me the tray with my sisters' meals on it and picked up the tray with her own meal and mine. She stood looking around the kitchen. 'I think we've got everything,' she said. 'I'll go first.' We went out the door and began making our way down the stairs. At the second landing the window was open. A black rocket with stumpy wings and a tail of bright orange fire was roaring towards us out of the grey sky. It was making a noise like a motorbike with a broken muffler. As we looked, the orange tail fire went out and there was silence. The black rocket sailed on towards me and my mother out of the grey sky for a thousand years, the whispering of the wind across its wings . . . My mother's shout was a distant echo I still hear in my dreams.

We dropped the dinner and ran down the last two flights of stairs, taking them three at a time. At the bottom of the stairs we ran out through the covered way into the long lane leading to our garden and the air-raid shelter, where my older sister was looking after my little sister. Halfway along the path the earth heaved up under us as if a volcano was erupting beneath our feet. We stopped and stood on the path holding our breath. Then came the ear-splitting roar and at once the sky filled with smoke and ash and pieces of debris. The air was still alive with papery pieces of stuff floating down around us like theatrical snow or autumn leaves at the pantomime when my mother said, 'The poor devils up the road have caught it. Go back to the kitchen, darling, and peel some more potatoes, will you? I'll go and see how the girls are getting on.'

2012

Learning to Fly

John Aylward was my best friend. After school, in the twilight of a winter afternoon, we did not go home but walked in silence together to a bombed house in a neighbourhood more well-to-do than the neighbourhood in which we ourselves lived. We stood side by side on a hill of fallen masonry and bricks in the remains of the front room of the destroyed house. The room had been the parlour of a rich woman. We had passed her house often on our way to the woods. The filleted rooms of the upper storey hung over us, stone lintels askew and on the point of falling free from the bricks, the walls leaning, the mortar shattered; ceiling lathes stripped of plaster had become the bare ribs of the house, in silhouette above us against the purple depths of the evening sky. When the woman had been alive, before the German bomb killed her and destroyed her house, the curtains of her parlour had always remained closed, even on summer days. Now her secret room was open to the sky. Standing there together on the hillock of rubble, John

Aylward and I were awed by the trespass of our errand. It was our intention to construct an aeroplane from the ruins of the dead woman's house. Our aim embarrassed us with its grandeur, and we had not dared to speak of it to anyone for the certainty of being mocked. We were from the council estate and our caste knew nothing of flight, real or lyrical. Our silence spoke of our knowledge that if we failed there would be no appeal.

It was dark by the time we left the ruin, a bundle of lathes slung between us across our shoulders.

I had never seen John's father sober and feared him. I don't know whether John feared his father, but I imagine he did. We had never discussed it. We walked along the lamplit streets, empty of pedestrians and without cars in those days, our bundle of lathes forming a kind of spring between us and forcing us to maintain in our step a rhythm suited to the step of the other.

2012

Boys Wanted for Farms

Along the footpath in front of him the paving stones are black and shiny with the rain. He sees something, something dark and green plastered to the footpath by the rain. When he comes up to this green square, a memorial plaque, it might be, set in the paving stone commemorating some past tragedy, he stands and looks down at it, the rain going down the back of his neck. He mouths the words as he deciphers them: BOYS WANTED FOR FARMS. He repeats the four words aloud, his voice solemn and intent, as if he is deciphering a code, a message from some exotic bard, an inhabitant of the empty road, lilac bushes over the garden fence swaying and thrashing about. Cold in his shoulders. His fingers sore from the factory. He squats and lifts a corner of the small green square of paper and slowly peels it from the surface of the stone. He has come into possession of his answer. He walks on along the quiet street, past the school gates, to the corner. It is a message from the gods. His heart is joyful. He will never return to the floor of the factory. He will never again endure the long day from dark morning till dark evening among the sound and the fury of the machines and the terrible men, and never again will he witness their torture of the hunchback and their lewd obscenities.

2012

My First Love

When I was fifteen, I left school in South London and got a job as a farm labourer on Exmoor. Which sounds easy enough. It wasn't.

My struggle at that time brings to my mind a cartoon I once saw in the *New Yorker*. The driver of a car has pulled into a garage and is asking directions from the pump attendant. A grid of freeways knits its way through the sky above them. Through a gap in the flyovers there is a view of a distant church steeple. The garage attendant is explaining to the driver: 'You can't get there from here.'

The teachers at my secondary modern school, whom I asked for help to get to Exmoor, gave me the garage attendant's advice. I didn't believe them, but I did discover that nobody where I was knew anyone who had ever been to where I wanted to go. It took persistence and twelve months of failure before I found my way from the South London council estate where I'd grown up to a job as a labourer on a West Somerset farm.

The friends I left behind on the council estate when I went to Exmoor didn't really know where I'd gone. I went off their screen. I had made my first cross-cultural journey. There was more than time and space involved. In a sense my teachers had been right when they'd advised me: 'You can't get there from here, Miller.'

So what was it that made me persist?

I was in love. We do crazy things when we're in love. When we're in love we think we're different from other people. We get this idea that for special reasons that apply only to us we can do things that the other people around us can't do. And we can. And we do. We don't listen to advice from people who know the limitations better than we do, people with experience of the barriers whose opinions we would respect if we were sane.

I was obsessed. It was no good trying to tell me anything. So people were glad when I left. They were relieved to see me go. I'd already ceased to be one of them. I'd become an embarrassment to my friends and family. As if Exmoor were a married woman luring me into a dangerous liaison, my schoolteachers warned me to abandon my obsession. 'Forget Exmoor, Miller. Get yourself a job where you belong, on a production line.'

But I was walking home from the factory in the black rain, being seduced by a vision of green fields and woodlands and pale heather stretching out beneath my feet in the sunlight. 'What's he smiling at?' I was earning a reputation for being lunatic, a weirdo, an outsider. 'Who does he think he is?'

In Australia, thirty years later, I wrote a novel based on the two years I spent working on Exmoor for Tiger Westall, the tenant farmer with a dangerous obsession for hunting wild red deer. The novel turned out to be a parable of the stranger, a meditation on the power the stranger has to negotiate a way into a settled community and to change the community forever. And the powerlessness of the community, despite its numerical superiority and assurance of belonging, to resist the changes the stranger brings. I couldn't have written that novel if I hadn't still been in love, with Morris and Tiger and Roly-Poly and the great black hunter Kabara and the wilderness of Exmoor and the mysterious old nott of Tivington.[1] Without love I couldn't have got to Exmoor in the fifties from Melbourne in the eighties.

Several years after I'd written the novel I revisited Exmoor for the first time since I was a boy. I was lucky I hadn't gone back before I'd written the novel. There was nothing left. Thirty years of change had erased it all. Where Tiger's farmhouse had been—an old stone building squatting in the groin of a lane—there was a self-service petrol station on a motorway. And they were all dead, the people I'd written about.

No one could even remember Tiger or Morris or Roly-Poly. Strangers had taken possession. There was silence and absence where I'd once ventured my little history. And while I was standing at the pump filling my hired Fiat Uno with petrol, I realised that, except for the absent pump attendant, the cartoon in the *New Yorker* had at last come true for me.

I was in the middle of it. I could no longer get to Tiger's place from where I was standing.

If I was so much in love with Exmoor, why did I leave? Why didn't I stay and see out the changes? Because I fell in love with somewhere else.

First, before anything else, in the mute state, we're a migrant species. First we set off on a journey. The journey of the story, however, is a different journey from the one we actually travel. For the story of our journey is always a fiction; it is always dealing with the past on the present's terms. We tell the story in order to free ourselves from the past so that we can move on, not in order to recover the past, which is merely nostalgia.

Travelling, moving on, seeking the future, is what we do. The journey is our reason for living. Our storytelling is secondary to our journey. Storytelling eases the way. The journey is the thing. In other words, getting to places people believe we can't get to from where we are. Which often makes us appear to be a bit obsessed with the transgression of boundaries.

I read a book when I was on Exmoor that began my love affair with Australia and made a migrant of me. It was a brown cloth-covered hardback with reproductions tipped into the text. The only photograph I remember clearly is of several stockmen lounging on the verandah of their quarters on a cattle station in the outback. The stockmen and the verandah are in black silhouette against the luminous sky, like a Matisse cut-out. The stockmen seem to be watching the horizon, which is an unhindered line.

The migrant's dilemma reflects the general human dilemma: Freud's discovery of the ambivalence of human emotions, that we can be in love with two opposing states at the same time. It's no easier to be in love with two places than it is to be in love with two people. These things often end in pain and suffering and in love turning to hate and to permanent scars and guilt and accusations and counter-accusations, even in litigation and sometimes total disaster. Betrayal and treason are trying circumstances. We all know, in the conduct of our rational lives, that two loves are not better than one. We all know that it is easier not to be in love at all than to be in love with two people at the same time.

But what is knowing compared to loving?

Everyone on Exmoor whom I asked for directions to the Australian outback gave me the garage attendant's advice. 'You can't get there from here.' But you could. And I did.

The bus left at noon. Morris, the labourer with whom I'd been living for the past two years, and whom I loved because he was the kind of man I wanted to be when I grew up—his own man—had gone to the pub to pick up the beer for his card night. 'Don't worry, I'll be back before the bus gets here,' he had said.

Today his attempt to reassure me has the portentous ring of an epitaph. The bus was a couple of minutes early and Morris was a couple of minutes late.

He was coming out of the door of the pub as I sailed past in the bus. He was carrying a case of beer in both his hands, so he couldn't wave. Our eyes met in the instant it took for the

Alex (left) and Morris Aplin, Exmoor, 1951

bus to go past. I know there was anguish in my gaze. I never saw him again, but I can still see the look in his eyes, a kind of guilty smile. It is unresolved. I find myself still reading that look. His anticipation of the beer and the cards later with his mates at the cottage. Was that it? Or did he really love me the way I loved him, with inexhaustible admiration?

I've got two snapshots. One of him and one of me. We're standing among the brussel sprouts in the garden at the back of his cottage. There's a bit of snow on the ground. In the picture of me I'm wearing twill jodhpurs and leggings and boots and a tweed jacket and a cheese-cutter cap over one eye, a costume identical to the one he's wearing in his picture. And

I've adopted his pose. So I guess I took his photo first, then asked him to take mine. In other words, I'm not the original. But I am a near-perfect copy. Only I'm not my own man. Trying to be like him, and he was like no one but himself, had made me as unlike him as I could possibly be.

When I reached the cattle station on the Leichhardt River in the Gulf of Carpentaria, I found myself surrounded by the uneventful horizon line: the perfect line that had lured me all the way from Exmoor. The stockmen were all Maigudung clansmen, all thirty-five of them, all mounted, all with long black hair and beards and all with skin that was shining in the sun as if they had oiled themselves in preparation for my reception. They rode up to me out of a cloud of red dust and stared at me in silence; calm and relaxed and curious and arrogant in their possession of the situation, the confidence of their belonging. One of them, who later became my first Australian friend, challenged me to reveal myself. 'If you're really English, where's your English saddle?' But I wasn't really English. It was more complicated than that.

He told me later, glancing at the horizon as he did so, that his ancestors had been living on this stretch of country forever. I'd arrived just as the end of his forever was beginning. Within a couple of years of my arrival, the equal pay judgment had given the lessees the excuse to exile Frank and the rest of the Maigudung from their land. It was the elaboration of one of those negotiated changes that strangers bring among a settled people, and which the settled people have no power to resist.

Frank said nothing at the time. He only looked upon the sun and drank the morning air.

Two years later I left. Everyone left. The thing changed. Frank's forever had come to an end. He stood in the dust on the station runway and waved to me as the plane lifted away. His arms weren't weighed down with beer, as Morris's had been, not yet anyway. And I didn't see the look in his eyes. So I can't see it now. I just see his last wave.

I'm still reading that wave. Years ago, before I'd learned that there is something immutable about the writing of fiction that will not admit of just any kind of lie, I thought I was going to write my reading of Frank Maigudung's last wave. It was going to be a story about the dilemma of being in love with two places at the same time. But it wasn't my story to tell. It was Frank's story. The story of the Maigudung exile. And I could never tell the story of the Maigudung exile the way it had to be told. The way all stories have to be told, with the passionate ambivalence of those who have made the journey. Only for them is the spirit of truth and the spirit of love the same.

1995

---

1   A nott is a stag without antlers.

EXCERPT FROM

The Tivington Nott

Morris and his wife aren't awake when I slip the latch on the back door and step out into the darkness. The moon is still bright enough over the oaks in Will's wood to cast their shadows across the close-cropped turf of Old Ley. Everything's sodden from the storm and the air is cold and still. I stand on the crest of the ridge and look down into the valley without a name that locals call the Black Valley, and I can see across a vast sweep of sleeping countryside all the way to the silvered waters of Bridgewater Bay and the outlet of the Doniford Stream. Everything is cool and clean! I can taste the air on my palate! There's the sound of water trickling out of a pipe under the hedge next to me. I have to go. As I turn I startle a blackbird from its roost and it flies out, flat and fast across the field.

From fifty yards away the farm could be abandoned. Dead. Deserted. A settlement left over from another era. The big dark shadows of the cattle shed, the barn, the stable and the house all joined together, their windows and doors facing inward to the yard. Blank walls to the world. Compact against storms and trouble, and against anything else that might come along. Expecting the worst. Their weathered grey featureless stone walls and their grey slate roofs not interested in anything outside. They don't want to know about it. Keep out! Silent in the autumn moonlight. Been standing there since who knows when? The odd bulge of the disused bread-oven poking out into the road like the bum of a giant squatting in the end wall of the house.

I've got a good two hours of work to get through before daylight. Finisher and his mate Ashway hear me opening the road gate and they whinny softly. This is enough to start the cows moaning, even though they know it's too early for them

The barn, Handycross Farm, Lydiard St Laurence, 1952

yet. I light the kerosene lamp in the stable and close the door behind me. The soft light reveals the cobbled floor and the ashen stall-trees, their wood polished to a deep honey gloss by the rubbing of generations of hunters and plough horses. It's warm in here. The air rich with the acid smells of horse dander, piss, dung and meadow hay. Kabara is stationary in the shadows. Watching me. Making no welcome. The two geldings lean out and stretch for my hands, glad to see me.

1989

Travels with My Green Man

I think dire need was my initial source of inspiration. When I was twelve or thirteen my young brother, who was around five at the time, was ill and had to be kept in a darkened room for a couple of weeks. I loved my brother and had seen his arrival in the world as a great gift. The gift of brotherhood. So while he was ill I stayed home from school and sat with him day after day. He lay there in the bed bored, motionless and suffering. I soon realised if I was to be of any help to him I'd better come up with something to distract him from his situation. So I invented a character who wasn't confined to a darkened room as he was but was free to go off on grand adventures.

For a reason I don't now recall I named this free-roaming adventurer the Green Elfin, but I do recall a dingy and mysterious pub not far from our house called the Green Man, and maybe that kind of place seemed to me even then a likely theatre for such dreaming. After my brother was recovered, the stories I'd told during his illness became known in our family as the Green Elfin Stories, as if they had an existence somewhere beyond my telling of them. I even had requests for more stories from my brother and other members of my family from time to time, but the dire need was no longer there and the inspiration was lacking.

Winifred Millar with (clockwise) Ruth, Alex, Kathy and Ross, c. 1946

From that time on, however, I did go along believing that I had the talent to be a storyteller if I ever had cause to draw upon it in dire need. This knowledge formed a kind of reservoir of confidence for me later, when I was wandering around the world on my own, and it often supported my morale through the years during which I was painfully aware of my cultural deprivation. There were bad times, when it seemed that there was nothing left but to tell myself a Green Elfin story, and by that means I more than once made my escape to a more congenial world than the one I was actually living in.

But you don't have to love, or even to like, the person who inspires you. Brotherly love doesn't have to come into it. The reality of a writer's daily life is, after all, not inspiration but hard work. And more so even for a writer as highly charged with originality of style as was Louis-Ferdinand Céline than for most of the rest of us. Though the impression of effortlessness is, of course, always the aim of the writer. Like plumbing, the hard labour of writing must be concealed from the consumer. Kurt Vonnegut said, 'Céline was so concerned with style that he could not let a sentence rest until he had assured himself that it would impress the reader as not written but spoken . . . and spoken spontaneously, without reflection.' Spoken, in other words, under the mysterious influence of inspiration. An influence which, in the popular imagination, often seems to have more to do with magic and the spiritual, the inbreathing of the animus, than with simple hard work. We love nothing more than to be mystified, and in fiction the bare truth is boring.

But for me Céline's sleight of hand of the seemingly effortless worked its magic. When I read his last novel, that astonishing blast of energy that is *Rigadoon*—completed in 1961 on the day of his death—I closed the book with the feeling that I'd just read something written at a single sitting under the influence of one enormous rush of inspiration. It was one of the best Green Elfin stories I'd ever read. It was also the impression of effortlessness, not the truth of the hard labour Vonnegut was to speak of, that convinced me I'd found a way to write my first novel, *The Tivington Nott. The Tivington Nott* was a story that required the galloping blood race of a hunt for a wild red stag on Exmoor. When I tried to write the book, however, energised and permissioned, as it were, by the example of Céline's *Rigadoon*, I found the effect of a spontaneous and breathless advance could only be achieved by an almost infinite number of assiduous rewritings at the specific level of word and punctuation.

During that arduous period of writing and rewriting I learned that rhythm—the most complex of all our literary effects—held the key to my problem. I learned that in the rhythm of prose, as in music, every black mark on the page is critical to the effect of the trick you're trying to pull. I learned that rhythm is the heartbeat of prose just as it is of music and poetry. Céline had achieved exactly the effect of spontaneity I needed, and in the heartbreaking effort to achieve that effect for myself I learned to write.

But each book demands its own solutions and the rhythm of one story will not do for all stories. We move on. And the new territory poses new challenges. It took me five years and numerous drafts to find how to write *Conditions of Faith* because I couldn't see the key to writing about the intellectual and emotional development of a sensitive young woman during a period of little over a year without making the story introspective and stationary. The problem for me was that *Conditions of Faith* was inspired by my reading of my mother's Paris journal for 1923, a time when my mother was a free-spirited young woman dreaming of her own future, long before she met my father or had any thoughts of having to look after me and my brother and two sisters.

My mother's journal—which my brother sent me from England after my mother's death—provided me with a magic keyhole view into her youthful interior life, but it didn't give me any sense of a narrative. I had lived in Paris in the early seventies myself, and in the weeks and months after reading her journal I often found myself picturing my mother as a young woman occupying the sixth-floor flat I'd rented in rue Saint-Dominique back in the seventies. Inspiration in this case was not a sudden flash of understanding but was a gradual realisation over a period of a year or more that I had a character and a setting and that I wanted to write about them. What interested me about the situation was the interior life of the young woman, her passionate dreaming of an independent life for herself. A dream that I knew was not to be. Kurt Vonnegut (here he is again!) has said his own writing life was an attempt to realise his mother's unrealised dreams for her after she was dead. So maybe *Conditions of Faith* was even more deeply a story about my mother than I realised. For my hero in that book, the young Australian woman Emily Stanton, finds a way to avoid the kind of stifling wifehood that locked my own mother into a destiny she had not dreamed for herself, and Emily reaches that free-spirited life my mother *only* dreamed of.

Although she was grief-stricken at the death of my father, after fifty years as his companion, my mother confided to me, 'I feel a little guilty saying this, but now he's gone I feel free.' And maybe in that guilty confession of the old lady there was the whisper still of the voice of the young girl dreaming her dream of freedom in Paris. For I am beginning to see these days that as we get older we come to understand that we have not travelled as far from our early years as we thought we had. We think we buried certain things long ago and forever, including one or two of our youthful dreams, until time begins to dig them up again and presents us in old age with the consequences of our abandonment of them.

At such moments of grim realisation I take cover in Vonnegut's favourite piece of advice to himself: 'Don't take it all so seriously.' And so maybe it's Kurt Vonnegut Jr, after all, who I have to thank for the inspiration to persist with the writing life, for certainly I do love the spirit of that man. But how to lay bare the threads of such a fine elusive thing as that without parting them? And if it is true, and Vonnegut has greatly inspired me, you won't find it in my work. For inspiration has nothing to do with mimicry, but is a thing entirely of the spirit.

2003

Once Upon a Life

As a youth I went to work as a farm labourer on the edge of Exmoor in the wilds of West Somerset. I fell in love with the life of the country at once, getting up before dawn and working until the evening seven days a week. And when the hunt was meeting I rode second horse for my boss with the Devon and Somerset staghounds. The life was all magic to me.

A year later, when the magic had become my routine, a fine-looking horseman rode into the wintry field where I was digging turnip shells for the sheep. He stopped beside me, his beautiful horse excited and uneasy with my closeness, and he said hello. This was unusual. But he was an Australian, my first. He told me he had come to England with the dream of retiring to the life of an English hunting gentleman but had soon discovered he was out of place. This wasn't the open society, he said, of the kind he'd left behind him in Australia, where anybody could decide to be whatever they fancied. On Exmoor the locals viewed him with distrust as an oddity and an outsider. I knew what he meant. I was an outsider there myself, and possibly his last resort for someone to chat to.

A couple of weeks after he came into the turnip field I was drinking a cup of tea with my new Australian friend and his wife in the kitchen of the small manor house they'd bought. He got up from the table and fetched a book. 'If it's the wild frontiers of this world you want to see,' he said, 'you should read this.'

The year was 1953 and the name Nolan meant nothing to me, but the fine black-and-white silver gelatin photographs captivated me. One in particular I still recall today with the smell and feel of those times, catching in its grainy image myself being that boy again. Three stockmen stand in deep shadow in various attitudes of ease on the verandah of a hut, the broad brims of their hats and the picked-out points of their spurs. They are gazing out into an empty landscape and seem to be waiting for something, the horizon an uneventful line dividing earth and sky, the only feature the wretched limbs of a dead tree in the middle distance. I read the caption, *You can ride for a month out here and never strike a fence*, and was gripped by the dream of finding Sidney Nolan's outback for myself. To ride with those nameless stockmen out into the emptiness of their landscape and over that mysterious horizon . . .

Almost a year later, on a grey November afternoon, my family stood in a close group on the platform at Liverpool Street Station, watching my train pulling out, waving me off for Tilbury and the other side of the world. I was not to see them again for ten years. In this last remembered image of my family gathered together in the one place, my little brother is standing between my father and mother holding my father's hand. My older sister and my younger sister are holding each other's hands and are standing up close against the skirts of my mother's coat. It is as if they fear that separation might prove to be a contagion. Forty years later, when my brother came out to Australia to visit me, I asked him if he remembered seeing me off at Liverpool Street. He said, 'Of course I remember it. We were all crying.' My brother's words surprised me. For although I was leaving a country and a family that I loved that day, I was too excited by the adventure ahead of me to fear that I would miss my country, or to notice that my leaving had brought great distress to my family. I was going to Nolan's outback to join the stockmen. The train was moving. The Australian's book was in my suitcase. I had acquired a new reality.

When I got off the boat in Sydney six weeks later I was still underage and was supposed to report my arrival in Australia to the authorities. But I was too impatient to reach the outback to bother with this formality and I set off at once with my suitcase. Walking north along the highway I thumbed down a truck. The driver was friendly. My story did not surprise him. 'You're doing the right thing, old mate,' he said. 'I should have done it when I was your age.' He drove me all the way to the southern Queensland coastal town of Gympie and got me a job on a dairy farm where he knew the farmer and his wife. The truck driver and I had become friends of the road and he had led me into the way of being Australian. It wasn't difficult for me. My mother's people were Irish and my father was from Glasgow, my parents' cultures the very ones from which the majority of white Australians had their origins in those days. Being Australian felt more natural to me than trying to be English ever had. With an intuitive certainty that is only available to us when we are young, I knew that my arrival on the other side of the world had been a homecoming. I had found the place where the outsiders had gone long ago and knew myself to be among them.

Gympie was hot, the vegetation subtropical, fierce taipans lurked among the flowering lantana, and death adders sunned themselves along the riverbank when we went for a swim. It was all new and exotic and it fascinated me, but it was only a stop along the way. A dairy farm in Gympie was not Nolan's outback. After a couple of months I showed my book to the farmer and his wife and told them my dream. They understood and offered to help me with the next stage of the journey. They had never been to the outback themselves, they said. 'Will you write and tell us what it's like?' Their curiosity was sincere and I promised I would write. But I never did. With that leave-taking I was beginning to accumulate my grown-up store of small regrets. There would be occasions for larger ones later.

He was gentlemanly and had about him an interesting air of melancholy, which I thought at once had something to do with a solitariness in himself. He liked to drink Pedro Ximenez black sherry in front of the fire in the evening—or even during the afternoon—and he loved to read. He preferred a beret to a broad-brimmed hat and was inclined to stay indoors. He was the owner of a sixty-four-thousand-acre cattle station in the open ironbark forests of the Central Highlands of Queensland, his domain set deep among the wild granite escarpments of the Carnarvon Range, his pastures watered by the abundant stream of Coona Creek. He was my new boss. I was shy with his youthful wife and addressed her respectfully as Mrs Wells, while I dreamed of being her lover. He insisted I call him Reg. There was little to be done on the station just then, he said, and he gazed out from the front verandah at the silver grass of the plain and the dark ironbark forests beyond and the rim of fortress hills, as if he dreamed of being somewhere else. I could spend my days reading if I wished, he said, and smiled and left us.

I explored the wilderness on horseback, camping on my own for days high in the escarpments, where the dingoes were so wild they had no fear of me. At Christmas Reg said I should fight in the boxing tournament in Springsure to raise money for the Red Cross, and I reluctantly obeyed him. With more enthusiasm I rode in the bareback and saddle bronc events in the rodeo, as all the other young stockmen of the district did. When autumn came we mustered the half-wild cattle, then together drove the steers to the market, riding behind the mob at an easy walk, making our eight-mile stage along the stock route each day. And in the sandhill country I smelled the heady perfume of the wattle scrubs in bloom for the first time. Reg and I camped under the stars at night, lying in our swags beside our fire, I talking of my dreams and he of his disenchantments.

'Here's a book to suit you,' he said one day, and handed me Sir Richard Burton's two-volume *Personal Narrative of a*

Pilgrimage to Al-Madinah & Meccah. Burton's journey inspired me with a new resolve to persist in my own journey. I knew by then that the Central Highlands of Queensland was not the outback, but I loved it on Goathlands Station with Reg and his family, so stayed longer than I intended. He and I often sat by the fire till late on winter evenings, reading, sipping sherry and smoking. He had been delighted to discover that I could shoe horses and ride, but it was not station work that was his first love. Before anything else I learned from Reg Wells the pleasure of reading, and something of its art. After two years I told him, 'It's only that you've been so kind to me that I've stayed this long.' He smiled; he had known he would lose me one day. He radioed his old friend, the manager of a vast cattle station in the remote Gulf of Carpentaria, a tract of country bigger than Wales.

I shook hands with Reg for the last time at the Springsure railway station, the family gathered to see me off. I was leaving behind me a scene that recalled to my mind my other, earlier farewell at Liverpool Street. This time I was more emotional. This time I had doubts. This time I wondered if what I was leaving behind might not be the very thing I had set out in search of. I left the Nolan book with Reg. It would sit nicely on his bookshelves among his accounts of travels.

Three days out of Springsure on slow trains took me to the far western cattle town of Cloncurry, a huddle of pubs and stores in those days, stained with the monochrome dust of the landscape. Not the famous red of the western deserts but a less distinct tone, somewhere between grey and brown.

Alex (left) with Reg Wells at Goathlands, near Springsure, Queensland

I picked up the mail coach, an old army blitz wagon loaded with drums of fuel and stores for the stations along the Leichhardt River, and rode it the three hundred miles north to Augustus Downs Station. There was no road, just wheel tracks through the savannah. Where these crossed the waterless bed of the river the mailman picked his own way among the rocks and treacherous sands.

The manager of Augustus Downs drove his jeep at high speed across the plain for sixty miles. We did not need to stop to open gates. There were no fences. This was Nolan's outback. The cattle camp was a tent fly and a smoking fire among the timber on the bank of the Leichhardt River. Under the fly a man was kneading dough on a board. When I greeted him he went on kneading his dough, mumbling to himself, ignoring

Goathlands homestead

me. Towards evening a group of about thirty horsemen rode into the camp, raising a cloud of dust. They formed a half-circle around me, not smiling nor offering a greeting. Two of them were white, the others were black, their hair and beards long and unkempt, their broad-brimmed hats and mounts covered with the same grey-brown dust that had clothed the buildings of the town. They were the legendary ringers of the great plains of the Gulf of Carpentaria, tribal Aborigines on their own country. We became friends. When I left the Gulf, I knew I would never belong in that country. Not as the Aboriginal stockmen belonged in it. No matter how welcome they made me, I would always be passing through on my way to somewhere else. And passing through on my way to somewhere else wasn't the life I wanted.

After I left the Gulf I did not know where to go. For some years I was lost. Nolan's outback had not answered something for me but had presented me with my biggest question: how was I to make sense of my life? In a boarding house for single men in the southern city of Melbourne I began to write of my uncertainties. Writing seemed my only way forward out of the despair into which I had sunk. Reg Wells made a reader of me, but it was Nolan's outback that made me a writer.

2010

EXCERPT FROM

Watching the Climbers on the Mountain

As the stockman squatted in the shade against the darkness of the beefwood, so still he would have been invisible to anyone passing, an afternoon cicada chorus began to scream suddenly, without warning, as if triggered by some mysterious alarm. The tide of noise rose and swept the hot and silent bush with oscillating waves of shrill intensity, passing back and forth and rising in layers upon itself until the sound reverberated inside the stockman's skull. The invisible insects flooded the enthralled afternoon.

A few minutes later the cicadas ceased their signalling as abruptly as they had begun it. In the deep shadows of the beefwood the stockman shifted his weight. Fragments of high-spirited shouts and laughter began to reach him from the direction of the creek. He rose slowly to his feet and moved back in the direction of the cattle track. There was a look of unhappy resignation on his face as he made his way towards the swimming party, and just before going down the creek bank he glanced back once over his shoulder at the dry level country spread out behind him. A trace of intense emotion resonated within him, but it was rapidly being overlaid by anxieties about the fight tomorrow evening—there was a dumb regret in him that he had not, after all, found a way to avoid that.

1988

How to Kill Wild Horses

It was a regulation two-man quarters. A bed each side of the door, and between them just space enough for a small three-drawer chest. There was nothing else, except nails driven into the wooden frame. An electric light bulb hung by a flex from the middle beam of the ceiling. Above the chest of drawers was a single-pane window that could be swung in or out. Outside was a three-foot verandah and two steps to the ground. Where the path carried on from the hut it passed a tin lavatory and ended at a hen run, in which there were a dozen White Leghorns.

Milky unrolled his swag and started putting his things away in the drawers. From the thin shade of a mimosa bush, two chained blue dogs watched his movements. When he'd finished he lay down on the bunk and stared up at the naked pink gecko that had suckers on its feet. The lizard returned his stare, blinking now and again. He wondered if it was waiting for him to close his eyes so that it could drop on him. But it yawned and swallowed as if it were sleepy itself, so he decided it was just passing the time like himself. Waiting. He could feel the heat coming through the fibro walls and the sweat trickled over his body. He lay still. The hens next door were making small troubled sounds and everything seemed to be waiting. In the distance a flock of black birds were going aah-aah-aaaaaah, as if they were suffering a bitter grief. Through the open door he could see where the bank of the creek went down. There was a big aluminium windmill on the far side, but it wasn't turning. And beyond that there was the dull silver plain, mile after mile of featureless spear grass. Far away, beyond the plain, the hills rose out of the mirage, grey and mysterious. Perhaps even cool. He would be going there with Mr Kelly to look for wild horses.

He closed his eyes—it was like being wrapped in warm pastry—and dreamed of being stalked across the silver plain by an insistent and sinister emu. The dogs woke him, barking and lashing the dust with their chains. He sat up and looked out the window. Coming up the road, which twisted through the dark wild lime trees, was a white Holden ute. He watched it. Behind the ute a horse float swayed through the pall of dust, like the prow of an unexpected ship breasting a grim fog. His heart beat faster and he wondered if he should go and meet the man or wait. He got up and went to the door. A hundred yards away the station homestead stood squarely on its stilts, green and white blinds drawn down over the verandahs and heat radiating off its shiny tin roof. The ute came on past the homestead towards the hut, swaying and jolting and driving the dogs into a frenzy. It pulled up in the dust next to the verandah and a short thin man stepped out. The dogs were silent, watching him intently. Milky went down the steps to meet him.

'G'day, I'm Milky,' he said.

'Moran Kelly,' the man said, and offered his hand. He was in his middle forties, a good half-head shorter than Milky, his face lined and brown and with a two-day growth of beard on his chin. Milky watched him unload his horse. They were a matched pair, man and horse, both short and scruffy. Liberated from the float, and without halter or bridle, the mare stood alert, watching Moran Kelly while he unloaded the rest of his gear from the back of the ute. Milky felt like an unwelcome observer of these proceedings so he went back inside the hut and sat on the edge of his bed. Perhaps Mr Kelly had not expected him to be there.

There was a brilliant moon that night, and Milky lay awake listening to the sharp sounds that carried through the still air. The dogs whined and snuffled in their dreams and the steady munching of Moran's horse stayed close to the hut. When they'd gone over to the house for a meal that evening, Reg Moffatt, Milky's boss, had asked Moran if he would mind Milky going with him on the hunt. Moran Kelly had not appeared enthusiastic but had shrugged and said, 'Why not?' They'd left it at that. Moran lay sleeping in the bed opposite. On the chest of drawers six metal clips lay in a black heap, the moonlight coldly outlining them against the scarred surface of the wood. Milky had watched him carefully file the points off sixty bullets and press them into their spring-loaded beds. He was not a man who made you feel like asking a lot of questions.

They rode across the river at first light and headed out across the spear-grass plain towards the hills, which looked closer and more twisted than they had during the heat of the previous day. Milky rode behind on the old brown gelding they called Beau. Beau rolled his head from side to side as he walked, lurching and swaying like an old barge anchored in a swell; not exactly a top-class pony. Beau had once been a gun horse, however, and knew what this was all about. Moran rode ahead, a dirty little hat perched on his head and his rifle slung over one shoulder. He was not an impressive sight.

Milky didn't see a living thing, and although Moran raised his hand once and seemed to point over to the left, Milky didn't see anything that you would point at. After nearly two hours of travelling in a straight line they started coming into a bit of low scrub which was crisscrossed with deep breakaway gullies, impossible to travel through without knowing the way. They followed a cattle pad through this maze, sliding and lurching down the steep erosions on one side and struggling and grunting their way up the other. Moran's pony stuck his head into it and did the job firmly and squarely. Beau farted and sighed and staggered about as if he might go down at any minute, but somehow he managed to breast each gully without actually coming to grief. Emerging from a particularly engrossing gully, Milky suddenly found himself among trees and for a moment he lost sight of Moran. Beau pulled up short, sensing the uncertainty of his rider, then waggled his head impatiently just as Milky caught sight of Moran moving ahead of them through the stunted ironbarks. The ground was rocky now, strewn about with great basalt boulders and lesser stones which tinkled under the horses' hoofs, a dry sound that carried in the morning air like the ringing of a small handbell.

They began the ascent, following the line of a ridge that dipped and rose and meandered deeper into the hills, climbing all the time until you could look back and see the miles of spear grass spreading out below, flat and still as far as the eye could see, cut by the irregular line of the river which arced out deep into the plain as if it had gone exploring.

They followed the ridge for maybe an hour and at last they came to a saddle, where Moran stopped among the trees and waited for Milky to catch up. Milky would have ridden into the grassy clearing, for a better view of what lay ahead, had Moran not motioned him to his side beneath the overhanging branches of a soft wild cherry tree. The hill fell away steeply in front of them, ending in a tangle of rocks and fallen timber at the river far below. Beyond the river more hills rose up, ridge upon ridge of grey and silent forest, like gigantic waves in a petrified ocean. Below them an eagle drifted across the narrow valley, turning his head from side to side, casting his gaze into the grassy pockets that dotted the riverbank at uncertain intervals. In one of those pockets Milky saw something move, sunlight catching the flank of a beast as it emerged from the shadow of the trees. He looked at Moran, but the man was rolling a cigarette.

'There's something down there.'

'Yeah,' Moran replied, not distracted from his cigarette. He examined the finished product, nipping the stray bits of tobacco from the ends and fastidiously turning it around in his fingers, as if he might yet decide to discard it. 'Yeah,' he repeated, putting a match to the cigarette and drawing in the smoke. 'I suppose we'd better go and have a look for these fucking yarramen.' And he turned his pony and headed carefully down the ridge at an angle, following, it appeared, a precariously marked pad. Perhaps he'd been following it all along. A few minutes later Milky saw some desiccated balls of horse dung.

Descending the bluff was a hazardous business, especially being perched on Beau's unsteady carcass, and Milky had no spare attention for the scenery until they came down, with a rattle of loose stones, onto the narrow flat which bordered the river. Here they encountered fresh horse dung and Moran got off to examine it.

Moran communicated no conclusions about this sign, and they rode on in silence for a mile or so until they came to a place where the river spread out over a shallow bed of loose stones. They crossed here. Coming out of the water on the other side they startled a calf, which had been planted by its mother under the shelter of some flood debris. The calf gave a panic-stricken bellow and raced off at full speed, its tail cocked in the air like a little banner. Moran cursed under his breath, listening to the snapping of twigs and crashing that marked the wild flight of the animal.

They did not follow the river, but cut up the side of a gully. About halfway up Moran turned off to the left and dismounted. He left his pony to graze on the small grassy shelf and made his way on foot. Milky followed. They soon came to a rocky parapet which was shaded by a thick-leaved hickory tree. Here

Moran sat down. The parapet overlooked a steep slope which was sparsely timbered and beyond which was spread out a large clearing. The clearing was well grassed, with here and there a sturdy old red gum. On the far side of this parklike meadow a cow and a young heifer grazed together peacefully. A grazing animal could scarcely have found a more agreeable place, with water close by, shade and plentiful feed. Milky wondered why there were not more cattle there. Moran was still and alert. He did not speak or roll a smoke, but watched the cow and the heifer, never taking his eyes off them. The two beasts moved slowly around the perimeter of the clearing, feeding from one choice patch of grass to the next, but never venturing into the centre of the clearing. The sun was very nearly overhead now, and although the day was hot the air lacked the heaviness which was common on the plain. The flies were less intense in their probing and there were fewer of them. The hills were a good place to be.

They sat there in the shade of the hickory tree for maybe an hour, neither speaking nor moving. Then suddenly the cow lifted her head and turned, looking nervously towards the river. The heifer stopped feeding also and turned with her. Moran breathed out audibly. 'Here they come,' he said.

The cow took a few inquisitive steps forward, paused for a moment, her nose lifted to catch the breeze, then turned and trotted off into the timber, the heifer close at her heels. For maybe two minutes the meadow was still and empty. Then a chestnut mare moved out into the sunlight and, after looking around, dipped her head and began to feed. She was soon followed by another, then another, until there were about eighteen mares, some with foals at their sides. Moran remained motionless, watching the trees from where the horses had come. There was a sudden flurry of movement among the mares, a nervous crowding and tucking in of the hindquarters, and into the clearing trotted a blood-bay stallion, his head held high and his magnificent body rippling in the sunlight. He whistled once and cantered around the mob, administering a nip here and there and ducking his head at any mare that looked like standing her ground. Then he trotted off a few yards and examined his brood.

Moran suddenly slid down behind the parapet and motioned to Milky to do the same. Milky's heart was thumping violently as he followed Moran down the bluff at a crouch, following carefully the precise movements of the older man. Without noise they made their way towards the river, then angled back into the hill, Moran stopping every now and then, his gaze never off the stallion for more than a second. Cautiously they moved from cover to cover, until they had reached the very edge of the timber and the mob of horses was no more than a hundred yards away. Here Moran lay down behind a slight rise and up against the trunk of a gum tree. The shelter was slight, but his field of fire was clear.

The stallion roved about restlessly, eyeing every bush and occasionally snorting and striking the ground. Clearly he was uneasy. Moran mumbled something inaudible and slowly slid back the bolt of his rifle, then pushed the shell home with a dry snick. The stallion stopped, stood stock-still, and stared right at them, searching for a telltale movement, as tense as a drawn bow. Milky felt that if he so much as blinked the stallion and all his mares would vanish.

At that moment a foal moved playfully across the stallion's line of vision and he dipped his head and trotted stiffly towards it. Moran raised the rifle to his shoulder and took aim. The foal wheeled from the path of the threatening stallion and Moran's rifle followed it. Suddenly a tremendous crash roared and reverberated around the valley and the foal fell on its side like a log. The stallion reared and screamed a wild warning. There was confusion in the meadow as the mares crashed into each other in their panic. Then they were gone, thundering into the trees from where they had come, the stallion at the tail urging and striking the last few. Milky heard them crashing through the timber and then splashing across the river. In a moment all was silent again. A light pall of dust hung in the air. Milky raised himself on his elbow, intending to get up and go and look at the foal, which had not moved. Moran gripped his arm. 'Stay down,' he ordered. 'They'll be back.'

They waited in silence, listening to the crashing of under-growth. Suddenly a mare came galloping into the clearing with the stallion hard on her heels. She whinnied desperately and raced straight up to the fallen foal, which she nudged with her nose, but the stallion struck at her and bit her so that she had to fight him off. Still, she wouldn't go far from the foal, and at last the stallion seemed to make up his mind and bolted away into the trees. The mare walked all around her dead foal, nudging it with her muzzle and pawing at the ground, all the time making a throaty coughing sound. Moran watched and

Milky watched with him. Then the noise of the other horses grew louder and in a moment they streamed back into the clearing with the stallion hard at them. He swung them around in a big circle and headed them at a full gallop straight for where the mare was pawing at her foal, and he drove them over her and carried her along with them. As they streamed past Moran took aim at another foal. The second foal did a somersault and stood up for a moment, as if wondering what had happened, then fell on its side and kicked a couple of times.

Moran reloaded and said, 'That big bastard's doing our work for us, eh?'

Milky saw that his khaki shirt was wet with sweat.

'Will they come back again?'

'They can't keep away,' Moran replied, never taking his eyes off the clearing.

And sure enough, within a minute or so the two mares came flying back with the stallion after them. He went from one to the other, lashing and biting at them, but no sooner had he got one away from her foal than the other returned. He fought this losing battle for maybe three minutes before again heading off into the timber in search of his brood.

'He's a great horse, ain't he?' Moran said appreciatively. 'I'll bet he's got a few colts bluffed around here.'

Milky swallowed the dryness in his throat. 'Will you kill him?'

'Good question, eh?' Moran said, wiping the sweat from his face with his sleeve.

And again they came back, wide-eyed and black with water from the river, flecked with sweat and staring wildly, bitten

and driven by their tireless entire, who rounded them on the
two mares and drove them ruthlessly with the mob.

Moran fired and reloaded and fired again. Another foal, about
twenty yards from the first two, and this time a mare as well,
scored into the ground as the blunt-nosed bullets struck them.
Milky heard the distinct smack of the impact. The situation
was now too difficult for the stallion, and when he brought the
blind mob back a third time he failed to get the mares to follow
through in the rush. Moran now fired one shot after another
steadily, picking his target all the time and never missing.

Each time the rifle went off the mob swerved like a shoal
of fish as the shocking sound washed over them and rolled on
around the hills. And each time the gun roared one of them
fell. Milky felt a touch on his arm. Moran was offering him
the rifle. He took it and put the butt to his shoulder. Resting
his arm along the bank he sighted through the open V on the
tip of the barrel. Beyond the V was a confused and dust-driven
view of flying legs and bodies. He could pick nothing definite
out of the blurred melee and his arm was quivering so much
that the barrel was unsteady. He closed his eyes and squeezed
the trigger. The stock smacked him on the shoulder and nearly
turned him over, and the acrid smell of burnt cordite made him
cough. Moran took the rifle and said quietly, 'Just behind the
ear, eh?' and he sighted off and shot another mare. The mares
were crazed with excitement; some were shot and some just
fell over, while others jumped them and kicked viciously at the
air. There was a wild squealing and shrieking, and each time
a mare made a break for the river the stallion drove her back.

The big horse finally got them all going around in a wide circle, and then he cut the lead and drove them once again into the trees. The air was filled with sunrays slanting through the dust and again the clearing was still. Five foals and nine mares were left on the ground. One of the mares lifted her head and looked to where the others had gone. She struggled to get up then fell back with a grunt and rested. Moran said, 'Well you stopped her at any rate.'

Milky was unbelieving. 'I didn't shoot her.'

'In the lung,' Moran said dryly. 'She won't last.'

And they came back again, as if they would never understand, one mare lashing viciously at another, grunting and squealing and digging wildly at the corpses of their foals, impervious to the blows of the stallion, who was now covered with foam, his coat blackened and streaked with runnels of sweat. And Moran picked them off as if he had all day to do the job. When there were only four mares left the stallion suddenly wheeled around and stared at where the two men were hidden. Milky raised himself a little on his elbow to see better and Moran said, 'You stupid cunt!'

The great horse came off his feet as if he was coming off a big spring, his lips stretched back off his teeth and his eyes white. The froth flew back onto his flanks and he raced towards them as if nothing would stop him ever. Moran stood up and aimed the rifle. He said quietly, 'Come on then, boy, come on.' When the wild horse was no more than forty feet away, he fired.

The stallion dived into the ground on his nose, spearing the grass and dust up in a shower, half his head shot away by the dum-dum. His one remaining eye was open and Milky felt it fixed on himself.

'Fuck you!' Moran said, for the other horses had cleared out, miraculously, as if a thread had snapped and released them. 'I could have got the lot.'

Milky got shakily to his feet, mesmerised by the eye of the dead stallion, breathing the smell of dust and blood that filled the air. He watched Moran go over and kick the horse in the balls, where they bulged out blackly, wet and slippery and still hot.

'Fuck you too!' Milky said.

Moran turned around and they looked at each other. 'Let's take a look at your mare then,' the older man said, and he smiled bleakly. 'You'll do all right.' He turned and walked over to the wounded mare. Milky followed him and they stood and looked down at her. Her eyes were open and she stared at them and snorted blood out through her nose and mouth. Moran took out his knife and he bent down and sliced her skin from rump to neck. She stiffened and blew out a mass of clotted blood.

'Kill her!' Milky said.

'Fuck her! Kill her yourself,' Moran replied.

'Give me the gun!'

'Use a rock.'

'Give me the gun, you bastard!'

Moran walked away, saying over his shoulder, 'She's yours, boy. You had the gun.'

Milky looked around and found a rock. He lifted it up and smashed it down on the mare's head, but she only grunted and stiffened again, and the rock just took off some hair and skin. Milky looked towards where Moran was bent over a foal, cutting open the hide and pouring in the pink strychnine powder that would kill the dingoes when they came later for a feast. 'Please give me the gun, Mr Kelly!' But Moran ignored him and went on working his way around the carcasses. Milky looked down and the mare looked up at him. She had a minute or two to live and she would watch him.

1976

The two-man quarters at Goathlands Station

Destiny's Child

I didn't become a writer until I was into my late twenties and had run out of other options. The truth is I became a writer because I couldn't think of anything else to do. Most writers I know, on the other hand, seem to have been predestined from an early age to become writers. To illustrate their predestination they recount an incident from their childhood. How, say, when they were six, or even three, they found a book like Stendhal's *La Chartreuse de Parme* under Mum's bed and taught themselves to read it in French in a week. Or maybe it was Sterne's *Tristram Shandy* they found. Some great work of literature, anyhow, that even most adults find a bit hard going these days. It's the destiny story. You know, the only girl whose foot will fit the glass slipper? It's not her fault. It's just the way things are. Or the only boy who can pull the sword from the stone? In the fairytales the handsome woodcutter's boy or the beautiful serving girl is found in the end, of course, to be of noble birth. No amount of modesty will hide this. So it is with most writers. Their gift was written in the stars and there were omens in their youth foretelling the great works of their maturity. Writers' festival committees love these stories and encourage us to tell them. Every true writer must have one.

Whenever I was asked about this business at writers' festivals I used to say I didn't have one of these destiny stories. I pretended I was above that kind of thing and claimed such mythmaking didn't interest me. But secretly the lack of such a story worried me. It made me wonder if I was really and truly a writer or just an ordinary bloke who'd only decided to write because he couldn't get a decent job doing something else. This, I suspected privately, was the dreadful truth. But who wanted to know it? My publishers and their publicity people turned away with pained expressions and refused to listen whenever I tried to tell them. Then one day I remembered Billy Bunter and the roller skates.

I was nine and it was a couple of years after the war. My father had been wounded and was out of work and we were poor. Everyone in London was poor. But I insisted that I must have a pair of the latest self-guiding ball-bearing roller skates for Christmas. These skates were the equivalent of a snowboard or a mountain bike now and were very expensive. I had a brother and two sisters and they wanted Christmas presents too. So my parents really had no hope of raising the cash to buy these skates. But still I insisted. Getting those skates had the intensity for me of a religious vocation. There was nothing else in my life. I moaned for them. I was Bernini's Saint Teresa. I would pine away to nothing if I did not get them. I took on the appearance of a doomed child with a wasting disease. There was no question; poverty or not, I must have the skates.

On Christmas morning there was a shoebox-shaped present waiting for me under the tree. Everyone was gathered around, silent and expectant, waiting for me to open it. I opened the box and there were the skates. Brand-new. Shining through the wrapping. Untouched by earthly hands. I put them on and skated away. I knew it was right for me to have those skates. I did not ask how it had been managed. It had been written in the stars. My family had been merely the poor instruments of a higher power. There was a messianic element to my possession of the skates. With the skates on I grew strong and bold.

For a month I skated.

All day and half into the nights I skated. I lived in a sweating exhaustion of skating mania. The lone figure of a boy flying along the footpaths of the neighbourhood and beyond. I went further and further. I left the familiar narrow streets of the council estate behind and penetrated deep into enemy territory, self-guiding along unfamiliar streets of red-brick Victorian mansions under the spreading boughs of mighty chestnut trees. On my speeding skates I dwelled in my land of perfect desire. My fantasy had become my reality. I went home only to eat and then immediately went out again, skating. I could not be stopped.

Until one day I was skimming along a peaceful boulevard in the beautiful riverside suburb of Richmond, miles and miles away from home, when I saw in the distance a boy walking towards me. As I got closer to him I saw that he was carrying something and was wearing the yellow and black private school scarf of the enemy. There was no one else about. The street was deserted and quiet. When he saw me speeding towards him the boy knew at once that he was doomed, that one of the terrible bully boys from the rat flats had caught him alone in the open. He stood still, a rabbit in the headlights, clutching a book to his chest.

I pulled up a few inches from him and said, 'What have you got?'

He thrust the book at me, no doubt hoping the barbarian would be appeased with this tribute and would spare his life.

The book was old and well used. The cover had fallen off long ago but the title page was still legible. *Billy Bunter Omnibus*, it said above a line drawing of a fat boy with a scarf. I began to read.

Time passed.

The boy waited.

A small shuffling movement from him woke me from my thrall and I looked up from the book.

'I'll swap you,' I said.

He gaped at me for several seconds.

Finally I kneeled down and, placing the book on the pavement by my hand so that he could not snatch it up and run away, I took off my skates and handed them to him. Without a word, he turned and fled.

I should say at this point, I suppose, that my parents had managed to buy the roller skates only because my sisters and brother had all agreed to forgo a present themselves that

Christmas. It was an astonishing sacrifice on their part. But I had not thanked them or wondered how it had been done. Destiny had been in the air for me with the skates. I had been sent on a journey. It was not of my own doing.

By the time I got home it was dark. My family gathered around me and my father asked, 'Where are your skates?'

'I swapped them for this book,' I said.

My father took the book in his hands and opened it. We were silent, watching him. After a minute of reading to himself he began to read aloud. My sisters and brother and my mother and I stood at his shoulders to see the illustration of the fat boy. My father read to us until he reached the end of the first chapter, then he closed the book and handed it back to me. 'It's a good book,' he said. There were murmurs of approval all round.

Such was the generous spirit of my family that not one of them—not even my older sister, who liked to bully me—ever reprimanded me for swapping the skates for the old book. They seemed to understand that the skates had been a worthy sacrifice in the service of a higher cause for each of us. And that's my story of how at an early age the book was received into my family as a mysterious and powerful sign.

2002

Living at Araluen

In 1967 I was deeply demoralised after working in the public service in Canberra for two years and needed to get out of the place. With the help of my first wife, Anne, I managed to get hold of twelve thousand dollars and bought a rundown, fifteen-hundred-acre farm in Lower Araluen. My reason for buying the farm was to have a place where I could write without the distraction of a nine-to-five job. Araluen saved my life. Another year in the public service would have killed me.

Lower Araluen is beautiful; wild forest, very steep, hilly, with nice little creek flats. The Araluen Creek ran all the way through my property and the southern border was the Deua River. This is marginal country. It's not country for people to make a lot of money on. Fortunately, I got the contract for the mail run, which gave me a modest monthly cash payment. I grew my own vegies and began buying a few head of breeding cattle at the Braidwood market. I knew how to deal with cattle in the bush. Horses had come with the property; I had once

Alex at his desk at Araluen, c. 1972

made my living as a horse breaker and a stockman. Over the next few years I built up a modest herd of Hereford cows and I grew tomatoes and pumpkins for the Canberra market. Together with the money from the mail run I had enough to live on.

At Araluen I wrote three pre-novels. In other words, I did my apprenticeship there. The first pieces of mine that were

Alex at Araluen with his dog, Blue, c. 1972

published in mainstream journals like *Meanjin* and *Quadrant* were written there.

I drew on my time in Araluen for my fourth novel, *The Sitters*, and returned to this landscape in my ninth novel, *Lovesong*, as the home of John Patterner. For me, John Patterner is a good Aussie bloke of the kind I knew in Araluen; a modest Australian with enough intelligence and curiosity to go to the university and make the journey to England. Like me, John Patterner also went to Melbourne University. He's got a lot of my biography in him. I know and love the places he knew and loved. I know the smell of his country and the feel of it. Like him, I loved Araluen and the time I spent there. I'm always pleased if I can get some reference to Araluen into my work.

2009

EXCERPT FROM

The Sitters

In her childhood bedroom in her mother's house at Lower Araluen there's a little blue china dish on the chest of drawers. The room is so small that Jessica doesn't need to get up from the bed in order to reach the dish. The little dish fits snugly into the palm of her hand. She taps the ash from her cigarette into the little blue dish, which she remembers from when she was a child, and she weeps. It's the first moment of her return. As the tears run down her cheeks she lifts her face to the ceiling and blows out the smoke of her cigarette. It is a confusion that is both sadness and joy that makes her weep. Then she stubs out her cigarette and she dries her eyes and blows her nose. And she replaces the blue china dish on the chest of drawers and she laughs and tells herself that she is an idiot. She runs her hand along the top of the chest of drawers. A piece, like a small bit taken from a pie, is broken from the bevelled edge of the chest of drawers. She inserts the ball of her thumb into the hollow of the 'bite' and rubs it back and forth. This is one of those idle gestures that are ventured upon involuntarily. There is something intensely familiar, something unexpectedly private and deeply personal, in the pleasure she gets from the feeling of rolling the ball of her thumb in the hollow of the wood. She is taken by surprise and she repeats the action. She rolls the ball of her thumb in the little hollow and searches in her memory for something. But it is like trying to remember a dream after waking. The harder she tries to remember, the more recessed the image becomes, until it is lost altogether.

1995

In the End it was Teaching Writing

The day after I received the Miles Franklin Literary Award in 1993 I had a call from Richard Friedman, who at that time was the Professor of English at La Trobe University. Professor Friedman, or Dick as he asked me to call him, offered me a job teaching writing. For many years I had been struggling, as most novelists must do, to balance a need to spend time earning a living with a need for clear periods of time in which to compose the novels I felt I needed to write. The conditions attached to the teaching job that Dick offered me were far more favourable to my writing than the conditions of any position I had previously held. So I accepted his offer at once—and Dick Friedman and I became friends and have remained friends ever since.

When they heard what I was going to do, my friends all asked me, as if the question had been poised on their tongues for years, waiting for an opportunity to be asked, 'But can you teach writing?' I didn't know the answer to this question, of course, and I think I responded with something like, 'Probably not, but perhaps I can offer students encouragement and give them a real sense of what it is like to take on the business of writing novels as the principal occupation of one's life.' The question of whether or not I could teach writing was one that greatly occupied my thoughts for the next few months while I prepared myself to begin working at La Trobe. I was anxious to know the answer.

Meanwhile, for a reason associated with the literary award and with publishers, I visited England. While I was in England I took the opportunity to stay with my mother in Dorset for a week. My mother was eighty-six and this, though we did not know it at the time, was to be the last occasion on which we were ever to see each other. My mother was in vigorous good health and we walked in the New Forest almost every day during my visit. On the last day our walk ended at a pub on the edge of the forest, and she suggested we have lunch there. We ate, and between us finished a bottle of a Spanish wine called Bull's Blood, then walked home arm in arm to her house in the village of Burton.

I had left my childhood home in London to come to Australia alone when I was sixteen, and although I had frequently visited England since those days and had often seen my parents, my mother and I had never before spent a week alone in each other's company. It was towards the end of the week that my mother pointed this out to me, as if she and I had at last stolen a week together. When I left her the following day to drive back to London in my hired car, we both pretended not to be deeply moved at our parting and sought to reassure each

Alex's mum, Winnie, on their last walk together

other, repeatedly, that we would be seeing one another again quite soon, when the two of us would spend another wonderful week together.

I had been teaching my two classes at La Trobe for three weeks when my mother telephoned me late one evening. 'I've had an offer of death,' she said. We both laughed and agreed it was probably the best offer she was going to get at her age. After her Irish beginnings my mother was brought up in a convent in Chantilly. A strict Catholic when she was young, she loved the nuns and had been treated by them with great respect, even with a degree of favouritism, and had always spoken of them as her family. Her memory of her time growing up in the convent at Chantilly was of a happy childhood. She was eighteen when she returned to England and met my father. From that day she had never revisited her faith and rarely spoke about it.

'It was a visitation,' she said to me over the telephone. And the moment she said this, I knew that she would not have told anyone else about the offer of death in quite this way. 'Two figures dressed in white came for me,' she said. 'They told me to fall back into their arms and they would take care of me through the darkness.' We were both silent for a long while. 'And you turned them down?' I said at last. 'Yes, darling.' She sounded a little sheepish at this admission. 'Do you think I should have accepted their offer?'

Two or three weeks later, when I was preparing work for my students' crucial seventh week of term, my sister telephoned me from Windsor and told me our mother was very ill and was in hospital. 'The doctor says she has heart failure and will not last more than a week or so,' my sister said. In fact, it took my mother six weeks to die. According to my sister's account it was a slow, painful and, in the end, terrifying experience for my mother, as her various systems shut down one by one, her poor heart retreating to conserve its failing strength, until at last she was blind and bloated beyond recognition.

I didn't go to England to see my mother during her final illness. I felt I had to stay with my students, who I felt were relying on me. The response of my students to the work we were doing together had been far more compelling than I had ever imagined it might be. There were not many of them and we had quickly become a passionately committed group of writers, knowing ourselves privileged to read the vulnerable early drafts of each other's work—a unique privilege, I believe, at that time, for most of us. We were all learning a great deal about the business of bringing a piece of writing out of its clumsy early stages and making of it a confident work. I didn't feel I could leave my students without betraying the trust and the hopes they had placed in me and in the process I had initiated with them.

Some years after my mother's death, I visited my sister in the small town in Provence where she was then living. I had always regretted not going to England to farewell my mother and had never resolved the feelings of guilt I associated with her death. I was eager to talk to my sister about my mother's final days and asked her to tell me everything she could remember. When my sister had finished her account she said, after a brief silence, 'Mum's last words were, *It will be all right when Alex gets here.*' She looked at me. 'Sorry,' she said. 'But Mum was waiting for you. That's why it took her so long to die.' My sister was not being cruel in telling me this, she was being honest, and I am grateful that she had the decency and the courage, and the faith in our love for each other, to tell me the whole truth.

When my sister had driven me to the railway station at Montelimar, and we were standing together in the forecourt about to say goodbye, she said, 'It's all right, you know. Mum understood that writing meant everything to you.'

'It wasn't my writing that prevented me from coming,' I said. 'It was the teaching writing.'

2008

The Last Sister of Charity

For Robert

Our family GP, Andrew McDonald, God bless him, picked up the big telltale pulse in my abdomen during a routine check. It was last March and I was leaving in three weeks for Paris and Provence for a two-month holiday with my family. Andrew sent me to John Gurry, who diagnosed a 4.7-centimetre aneurysm of the abdominal aorta. 'They don't usually burst before five centimetres,' John said. 'Enjoy your holiday. Call me when you get back.'

It was John Gurry's use of the imprecise 'usually' that nagged at me, as well as the scant three millimetres of leeway. But it didn't spoil the holiday. For the most part I forgot to think about it. Wandering around the Musée d'Orsay or going to the ballet in the crazily overdesigned Palais Garnier, or practising my French and enjoying the wines and cheeses of Nyons in the golden sunlight of Provence, I had become the old invulnerable me once again. It was only when I woke in the early hours in our apartment near the Madeleine and lay in the eerie glow of the Paris night, feeling around with my fingers for the thing thumping away below my ribs, that I sensed an edge of panic. *If it bursts I'm dead!* My wife lay sleeping beside me, but I was alone in the dark. She had assured me, 'If it bursts, darling, I'll rip you open with a kitchen knife and grab it.'

I'm sixty-three, I'm lean and fit and I've never been ill. My body had always been utterly reliable—I had secretly exulted in its perfection! I'd stood in hospital wards at the bedsides of less-fortunate relatives and friends, young and old, who had undergone what used to be called heroic surgery but which nowadays, with the high-tech and drugs, rates only the prosaic adjective 'major', and had felt impotent to offer either comfort or reassurance through the pall of chemicals and pain that lay between us. I'd watched them weep with gusts of emotion that caught at them helplessly, and I'd been glad to get out of the hospital and away from them. I am ashamed to say they seemed to have lost something of their reality for me, these people hovering at the edge of death. There was just a hint of superiority, of the hubris that it could never happen to me, in my attitude. Not overt cruelty, not a lack of feeling, but a desire to protect myself from their pain and their excessive emotion; a decision that there was no way of responding to these terribly ill people that would mask my own inadequacy. I waited for them to get well again, to get *real* again, as if communication between us was not possible until they did so. There was a secret guilt in my relations with them. I knew I could have done better.

I did not understand people who could counsel patients suffering this kind of distress. I did not understand how anyone could be counselled in such circumstances. I couldn't imagine ever responding to such counselling myself. I was certain of my emotional strength. It was one of the few certainties on which my sense of myself was based. I had always seen my own way through crises unaided. I believed I always would. I thought there was a hero inside me.

This certainty about the autonomous durability of my emotional life was as chimerical as my exultant belief in my perfect body had been. But I didn't know that yet.

I took three books and plenty of writing materials into the hospital with me. I'd decided to make my hospital stay a reading and letter-writing holiday. As I settled into my private room that first evening—a view over the city, the late-winter sun gilding the cupolas of the Exhibition Building, a view not utterly unlike the view we'd enjoyed from our apartment in Paris—I had only one pressing question for the nurse: Did the hospital serve wine with dinner? Of course, the nurse reassured me, I would be served wine if I wished. She withdrew the first needle from my abdomen. I was alone in the small pleasant room. Books, wine, peace and quiet away from the email and the phone and the PC. No visitors. I'd told my friends, *I'll see you when it's over.* I settled down in the armchair by the window and began reading James Bradley's *Wrack*. It had been on my list for some time.

I went into theatre at three the next afternoon and returned to the ward at eight, after spending a period in recovery. I'd had an epidural but couldn't remember much: a green sheet in front of my eyes, figures moving, voices, lights. Did my wife visit me that first evening? I can't remember. John Gurry, the surgeon? I imagine so. I remember the nurses coming and going, attending to the drips and catheters, giving me injections and taking samples of blood. But more than anything I remember the blinding headache and the nausea.

For the next three days the headaches didn't go away and the nausea became worse. I didn't know it then, no one did, but I'd always had a tendency to migraine and the epidural had triggered a major series of these terrible headaches. I couldn't eat or sleep and the painkillers they were giving me for the wounds had no effect on the headaches. I took anti-nausea pills half an hour before mealtimes. But the smell of food, even of orange juice, made me retch. Even plain water had a revolting metallic taste to it. The operation, however, had been a success and I was doing fine. I had nothing to complain about. I didn't complain.

The afternoon of the third day, I think it was; one of those rare moments when I was alone and undisturbed, lying in my misery staring at the ceiling, *Wrack* and the wretched old man at the centre of its action long forgotten, scarcely able to believe that the headaches and the nausea and the pain in my body would ever go away, suffering my own wrack. A young man came into my room. I prepared myself to give blood or to be given an injection. The young man leaned down and touched my arm. 'It's all right,' he reassured me. 'I'm Robert. I'm a counsellor.' I made to speak to him, to tell him he was welcome, but an irresistible tide of emotion flooded my chest and I burst into tears. I clutched Robert's hand, laughing and weeping with inexplicable joy. I'd had no idea that this enormous reservoir of emotion had been gathering in me. I was taken by surprise. Robert stayed. We talked about literature and philosophy and people, our lives and beliefs. He was training for the priesthood. He had decided against a study of the scriptures in favour of becoming a counsellor. A study of people. I said to him, 'You counselled me. You have a gift.' We were both delighted. I was sad when he left. I had never wept before with a stranger. With another man. I was astonished to realise that my life, my spirit and my existence, had acquired a new dimension. Counsellors seemed the most wonderful and necessary people.

The next day an elderly woman came to see me. She was dressed in a pastel pink dress and a lace collar. Her manner was tentative. She gave me a pamphlet. 'I'm with the pastoral care unit,' she explained. I said, 'You're one of the Sisters of Charity?' She was reluctant to sit down. I pressed her to stay and talk. She sat uncertainly on the edge of the bed and I asked her about her life. I felt her need for reassurance. She told me, 'There used to be one of us to each floor in this hospital. We were a community.' She stood up, ready to leave, unable to stay and talk. She looked at me. 'I'm the last Sister of Charity,' she said. I wished I could have done more to reassure her. I wished I could have done for her spirits what Robert had done for mine. But it wasn't so easy. There was more to counselling than the simple desire to reassure.

On my last day in the hospital I sat in a wheelchair dressed in a grey dressing-gown with a blanket over my knees. I had become an old man in a wheelchair, one of those people I'd been unable to offer comfort to. I felt the justice of my position.

I was waiting in the cold basement for the CT scan that would either confirm the success of the operation or condemn me to more surgery. A nurse wheeled in a man on a bed and stood waiting with him beside me. I looked up at the man, intending to say hello, to make contact, to offer the precious human contact that Robert had offered me, like a beautiful gift of belief. I wanted to use the gift, to see if I really possessed it. The man in the bed beside me was young, in his early thirties. I saw at once that he was dying, that he did not have far to go. And I saw that he was thinking of his young family waiting for him at home. The young nurse was holding his hand. They were holding hands, the two of them, silent and together. Sensing my attention the nurse looked down and smiled at me. I didn't speak. I didn't break the sacred silence of their moment.

Later that afternoon I walked out of the hospital with my wife. A few steps beyond the doors I stopped, the wind and the sun in my face, the touch of my wife's hand on my arm. I couldn't go any further. I stood there weeping. When I could speak I told her, 'I'm not crying for myself. I haven't had any suffering. I'm not crying because I'm sad. I'm just moved by the beauty and the mystery of our lives.' Then I told her with difficulty about Robert and the last Sister of Charity and the dying young man in the cold basement holding the nurse's hand. When I'd finished we looked at each other. 'There's nothing to say,' I said. 'I'm not going to try to explain it.' Arm in arm, we walked together to the car.

2000

The Rule of the First Prelude

September of 1982 was an unusually brutal month for the unit. On the fifteenth, a Wednesday and the middle of what had been up until then a quiet week, a young client committed suicide at ten in the morning by slicing open her throat with a serrated Solingen bread knife (the policewoman said the detail was important). The young woman performed this gruesome operation on herself in the corridor between the waiting room and Marie's office. The worst part about it for Marie Elder, who was first on the scene, was that the young woman died smiling, her lovely blue eyes gazing up at Marie for an eternity from the innocent linoleum of the hospital corridor.

A trauma counsellor was called in for a session of group therapy for the members of the team on the Thursday afternoon. Then the following Monday, just when everyone was more or less getting back to normal, a deranged male drunk—a boner at the abattoirs when he was not incapacitated by drink, and a man well known to Marie and the team—felled the security officer on the door with the bronze nozzle of the fire hose and put him in the ICU, where the security officer clung to life for three days before giving up the ghost. The security officer, whom Marie and the other members of the team knew as Nick, was married with three young children. His father and mother had migrated from Greece thirty years earlier to give their children a better chance at life in the land of opportunity. When the police arrived on the scene the boner was kneeling in Nick's blood, weeping.

Marie felt the threat to herself deepened by these events. The threat, that was, to her ability to go on alone. She was sure that her colleagues in the unit, and even one or two of the more observant doctors, had noticed that she had taken these events personally. But she couldn't help it. She felt knocked sideways by them. At least, she said to herself when she was alone in the canteen drinking a cappuccino and staring out the window at the car park, Nick had a family. At least he had been loved by his wife and children while he was alive. Nick had been a real man with a real wife and real children. A normal family man. One of *them*. Nick's brutal death sickened her, but it also fired a shot into her heart that wounded her in a way that was deeply private. Supposing *she* were to be bludgeoned to death tomorrow by a crazy drunk, or to cut her own throat—who would be left to mourn her passing but one or two of those old friends with whom she had kept in contact over the years? Friends who themselves were married with families. She didn't envy either Nick or her friends, but she did pity herself.

Marie's pity for herself arose from a complicated source. She would never speak of it. To whom could she speak? All this brutality and sudden death focused her fragile emotions on her own fragility and failure. Not on her failure to get married and have children—she had never wanted marriage and children—but her failure at the age of thirty-seven to have found the friend and lover she dreamed of finding; her failure to establish the meaningful life for herself that she had determined on as a senior girl at school. She didn't have it. Despite everything. The friend, the man, with whom she might share her anguish and her joy. Her ideal friend. She *saw* him. He was tall and modest, as she was herself. He was an artist of some kind. A man who, unlike the husbands of her friends, insisted on a meaningful life for himself too. A loner, just as she was. Perhaps he was a musician or a writer or a painter. It didn't matter which. In company he sat quietly and listened and observed and never attempted to dominate the conversation with the events of his own life and his accomplishments. But he was intelligent and reflective and curious nevertheless. And he was effective. A cultivated man who did not need a wife and a mother and children but who was deeply self-reliant. She had never met such a man. Never. None of the men she had met had ever come near to it. Now she was nearing forty and had begun to fear she never would meet this friend but would become the solitary professional woman, like Ellen Alworth, the senior social worker in charge of the unit.

Did it have to be one or the other? Did she have to stake her happiness and her fulfilment in life either on love or on her work? Couldn't there be this other choice? The friend and lover of her girlhood dreams? The intelligent sensitive man who was her friend? The amorous friendship, the French called it, with the emphasis on amorous. But it wasn't that. Her emphasis was on friendship, not on love or sex. Marriage was easy. Everyone did it. Staying single and giving your all to your job like Ellen Alworth was evidently just as easy. Why must her own choice be so difficult? To wake up in the morning with something exciting to look forward to in her life, instead of another trip to the hospital on the tram. She didn't want to go on doing it alone. She was tired of it. Sick to her heart with it. When she looked in the mirror she saw how suddenly aged her eyes had become. She knew she was closer to the edge than she had ever been.

She couldn't help thinking of poor Nick. It was all so meaningless. So empty. So pointless. The voice within her cried out to her its despairing appeal, for which she had no answer: *What about me?*

At home in the kitchen on her own that weekend she abandoned her plans for a small roast chicken and she wept. She felt so desperate sitting there on her own in the kitchen that she decided to call one of her friends. But when she wiped her eyes and pulled herself together she realised she didn't want to hear her friend's voice, bright and cheerful and busy with her kids' weekend sports and her own frenzy of activity.

Marie went back into the kitchen. There was nothing to be done. Nothing to be said. She stood at the back door looking out into the tiny yard with its single camellia bush. All she wanted was to come out of this lonely darkness into the sunlight with him and to laugh and be the woman she knew she was.

Marie is looking out the window of the tram at the passing street. The sun is low and is glaring off the dome of the great railway station. The crowd of humanity is going in one direction, making for hearth and home, or for a rendezvous in a bar. The novel in her lap is unopened, her left shoulder is pressed painfully against the hard lip of the window. The air-conditioning has failed and the tram is hot and sweaty and smelly.

The woman squeezed in next to Marie sneezes again. The convulsive thrust of the woman's shoulder presses Marie's tender upper arm against the jutting lip of the window and she winces. There is a rancid smell of rotten meat. It is the smell of wretched humanity. Marie feels the touch of a hot needle at the back of her throat and fears she will also begin to sneeze. Her past is rushing away behind her. The tram dings its bell rapidly several times, angrily, the driver stomping on the bell pedal, and the tram stops abruptly. The standing passengers lurch forward and recoil, like a wave hitting a sea wall. A man flings a curse into the ears of those pressed against him. He has borne enough and the curse escapes him. The tram dings its bell twice and moves on again. A young woman laughs and is answered by the laugh of another young woman. The press of them, swaying and sweating, tortured, the man's curse falling through their minds. He might as well have wept. Perhaps someone would have been kind to him. Now he has irritated them. But they are stuck with him. The woman beside Marie sneezes again, then again. She murmurs a choked apology.

Marie closes her eyes then opens them. The world has shouted, has laughed, has sneezed and has moved on, churning the wild waters around her stillness. There had been men, plenty of them, when she was as young as those women who just laughed, men who would happily have married her. She had had her chances. They had not interested her.

The tram waits, ticking and creaking, its iron wheels gripped in the jaws of the brake dogs.

Marie's face at the window looking out as the dogs release their grip and the tram glides on over the river. She is sweating. A long boat of tourists passing beneath the old bridge in stately isolation. The tram rocking, leaving the slow brown river behind, accelerating along the fine boulevard of trees and parks, soft green of elm leaves translucent in the last of the golden sunlight.

Marie's hands tremble. Her fine fingers cling to the book in her lap. But the tremor is within. Something has given. Refused the solemn oath of calm. It leaps back, flashing again into her unshielded gaze, her blue eyes wide.

Marie stands a moment on the footpath and looks at the tram going away from her, locked to its rails, the sudden smell of the sea in the air, freshening towards her, seaweed and fish from the bay carried on the light southerly. Mrs Snee is leaning on the railings at the front of her house watching Marie approach. Marie greets her and stands with her to watch the frenzied

Scotty frolicking with a silken greyhound in the triangle of park opposite. At her own gate Marie collects her mail from the box, the iron gate clacking against its broken hasp. A last faded cluster of blossoms on her rose. There is one more bud. Fragrance in the air at her door as she inserts her key into the lock and passes from the outer world into the stillness of her home.

Marie sets the novel and the mail beside her bag on the table in the hall and climbs the stairs to her bedroom. She stands at the window and watches as the Scotty and the greyhound leap around each other, a sharp bark of sudden fear from the Scotty that the game will go too far, will become violent. She stands looking out for a minute or two then takes off her clothes and crosses to the bathroom. She leaves the bathroom door open while she stands under the shower.

She dresses and goes down to the kitchen at the back of the house and turns the radio to the classical music program. She ties the strings of the blue and white apron she brought back from China last year and gets the chicken breast from the refrigerator. She takes her sharpest kitchen knife from the block and slices the yielding flesh of the chicken as easily as the young girl sliced open her tender throat. She thinks of the girl's parents. Their lives destroyed. It is all so pointless. Her tears fall onto the bloodless meat.

There is a handwritten note from her boss on her desk when she gets back to her office after lunch the next day. *Drop by and see me when you have a chance, Marie.* The note, folded for discretion, is written in blue ink with a fountain pen and signed, *E. Alworth.*

From behind her desk she examines Marie over the rims of her glasses for a considerable time, a thin absent smile on her wooden lips (unpainted), as if her thoughts are elsewhere, entangled in the endless administrative problems and tasks that beset her in her position as leader of the Alcoholism and Drug Dependence Unit. Recollecting herself with a sudden awkward abruptness, Ms Alworth says, 'Yes, I really think you should consider taking the first half of next year off on half-pay, Marie.'

Marie is not altogether surprised by the suggestion. She thanks Ms Alworth for her concern. 'I'm okay. Honestly. I just need a long weekend.'

But Ms Alworth is done with smiling. 'Consider the matter *over* the weekend, Marie, and see me first thing Monday morning with your decision.' Ms Alworth resumes writing in the file on her desk, her old-fashioned fountain pen in her right hand, her head bent to the task before her.

Marie has seen Mrs Allen and the Black Cowboy sitting on the bench in the corridor outside her office, shivering and trembling, nursing their resentments at the delay she is making them bear, the world conspiring to defeat them, the high threatening whine of Mrs Allen's pit-saw voice berating anyone incautious enough to catch her eye, the Black Cowboy studying his hands, shaking his head slowly from side to side, knowing what a man has to do but never being able to do it, his worn features lit suddenly by a thought, and there for an instant the bright jewel of a youthful smile, a glimpse of the lost boy inside him, before the shutters come down again. The way he shakes his head, his dreams of vengeance never enacted with those hands.

Instead of going back to her office and seeing these people of hers (Marie refuses to call them her clients), after she leaves Ms Alworth's office she walks down the passage to the hospital canteen and joins the coffee queue. Is six months off on half-pay a prelude to dismissal? Everything, after all, is a prelude to something. Standing in the queue she says to herself, I once found satisfaction in my job and would find it again if I had my friend and lover.

But there was something else, something even deeper than this. Ms Alworth's suggestion that she take time off has reduced the gap between where Marie stands and where she will fall. She is thinking of the nightmare of her father's last days. She was seventeen and a boarder at Ascham School in Sydney, studying for her fifth-form exams, in love with her literature teacher, Miss Wendell, and secretly writing love poetry of her own. In the middle of a clear spring day, lying on the grass with her friend Betty Arnold, Marie was called to the headmistress's office and informed with the keenest sorrow that her father had been taken seriously ill. She left for home at once. And suddenly she was at home with her father. He was fifty-seven. Within weeks this loving kindly man, her friend and confidant since childhood, was transformed into a grotesque stranger bound to his familiar old cedar bed by sickness, the carved bedhead with its row of koalas among the gum nuts mocking his disaster, his limbs and head swollen with oedema. Blind, paranoid, moaning and weeping, her loving father was a man abandoned by his failing body and swept by panic. The sanest of men had become mad, lost in a black whirl of horror—until that final terrible night when he emerged from his delirium in the early hours and clasped her hands in his own icy grip and with sobs confessed to her his unspeakable betrayal.

Everything, she thinks in her loneliness, everything is ineradicably connected. If you touch one thread of the web, the entire web trembles and then the black spider of despair is roused and it rushes out and clasps you to itself and sucks out your life and leaves you old and dry. She laughs. The whole delicate construction—of her life, that is—is tremulously interconnected. She carries her coffee to an unoccupied table by the window and sits down. She sips the hot sweet coffee and stares out the window at the rain falling steadily on the central compound, an open space originally intended by the architects as a treed recreation area for staff and ambulant patients, but commandeered by the hospital management for use as a temporary car park. She could do with something stronger than the cappuccino. She finishes the coffee and gets up. People whose lives are seriously out of control are waiting for her. People who believe themselves marked by fate for defeat, no matter what they do. People who believe the hospital owes them something because they have set out on a path of self-destruction. Marie does her best. It is not enough.

She loves them and she hates them. They repel her. They are everything that human beings are. She longs to help them and knows there is no help for them. Their defeat is her own defeat. They tell her not to worry. Don't get upset, they say when they see she is moved to pity by their state. She will never be a real professional, a truly objective social worker like Ms Alworth. She despairs for them, her patients. They will not leave her at night when she is alone and sleepless in her bed. They are part of her problem. It has taken years for this to happen but it has happened. It is they who are her company. Her companions of the night.

Mrs Allen has seen her coming and she stands up, her mouth open, words tumbling out of the broken hole of it, gasping for breath to tell her latest tale of injury and injustice. To tell again of how unfair it all is. To ask again, Why do they all pick on me? What have I ever done to them? The neglected and abused child she has been, confused and lost still, and she nearing her fiftieth year. She looks like a skinny old woman of seventy. Marie sees a bare-kneed kid in a school yard with no big brothers and no mother to defend her, a kid who has by some strange influence of life's process become this broken woman, Mrs Brenda Allen.

Mrs Allen is ready for her at the door but the Black Cowboy doesn't look up as Marie approaches the bench but shakes his head slowly from side to side.

'How are you, John?' Marie greets him as she ushers Mrs Allen into her office.

He raises his head at the sound of his name and lifts his hand to touch the curled brim of his black cowboy hat. 'Yeah, I'm good, Miss. How youse goin?'

'I'm good too, John, thank you. I'm sorry to keep you.'

Everything is good. We are all good.

'You're right, Miss. No worries.' This cowboy of the old West resting on a bench outside a bar on Main Street, watching the horsemen and the fancy girls go by, fancy boots crossed at the ankles, big Mexican spurs resting on the dusty boards. Is this not him? But the smile fades even before he turns away, the catatonic rove of his head binding him again, his gaze turning inward. For him, she knows, the story is over. There will be no miracle. Soon enough he will be dead. Finding death at night in one of the abandoned city buildings. His case notes closed and filed. He knows it too, but attends his appointments all the same, out of habit or from some faint residual hope, or because there is nothing else to do and he knows she will be there to listen to him. They are both captives of the same dream, after all. There is nothing to be done. Marie closes the door of her office. There is no way out for her either.

Mrs Allen is sitting across the desk from Marie telling her story. It is an old story retold again and again. It is the story of this beaten woman shuffling through the ashes of her landscape looking for something, some lost thing or memory overlooked before, some small thing here or there that might restore her to herself, some shining trinket among the blackened shards that might contain the power of redemption, revisiting the familiar scene of her apocalypse, the abandoned place of her tormented past in which something of her future was revealed but she doesn't know what it was. It's here somewhere. It must be. It has to be. There is nowhere else for it to be.

While Mrs Allen's voice goes on and on, Marie's thoughts spin out into her own story, following a wider parabola of consequence than the meagre span of her patient's bitter lot, which she knows by heart. She nods in sympathy and murmurs encouragement. Beware of pity, Ms Alworth told her when she joined the unit.

Marie is thirty-seven. An only child. She was born in Chartres. Soon after her birth, Marie's mother and father moved back to Paris, taking with them Marie's nanny, Sophie. Then, on 4 July 1948, her father and Sophie set sail with her for Sydney from Marseilles.

Marie's mother did not sail with them.

Marie never saw her mother again. There were relatives in England whom she wished to see. While there she had been killed in the Chillingworth rail disaster.

Marie's father had loved his wife. There was never an outlet for his anguish.

One evening, when Marie was home from school for the holidays and they were sitting together on the verandah looking at the lights on the harbour and guessing what each light signified, she looked at her father and saw there were tears in his eyes. She got up from her chair, put her arms around him. She felt that she understood him. They were both conservative people who believed they owed society a return for their own good fortune. They were old-fashioned. They held to the beliefs and tastes of a former generation. But so did most of their friends and they did not feel out of place with their beliefs.

When she was in fourth form at Ascham, an intense and intelligent girl of fifteen, on tiptoe to claim her womanhood, eager to demand a meaningful life for herself as her birthright, their wonderful, beautiful, mystical English teacher, Miss Wendell of the long black tresses, introduced them to the poetry of Emily Dickinson. And one evening, when Marie was reading alone in the dormitory the poetry of this strange reclusive woman who never published her writings, she came on the phrase, *The craving is upon the child like a claw it cannot remove.* And there it was! A gunshot in the silence of the dormitory. The poet speaking directly to her of her own secret anguish. *Knowing* it. Knowing it. Something for which there was no normal phrase in the ordinary language of people. For a mother's love withheld. Denied. Forfeited. Lost. The poet had found the secret words. The words of fire. *The craving is upon the child like a claw it cannot remove.* Words outside the normal voice of speaking and thinking. The voice of poetry. Marie's mother's name had also been Emily. It was a moment of sudden, almost hallucinatory intensity for Marie. A life-altering moment. A secret message encoded from beyond the grave from her mother direct into her own heart; the sharp sting of poetry's truth. As she lay there on her bed in the dormitory Marie was moved by the poet's words and she loved her and hated her and she wept and could not have said why she wept. At fifteen her idealism was pure.

In that moment of poetic revelation, Marie's mother and the reclusive Emily Dickinson in her house in the little American town of Amherst spoke through each other. They were not distinguishable, one woman from the other, poet Emily and mother Emily. Their voice, their message, opening to her at last the precious site of the mystery that torments her still, it was the one voice.

The *site* of her anguish opened to her that night.

That site, which had remained unsaid till then, was spoken. The telling of the site. She repeated the precious phrase again and again: *The craving is upon the child like a claw it cannot remove.* She copied the whole poem out in her best hand in her notebook, the one with the gilt top edge.

Alone in her bed that night in the familiar dormitory, breathing the air in which was the smell of perfect friendships, and more than friendships, the faint beautiful clinging smell of love, unsleeping, in the fierce unfettered theatre of her imagination, Marie enacted the scene and re-enacted it; the young woman, her mother, beautiful, mysterious, excited at the prospect of regaining her freedom, flushed by the audacity and the danger of her solitary decision. 'You go on to Sydney, darling. I'll go to England and will follow you shortly.'

Her mother, herself. Suddenly she understood it. Not visiting relatives but leaping to freedom. Terrible and wonderful. Her mother claiming the freedom of her womanhood despite her family. Despite her child. Her precious child. Leaving her family for freedom's sake. Simply in order *to be*. And Marie wept again, but silently, and she knew she was close to her mother and she forgave her. Her mother a free woman before she died. A mother she could be proud of, and whom she might yet emulate. No longer mother and wife, but herself.

By the time the yellow Sydney dawn had begun to lighten the dormitory curtains, Marie had exhausted herself and had acquired the first signs of those dark circles under her eyes that would never leave her but would grow darker and deeper with time. That night, Marie believed, she became a woman and ceased to be a girl. It was the night she received into her understanding the gift of her mother's pure and perfect act. The night during which the possibility of the greatness of life was revealed to her and she saw that life, like poetry, might soar beyond the commonplace and be something sublime. She wrote it all in her journal. The words flowed out of her as if a spring dammed for centuries had at last burst from its confinement. Had she not found her *source*? Her voice? She decided that she, like Emily, was a poet and would live a solitary life in conversation with the gods. Solitariness would be her goal. She did not think to ask that night what the price of such solitude might be.

Well, after all, she was only fifteen then, and was overwrought and things got a bit exaggerated for her that night. Other nights followed, of course, and days. Many of them. Calm returned. Life, her day-to-day life, went on. She did not forget that night but such intensity could not be sustained. Poetry had not really *called* her after all. She wrote, to be sure, but she had always written, adding every evening to the growing hoard of journals and diaries, kept since she was seven or eight (still illustrated, but no longer with coloured pencils), the elaborate and often confused account of her imaginary relationship with her mother, the account of the progress of her soul, her dilemma and her anguish, her search for the certainty of meaning and purpose, her belief in the meaningful life. The lined notebooks filled with conversations with her mother, with her teachers, with the poets and with friends, accusations, loathing, love and longing. And those secret conversations with herself that she could not have with others. But it was all in prose these days. Everyone has a mother, after all. And whether they have met her or not, she is the only way into this life. Marie refused to be denied her mother.

Then, abruptly, on that final night of his illness, her father roused from his delirium and clasped her hands with his icy fingers to tell her, 'I did it to save you the anguish of knowing.'

'Did *what*, Dad? What did you do?'

'I never gave your mother room to move. Never. I forced her to make a choice between us or her freedom. I could have given her time to test herself. She could have tested her gifts. It was my fault. It has all been my fault. I forced her to choose. And she made her choice.'

'Dad, it's all right. Just rest.' She was confident she had already dealt with all this. Had indeed won her own woman-hood from her understanding of her mother's astonishing choice of freedom.

She heard her father say, 'Your mother didn't die.'

It was as if he shot a bird from the sky and with his blind eyes watched it fall to earth.

He sucked air into his lungs with a terrible whistling and sobbed, his mouth gaping, his blank gaze roving the blindness of his vision.

A stillness invaded Marie.

She felt age creep over her, someone gently placing a coat over her shoulders to shield her from the chill. By the side of his old cedar bed, his freezing hands gripping her own with the grip of a madman. The cold of his fever in her own blood now.

'What do you mean she didn't die?' Her voice was steady. The voice of a woman who has entered life and must bear whatever life brings to her, be it her dead child or her suddenly not-dead mother. Far off in the night a train whistle punctured the suburban calm. Screaming in her head. Outwardly she was calm. Unmoved. She felt the presence of her father's death now like another person who has waited for this moment to enter the room of her life, always the shadow at the door.

'There was no rail disaster. There's no such place as the Chillingworth cutting. I made it up to save you from the pain of her abandonment. No child should know she has been abandoned by her mother.' He removed his hands from hers and tried to sit up but hadn't the strength. 'I put her letter in one of my books. It will still be there. That's all I have kept. She sent you letters for years, for the time when you would be grown up enough to read them and to understand her. She entrusted them to me.' His shallow breath whistled and he choked on his phlegm. 'I read each one as they arrived and then burned it. Years ago they stopped coming. I don't know why. I think she really did die then or she would not have stopped writing to you. Your mother loved you.'

His words were draining her.

'I burned them all, every one except the first one, to save you the anguish of knowing you had been abandoned. To save my*self* the anguish of it. My vengeance on her. Once I'd started there was no way back. Forgive me! I thought I was being strong.' He wept like a punished child. 'I've betrayed us all.'

Marie heard herself ask, 'Could she be alive? How can I get in touch with her?'

He gestured. 'It's in a book. It's all there is.' He reached out his hand for her, searching the air, but she evaded him and stepped away from his bed.

The following morning, after the undertakers had removed her father's corpse from the house and taken it to the crema-torium—there would be no funeral—she continued her search through his books. At four in the afternoon on the fourth day she found her mother's letter folded between the pages of the Rev. J. Milne Curran's *The Geology of Sydney*, its presence discolouring a sketched diagram. She carried the letter out to the kitchen. She felt a peculiar reluctance to unfold the letter and read it. She put the letter on the kitchen table and made a cup of tea, her eyes going to the small square of blue writing paper. Next door's cat came to the window and she let it in. It jumped down from the bench and rubbed itself against her legs.

With her cup of tea Marie sat at the table in her father's house and unfolded the two sheets of her mother's letter. It was dated six months after they had left Paris for Sydney all those years ago. Her mother would have been not quite twenty-three and Marie herself almost three by then. The ink was browned, the paper dry and nearly ready to disintegrate at the edges. Her mother's hand was confident and generously rounded. The hand of an educated woman. Marie sipped the tea. Her mother. It was a moment in her life the like of which she was confident she was never going to experience again, poised on the divide between before and after. Surely she was already changed by it?

Today for the first time my journal begins 'My Dearest' because I have understood that I am not writing to myself. Can one ever really write only to oneself? When I sat down a moment ago to begin my journal entry for today, I acknowledged truthfully for the first time that it is to you that I am always speaking in this record of my thoughts and emotions, and that this is the reason I have been able to keep this daily account. For you and I there will be another way to be a mother and a daughter than the way that is laid out for us. When you are ready, your father will let you come and stay with me at my little apartment in rue Saint-Dominique and soon we shall be friends. One thing you must be forever certain of: I do not regret becoming a mother. Your life is more precious to me than my own. Before you were born I did not know such a feeling was possible.

So you will ask, How does a mother who can say these things with sincerity reach a point of such estrangement and selfishness that she abandons her child in order to pursue her own dreams? How can I expect you to understand this? To dream is the right and even the necessity of all humans. For me to dream of a life beyond my family was forbidden to me by your father. So I have changed that. I have broken that chain. Believe me when I tell you that there is no sudden leap to such a radical place, but a daily increment over time. One goes by small degrees, one step at a time, until one stands at last on the place from which one refuses to be moved. And if the other will not be moved, then there is nothing for it but to act. And one is more astonished than anyone to see it is oneself who does this. Yes, astonished. The feeling that the person who acts is not oneself but is another whom one has brought into being. The dreamer become real. The dream made flesh. Is that too much? When you are a young woman and have read all that I intend to write to you of myself and of my way through life, you will know then that my terrible decision was not the end of our love, but was its difficult, unorthodox and painful beginning.

You are never forgotten, my darling, but are with me every hour of my life. You will always be my daughter.

She read the letter again, and then again, aloud in the silent house in a voice charged with anger, almost with violence. Marie was so angry the tea she had drunk made her feel sick. The loss was incalculable. A great black gaping hole. No, she did not *understand*. Her mother was right to say she would ask how any mother could do such a thing. Too right she would ask. There was only one way to be a mother and that was to stay close to your child and nurture it and love it and be its very best friend all through your life. And if you didn't want the tie of children then don't become a mother. How obvious was it? Her mother's great leap to freedom had been at *her* expense. It was she, Marie, who had paid the price.

And yet . . . 1948. Early days, just after the war when women had learned they could come out of the house and be in the world. Had she been alone? The twenty-three-year-old. Her mother. What had she done with her life, with her extraordinary freedom? Or had she just learned to wear it like the skin of a man and done nothing special with it? Was that it? After all, did she *have* to do something special with it just because she was a woman? Or could she have it the way *they* had it?

Marie was two and half years of age when she last saw her mother but has no memory of her. Not a thing. Not one fleeting fugitive image. None of those remnant memories people talk about.

It is twenty years ago now since she sat at the kitchen table in the empty silence of her old home in Sydney, orphaned at the age of seventeen. She had hated her father for his deception, for his betrayal of what she had believed all through her childhood to be their perfect trust, their unique deep perfect trust. For years after his death she had been unable to think of him without anger, loathing him fiercely for dying the way he did and leaving her with the tattered ends of it all to deal with on her own. But of course that didn't stop her from loving him.

It just made loving him more complicated and painful. She had determined then that she would never stake everything on love. Even now, at thirty-seven, she still needs to believe her mum and dad were good people. So she keeps it all locked up inside herself. The truth. The price she was made to pay. And every now and then—in fact, often, lately—something triggers it and the whole thing opens up and swamps her once again, leaving her washed out and wanting to cry. To cry like a baby in its mother's arms.

Marie tries to stop thinking about herself and to focus on what is going on in front of her. The thing they are paying her for. But she is so very tired of the fallen state of these people she finds it nearly impossible to stay focused on them for more than a few minutes at a time. As irresistible and persistent as waves they are, a sameness about their differences that makes her forget who it is she is talking to. She has been known to confuse one for another. An awkward thing to do. Dangerous even. They are on the lookout for any lack of respect, ever watchful of their dignity, ready for a fight, which usually means nothing more hazardous than a screaming session of abuse. The same old abuse. They never think of anything new. They would be dumbstruck for punctuation without the word *fuck*. She is too used to it to care.

Mrs Allen left a while ago. The afternoon has moved on. Marie is tired now. She needs a drink. It seems to have been an extra big day. About this time of the afternoon this is the usual feeling every day. *Another* big day. Are there ever going to be small days? *Oh, what a small day I've had!* She is staring emptily at the Black Cowboy, a tight band of pain around her head, her bowels making complaining noises.

He is sitting across the desk from her talking his talk, posturing his postures, being the man he knows he is not, the broken giant, the helpless little boy. Her attention wanders from him again and she finds herself remembering Ms Alworth looking at her over her glasses with that so-hard-to-read expression in her eyes; *I really think you should consider taking the first half of next year off on half-pay.*

In her final year of social work at the university, reading the history of the idea of juvenile delinquency, Marie came across the work of the nineteenth-century French social philosopher Henri Gaillac. It was in his *Les maisons de correction* that she first encountered the idea of people addicted to running away for its own sake; people for whom to run away is not an act of necessity, people who are not escaping material or emotional neglect or deprivation or cruelty, but who do it from what Gaillac called 'a need for freedom, for carefree hours, for new emotions, which is never satisfied'. He spoke of this need to run away as 'a violent, irresistible passion: in order to abandon themselves to this pleasure they flee the pleasures they enjoy in the breast of the family'. Had her mother, she wondered, been a freedom junkie of the kind described by Gaillac? Was there a medical diagnosis, Gaillac's Syndrome?

Her mother the freedom addict was a phrase with a nice ring to it, and she didn't feel like dealing it out of the range of possibilities. In fact it remained her favourite. There are duty addicts and there are work addicts, after all, so why not freedom addicts? The rush of ridding oneself of the accumulated responsibilities and encumbrances of family life in one grand leap! My God, imagine it! There one day, gone the next. Out the door one sunny morning and never seen again by the husband or the kids. To experience this rush, however, the freedom addict must first establish the situation of responsibilities and encumbrances from which the temptation to free herself eventually becomes a compulsion too strong to resist. She has to create the conditions for it herself. And surely getting married and having a child is just about the most encumbering condition a young freedom-loving woman can create for herself. And abandoning it the most liberating.

How often did her patients stare at her and tell her, 'I just felt I had to do it,' bewildered by the mysterious source of this irresistible compulsion to do the wrong thing?

She focuses once more on the Black Cowboy. Suppose she were to stop the flow of his talk with a counter-flow of her own? Let him have the lot. The whole great dammed-up tide of her own elaborated interior life breaking over him. Let the Black Cowboy have it between the eyes! She hasn't dealt with any of it. There *is* no interior order to it. How can she ever expect anyone to know her story as she knows it herself?

Impatient suddenly, she stands up.

The Black Cowboy falls silent, his mouth open. He stares at her.

'Sorry, John, time to go.'

She manages to get a seat on the South Melbourne tram. She has bought the *Age* but can't remember a thing about what she has read the minute she folds the paper and closes her eyes. No idea. There will be plenty of time during her six months off for some of the other things she is always promising herself she will do. For one thing, she will reread *Middlemarch*. A smile touches her lips at the thought of the pleasure this will give her. She imagines herself sitting by the window in the yellow armchair downstairs in the middle of a weekday morning, slowly turning the pages of that vast and wonderful book. The joy of being a real reader again, returning to a familiar ample landscape of the imagination, returning home to the voice of Miss Wendell of the long tresses reading to them from the books she loved and taught them to love. Bringing together at last the promise of those wonderful school days. She will get back to the piano. Every day for two hours. Chopin's Études and Beethoven's Variations in E Flat and in C Major. And, of course, she will add to her bunch of Bach preludes and fugues. As many as she can manage. And she will travel. Somewhere different. Bulgaria or Turkey.

The tram crashes its way over the points at the junction of Park and Clarendon and she opens her eyes. She gets up and makes her way to the door and waits with the other passengers to get off. She steps down onto the road and walks along Park Street past the dentist's and turns into her own street. The late afternoon is hot, the sound of children playing in the Housing Commission block, the tram going on along Park Street, the cars accelerating to overtake it before it gets to the next set of lights and holds them up again.

So after the Christmas–New Year break Marie doesn't report for work at the unit but stays home. She lies in bed listening to the uncanny silence long after she would normally have left the house. Everyone but the very old, the infirm and herself have gone to work or to school. After her shower she finds she is tending to creep around the house, as if she is an intruder. All day she can't shake off the feeling of being a person who should not be there. She doesn't feel the liberty of her situation and she supposes it will take a day or two for the routine of her normal life to let go its hold. This sensation is obvious, but she hasn't expected it. In the kitchen she turns on the radio for a bit of company but the constant blather of it jangles her mood and she turns it off again.

After lunch she can't make up her mind whether her first priority is to begin reading *Middlemarch*, which she's taken down from the bookshelf in the front room and laid ready on the low table beside the yellow armchair. She stands in the front room looking at the book lying there on the low table. She steps over to the window. It is another hot day. The grass in the park is parched to the colour of dead skin.

She flexes her fingers but doesn't open the lid of the piano.

Not yet. There will be time for that. And anyway it needs dusting, and probably tuning. It will take an enormous amount of practice before she is able to play anything near well enough to give herself pleasure.

She stands looking out the front window. She decides she needs to get out of the house. She puts on a headscarf to keep off the sun and writes a shopping list, flowers to brighten up the place essential, underlined. She walks to the South Melbourne market. She is making her escape, she knows it. She can smell the summer heat coming up from the tar and the eucalypts lining the footpath. She feels better walking. There are very few people about, but there are cars and the shops are open. A few old women in black and the men sitting outside the Greek cafe. There is no reason at all not to be happy. She has forgotten that the market isn't open on Mondays. That is why everything is so quiet.

There is no other florist, so she walks on along Market Street and looks in the windows of three new shops. Not really *new* new but refurbished Victorian shopfronts scraped back and redone. They are all to do with furnishing the home. Tasteful and expensive things looking more or less as if they have come from France or Italy. Who will buy them? She stands outside the last shop before the corner of Clarendon Street looking at an old square-sided wooden bucket, from a peasant's yard somewhere in France no doubt. The bucket stands on an iron table and is filled with an enormous bunch of white daisies with rich yellow centres the colour of egg yolks. Sensing a possible sale, the woman inside the shop steps towards the door and smiles. Marie smiles back and walks on around the corner into Clarendon Street. As she passes the newsagents she sees it is 14 January. She is suddenly aware of time passing, her six months of freedom already being measured out and eaten up, her little allotment being doled out a spoonful at a time.

Astonishingly two weeks slip by and she has still done nothing.

She doesn't call up any of her friends. Most, though not quite all, are at work during the day or busy with their children, but it isn't just that. It is that she believes she has to deal with this business on her own, whatever it is. So although she is rather intimidated by her solitariness, especially around the house, she does nothing to soften her situation and make things easier for herself. Something is going on and she has to see it through alone. She wonders if she is being seriously unbalanced about it all.

Even for Melbourne the summer of 1982/3 is hot. According to the weather forecasters it is going to get hotter. Marie reads the travel section in Saturday's *Age* while she is having breakfast at a cafe in Clarendon Street. She wonders if she should buy a ticket to the cool of the northern hemisphere. They are advertising winter specials to almost every European capital. Singapore Airlines has some enticing offers to Paris. But she doesn't consider Paris. She doesn't even read the ads with the Eiffel Tower on them but lets her eyes skip over them. Paris is too troubled by family ghosts. Paris will confront her directly with questions. *Why have you never gone in search of your mother? Why has your mother never come to Australia to look for you?* If she were alive, this year her mother would be sixty.

Not at all old these days. In Paris the painful questions would arise to condemn her and nothing would stop them.

No, she will not even consider Paris. Not for a second. She orders another cappuccino and reads about the Grand Canyon.

She is still lying in bed after ten in the morning, cocooned in the cling wrap of unbroken stillness, when she realises with a little shock that it is the first day of February. The shortest month.

She gets up at once and has a shower and dresses.

Without waiting to have breakfast she hurries around to the newsagents in Clarendon Street and puts a notice in the window: FREE PIANO LESSONS FOR GENUINE BEGINNERS, STUDENTS MUST BE ACCOMPANIED BY A PARENT. She leaves her phone number and returns home. She feels quite breathless. She dusts the piano and calls the tuner. She sits at the piano and plays scales for an hour. By the time she stops playing, her wrists and the muscles of her forearms are on fire. She listens to the fabric of the house resonating, like a tall Italian belltower after the thunder of the bells. She is elated by what she has done. She has taken herself by surprise.

Then the phone rings.

Within the space of three days Marie has four students and a fifth promised. People are obviously price sensitive. The tuner comes on Tuesday; not the man she has used in the past but a new and younger man. Her first impression was that he was a not unattractive man and it pleased her to think she would see him every so often. When he is removing the front panel from the piano she says to him, 'Someone once told me it was figured walnut. Is it?' She is not just making conversation, though she is doing that as well, but really wants to know. He says bluntly, 'I don't know anything about the wood. I just tune them.' She finds his response disappointing and begins at once to think him an unintelligent man and not at all interesting. She says, 'When you've finished, come to the bottom of the stairs and give me a call.' People are disappointing. She wishes she hadn't spoken to him about the figured walnut.

He calls, 'You there, Miss?' She comes out of her bedroom onto the landing. He stands at the foot of the stairs looking up at her, his black bag of tools hanging weightily from his hand, the ropey muscles of his forearm tensed. A vast growth with a life of its own slowly ingesting him, that black bag. That's how she sees him, standing there looking up at her as she comes down, something in his eyes she doesn't like.

The tuner, she decides, is the victim of his own meagre labours, the entrails of his allotted time eaten up slowly year by year, lost to the mouth of that sagging black bag. For an instant she fears him, his brutal presence. She reaches the bottom of the stairs and counts the notes into his hand, not meeting his eyes, wherein lurks his sardonic knowing. She follows him to the front door and closes it after him.

She goes into the front room and stands at the piano and plays a few chords. She has to stoop only a little to see in the mirrored wood her fingers undo the top button of her dress. She examines the effect of her open dress in the blurry reflection; the tone of her naked skin is favoured by the lambent glow of the precious timber. She straightens and does the button up again. Was she once beautiful?

After the second lesson she decides she isn't a natural teacher. But they are getting it for nothing, so the parents can hardly complain. None of them do. Indeed she is surprised to find they are in awe of her abilities. Her students are all young children who attend primary school until three-thirty in the afternoon, except the fifth student, whom she has not yet met. For some reason his mother says she can bring the boy at two o'clock. Marie doesn't ask the woman why this is possible. She doesn't care why. She buys a notebook for each student and puts their names on the covers, otherwise she knows she is sure to forget where they have got up to in the previous lesson.

The parents (all mothers so far) perch themselves on the edge of the sofa in a state of listening during the lesson, leaning forward and jiggling a leg, gazing anxiously from her to their child. She decides parents should not be in the room during the lesson and makes this a rule. She is surprised to find the mothers all accept the rule as if they believe in her authority to make rules. Each mother seems to think her child is a genius and will be playing like Mozart within months, if not days. One asks her at the end of the first lesson, 'Has he got it do you think?' Marie is bemused by the question. 'Got what?' But the woman is talking about It, genius, a gift. 'It's not a gift,' Marie tells the woman severely. 'It's the result of years of hard work. You have to live your art.' The woman gives her a funny look and Marie feels sure she isn't going to last. She wants to say, Why the piano? Why not basketball or footy? But she doesn't. Marie doesn't mind the children—they believe in her and in themselves—but five minutes with one of the mothers drains her tolerance to zero and is exhausting. So she begins claiming the children from their mothers at the door and not letting the mothers in at the pickup either.

Marie is standing at the window, leaning to see along her street to where it joins the main road. The fifth student is due. The drift of air from the fan caresses at intervals the back of Marie's dress and might be the light touch of an intimate companion. But Marie is alone and waiting. It is a few minutes after two on the afternoon of Tuesday, 8 February 1983, and at 109.8 degrees in the old measure (43.2 in the new) it is to be the hottest February day ever recorded in Melbourne.

The boy and his mother (she assumes it will be his mother who brings him) are only a few minutes late, but they are late all the same. It makes her nervous when people are late. A car turns into Marie's street at that moment and she pulls back from the window so as not to be seen, but the car sweeps past without stopping. There is only a driver. Then another car does the same thing. After that the street is empty and quiet again, as it invariably is at this time of a Tuesday afternoon.

Marie looks out at the terrible day. It seems to her the sun has not moved for hours but has hung there, stationary, at the highest point of the sky, refusing to relent, refusing to begin its descent towards the horizon. The sun god in revolt against humankind and their earthly endurance. Enough is enough! The laws of nature refuted. The eternal web of reality unfashioned. From Marie's downstairs front room window the horizon is in fact the flat roof of the Housing Commission tower block that rises behind the row of Victorian terrace houses on the other side of the park. The day is still and the city unnaturally quiet. Mesmerised by the stillness and the heat, Marie stares out at the day as if she expects the foretold hour when the first crack will appear and creation will begin to disassemble: trees without leaves, earth turned to dust, the sovereign sky a molten furnace in which no bird can live. Her memory presents her at this moment with an image of falling birds. Small black things falling against a malevolent yellow sky. A newsreel image she saw as a girl of the British atomic tests at Maralinga in the desert. The wind that passed over the watchers there, snatching at their military caps, and they not knowing themselves changed by its touch.

She feels sorry for the poor European poplars out there in the park, unshielded from the nuclear blast of the sun's rays, their leaves grey and withered, curled in upon themselves like beaten men. Those sad trees are not made to withstand this sort of exile but are made for the cool tonalities of Corot's landscapes. Oddly, right at this minute, staring out at the blistering day, she feels happy. She goes on with her Corot image. A grey drift of misty rain on a deliciously chilly northern autumn day, the deep greens of shade beneath the overhanging branches where they form a bower by the bank of a river. She insists on the image, and manages to steady it before her mind for a few more precious seconds before it too withers and withdraws, leaving the comfortless street and the dusty park and the blasted trees in the awful heat of this never-ending February day.

Despite the regular sweep of the fan, sweat is beaded on her skin. Droplets course down her neck from under her hair into the top of her stylish blue and white linen dress. She fingers the wetness on her skin where the sweat tickles and she closes her eyes. Perhaps the boy and his mother aren't coming after all. She can hardly blame them if they don't turn up on a day like this. But all the same she doesn't like it. His heat limit, or his mother's, she supposes, has been reached. She opens her eyes.

Across the road a man is sitting on the only bench in the small triangle of park reading his newspaper, the tabloid square of grey-white opening and closing as he turns the pages and folds them back, as if he is semaphoring a message to her. Is it an SOS? He is without a hat and is wearing only a singlet and shorts, his bald head glowing like a molten ingot. His dog (she supposes it is his dog), a low thickset white animal with a naked pink face and a swinging pizzle sac, is doing the rounds of the trees, snuffling at the base of each trunk then turning aside and lifting its leg, a look of dumb obscene bliss on its flat ugly face. She hates looking at the dog but can't take her eyes from it. When the dog squats to unload its bowels, its goggle eyes bugging with rapture, its jowls trembling, Marie makes a small dismayed sound and switches her attention abruptly to the burning man. She has never seen the man before. Or perhaps she has seen him but does not remember ever having seen him. She would remember if she had seen his dog. The pair of them are evidently members of a species that come into the open only when it is too hot for ordinary humans to endure. It occurs to her then that it is the likes of these two who will be not the burnt ones but the survivors when the last bird falls from the sky. A heartbreaking event they will not notice.

She turns away from the window, crosses the room and lifts the lid of the piano. It is a tall instrument made in the workshops of Carl Rönisch of Dresden in the first decade of the twentieth century. The instrument was chosen for her by her music teacher. She has owned the piano all her life. Its top is level with her breastbone. She examines her reflection in the front panel, seeing there a woman in the mysterious lamplight of a romantic interior, the edges of her form softened, the contours suggestively broken and dispersed, the tones blending her into the tapestry-like background of the room, the picture on the wall behind her, the motley of the tall bookcase beside the fan in the corner, a highlight from the window catching the deep yellow fabric of the armchair by the fireplace, the dark cavern of the Victorian grate beside the chair.

It is the figure of an anonymous woman that she sees in this softened world. A woman living happily in an indeterminate other time and place than her own, a character from Chekhov, an inaccessible time and place that is both timeless and place-less and forever, the place of *Middlemarch*, the place of novels she has loved, movies she has loved, stories she has read and not forgotten, the imaginary place of Emily Dickinson's claw in the flesh. Why can that place never be *here*?

There is the sound of a car door being slammed outside, then another, and a woman's voice. Marie walks out of the room, leaving the door open, and along the passage to the front door. She waits a breath or two after the bell rings, composing herself, then she opens the front door.

The woman is young. Perhaps twenty-five. She is slim and looks fit and as if she takes good care of herself. She is wearing a soft grey shirt with breast pockets, a fine wool and cotton mix of some kind, the top three buttons undone. Narrow shoulders and small pointed breasts. No bra. And blue jeans. Indian sandals on her tanned feet. She is without makeup. Her skin is clear and fresh and lightly browned. She is a homemade loaf. She smells fresh. The pupils of her eyes are a deep velvety brown, their expression kindly and concerned. She is hoping to be liked by the new piano teacher. The woman holds out her hand. 'Hi, I'm Anne. We're not late, are we? I hate it when people are late.'

Marie takes the young woman's hand lightly in her own.

'This is our Maurice. He's seven. Seven's not too young, is it?'

She looks at the boy. He is carrying something called *Pianoforte Book 1*. He holds it tucked tightly under his arm. Marie sees that he is an old barrister carrying a slim and familiar brief. A studious little chap from a back lane in Dickens. She sees indeed that he is an ancient little boy and she is amused, and feels for him a fear she can attribute to no cause. His dark expectant gaze on her face is grave and serious, a composure in him she envies. In his eyes she sees that the piano, after all, is his idea and not his mother's.

Marie does not resist the impulse to take his hand in her own. He willingly permits her to lead him along the passage and into the room with the piano. She forgets to bar his mother, who follows. And isn't all this exactly as he has dreamed it would be with his new piano teacher today? Old age, she knows, is not encased in the passage of the years but is embraced by experiences that are private and unacknowledged, ineradicable; the hidden life of the soul, she might have called it had she believed enough in souls just then. She knows it, just as the young soldier who sees death knows and is suddenly old. Not everyone is destined to experience the antique in themselves. For many it will pass undetected. The boy has it.

They stand side by side, she and the boy, holding hands in front of her beloved Rönisch. 'It was my grandfather's,' she says, and cannot imagine why she has invented this lie, except perhaps in order to have a sense of family.

'It's taller than ours,' the doomed boy offers.

'They don't make them like this anymore.' She would tell him that the Dresden factory where it was made no longer exists but she doesn't. She reaches with her free right hand and caresses the precious veneer. 'I play Bach, but Herr Rönisch is not a Bach piano. Bach loves a bright tremulous sound. Herr Rönisch is a Beethoven piano. His voice is enormous. It is rich and warm and is all the grand and mysterious things that come after Bach. It is not in my nature to play him as he should be played. Perhaps you will one day give him the chance to become the storm in the mountains again, as my grandfather used to do.' She is aware of having begun a lie that she must persist with or confess to now, before it is too late, the lie that gives her beloved old music teacher's place in her life to an imaginary grandfather. Robert would have been amused.

She is wasting time. The boy's warm hand in her own hand is close and still against her—a mouse safely home in its nest. His trust is palpable. The throb of his pulse. The boy's presence is calming and she cannot deny to herself the deep pleasure of his handclasp. He has placed himself in her care.

'Herr Rönisch sulks when I play Bach,' she says and laughs.

'You love him,' the boy says, 'because he was your grandfather's.' His hand moves in hers.

Impossible now to disillusion him with the truth. Should they be friends for twenty years, it is already too late to undo her lie. The imaginary grandfather already has a life with the boy. She will defend its truth. Her father's lie was precious to him too. Can nothing remain simply itself? Does fiction always triumph over truth?

She is suddenly happy and wants the moment to go on and never end. She loves the boy. Their little Maurice. *Her* Maurice.

She might have said his hand nuzzles in hers, but it isn't quite that. *Where there is hatred, let me bring you love.* 'I play Schubert too. Schubert always cheers him up. Schubert used to see the great Herr Beethoven in his local coffee shop, but Schubert was too shy to approach his hero and so they never met. In that situation I would be like Schubert too. My father called it the woman's disease—my modesty, he meant—and was impatient with it. But it is not only women who feel like that. Men feel it too. Artists feel it. People who believe in something greater than themselves feel it.' She stops herself from going on and looks down at him, allowing the boy his modesty.

'Did you love your father?' the boy asks. His question is quiet, sudden, impeccable. He is looking up at her as if, were she to say, 'No, I hated my father,' he would not be perturbed or surprised but would simply know from that time on that some people hate their fathers. Does he have a father himself?

She is moved and grateful for the wisdom of his innocence. 'Oh, yes. I did. Very much.' The boy doesn't ask her about her mother. Her friendship with her father was her best truth for so long. It was the best truth anyone had ever known. Then, at the end, the other truth came out of him. He kept the other truth to himself until his last day, as if it had belonged only to himself and had not been hers too. Until the despair of his dying drew it out of him. His tortured cry of regret as he went over the edge into death everlasting. 'Yes,' she says, and feels in her chest a stirring of the anger against her father she felt then for his betrayal of their perfect trust. The bitterness that is not dead in her soul but which has resisted decay, attendant upon its resolution in an action as yet unconceived by her, as yet undreamed, an action she has yet to imagine. 'I loved him and he loved me. I'll play for you,' she says. And such is the slippage between words and meanings, to the boy's ear his new teacher might have said, 'I'll pray for you.' He waits beside her while she settles herself on the stool.

She turns to him, her eyes on a level with his eyes now. 'Schubert's Impromptu No. 4 in A-flat major. You will hear Schubert's modesty too. My father was mistaken when he called modesty the woman's disease.' She does not require the music. The piece is an old friend. It lives whole in her memory. She is unafraid of not playing it well for the boy. She is glad she has had the piano tuned. She will never betray this instrument. Her teacher Robert sits at her shoulder. She closes her eyes and plays.

While the last note is fading into the sublime silence which the music has carved out, like a perfect negative shape in an old-master painting, even before Marie opens her eyes, the boy's mother says, 'Oh, that was so beautiful,' and she gives two uncertain little claps.

Marie has forgotten the boy's mother is with them.

She draws breath and says, 'We should begin your lesson, Maurice.'

The boy does not applaud her but stands entranced, himself his own wooden effigy. An odd little person.

Marie sits there, seeing the boy has joined her now in her secret place within the reflected room, standing beside her deep within the enchanted landscape of the disfigured walnut.

'I can see us in the piano,' he says.

Has she ever been so happy?

Her own first piano lesson at this boy's age; Robert, her teacher, a tall deep-chested Viennese, his long hair flinging out of his great round skull in every direction, falling over his eyes as he plays. A beautiful man, he tosses his hair back like

117

a horse tossing its shining mane, vigorous and impatient with the uncomprehending world around him. At that first lesson he sat at his princely black Steinway and played for himself Bach's first prelude.

When the brief simplicity of the prelude had been brought to its end, a tremor remained in Robert's hands, poised above the keyboard like a pair of skylarks trembling on air, and for an instant she expected him to continue. But he stood up, abruptly and with a kind of violence in his action, and stepped away from the piano, as if this sudden physical wrench was needed to disengage himself from the charm of the instrument. According to Robert, Bach's Prelude and Fugue in C Major was the single greatest moment in the entire history of music. Marie believed him. She believed everything Robert said. She had never before encountered such an authority as his. She still believes him now, today, here at her piano with Maurice standing beside her, the pair of them mirrored in the figured walnut of the Rönisch and dear, dear Robert dead years and years ago.

Marie turns to Maurice. 'Now I'll play Bach for you.'

Her memory of her first lesson is that Robert played for her on that occasion (when she was seven) without saying anything. Not a word. Now here she is talking when talk isn't needed, failing to trust to the moment and to the boy's intelligence. 'This is the simplest and most beautiful work ever written for the piano. Everything that comes after it is foreshadowed in it in some way, either in a hidden way or in a manner to celebrate it. But of course it wasn't written for this great masculine instrument, but for a lovely feminine clavichord.'

She plays the prelude. It lasts barely three minutes. Three minutes of eternity.

She turns to the boy and doesn't wipe away her tears.

'You cry when you're happy,' he says. 'Like Mum.' He looks to his mother, who steps forward and touches him.

Marie says, 'There's only one rule for us to follow. We must love what we do. That will be our one rule. And if ever you or I forget it, we must promise to remind the other of it. Let's call it the rule of the first prelude, shall we?'

'The rule of the first prelude,' the boy echoes, and he smiles, knowing he is embarked now and has learned something from this strange woman, though if his mother were to ask him later in the car what it is he has learned he would not be able to tell her. He has already begun to bestow his love on this woman, too, without knowing it.

There is a sudden noise outside in the street. Marie stands and goes to the window and looks out. Something has fallen.

Rising for thousands of feet above the roof of the Housing Commission tower a deep red cloud approaches, its leading edge boiling with energy against the hard blue of the sky.

Anne comes and stands at Marie's shoulder, the boy beside her, the mother's arm around the boy's shoulders.

'God! What is that?' Anne says.

The man on the park bench has his back to the approaching cloud. He is struggling to fold his newspaper against the snapping and sucking of the wind. The wind is too strong and the man lets his paper go with a flinging gesture of anger, as if to say, Well fuck off then! The white pages fly like maddened birds into the air, the dog chasing after them, barking and leaping.

'Is it smoke?' Anne says.

An image of the young woman has come into Marie's mind suddenly. She stepped out of her office that day thinking of something and the girl was lying on her back in the corridor with her throat gaping, a terrible smile of triumph and despair on her stricken features, the bread knife still clutched in her left hand, as if she clutched her life still, the vast pool of blood a cloak flowing out from her small girlish shoulders. She had seemed to Marie not real but an actor in a tragic role in a school play. Then the truth of it came, like this great red cloud, and there was nothing to do but watch.

The cloud reaches the edge of the sun and the day suddenly goes as dark as evening. The poplars are being whipped and bent by the wind, leaves and twigs, and bits of rubbish rattle against the window. The light of the world after the apocalypse. Why is it, Marie wonders, that all stories of the future are cast in the ash and gloom of a destroyed civilisation? The wind strikes the house then with the force of a blast. The man and his dog have gone. The air is now so thick with the whirling red dust that she can hardly see the terrace of houses on the other side of the park. The wind roaring against the house, shaking it. The Housing Commission block is a black tower rising to fantastic heights, its upper storeys lost in the swirling cloud. Marie expects to see a shaft of light driving down through the tormented sky as it does in old paintings, but there is no shaft of light, only the thickening darkness of the dust cloud as it roars across the city.

Marie says, 'It's a dust storm. That's all it is.'

Anne touches the sleeve of Marie's dress. 'We should move away from the window.'

Marie hopes secretly, perversely, that this is the beginning of something irresistible and vast beyond imagination or experience. Something so powerful it will sweep away everything familiar, until beyond the window there is only the landscape of the apocalypse predicted by the writers. She wonders if she has expected it. Perhaps everyone has expected it. Perhaps the predictions are all true. She hopes to see the beginning of the fire through the thick brown gloom of the astonishing day, the roaring of flames through the thunder of the hurricane wind, great tongues of flame bellowing and devouring. There will be no stopping a fire in this wind. She wants to stand outside and hold up her face and look into the obliterating Martian storm and know that this is the end of everything. She can feel the grit between her teeth; fierce eddies of red dust from the parched hinterland spin in the corners of the window. A long branch detaches from one of the thrashing poplars and falls across the bench where the man was sitting reading his paper. In the city there will be few survivors among the black ruins when the storm has passed, the red dust settled like dead snow over the silent streets. And in a wonderful way she knows it won't matter. None of it. The beautiful young woman cut her throat and tossed her young life away with that terrible fierce smile of impossible dismay that Marie will never forget so long as she lives. She covers her face with her hands and weeps.

2014

On Writing *Landscape of Farewell*

Landscape of Farewell is a celebration of friendship between two men of my own generation. The novel speaks of the shadow of the past they have each lived with in silence for the whole of their lives. It is the story of how their friendship empowers them to penetrate that silence and to give voice to it.

I first heard the story of the Cullin-la-Ringo massacre when I was a boy of sixteen and was newly arrived in Australia from England. I was working in outback Queensland as a stockman on Goathlands Station in the beautiful valley of Coona Creek, south of the Central Highlands town of Springsure, not far from Cullin-la-Ringo Station, where the massacre of nineteen white settlers by the local Aborigines took place on a lovely summer morning in 1861. Over the years since then I often wondered how I might write the story of that massacre without setting it in an historical reconstruction of the times in which it took place, when European pioneers were first penetrating that country with their vast flocks of sheep and dispossessing

A cave high in the escarpment, 1954

the local Indigenous people of their traditional homelands, which until that time they had enjoyed without challenge since before the beginning of time.

My inclination has always been to write of my own times, or at least the times of my family and friends. The idea of writing about Cullin-la-Ringo, however, continued to pester me. When I was in Hamburg in the autumn of 2004 at the invitation of the Gesellschaft für Australienstudien (the German Association for Australian Studies), I met and became friends with Dr Anita Heiss, one of Australia's foremost Indigenous writers and intellectuals. Anita was teaching Indigenous Studies at UTS at the time and told me of her admiration for my novel *Journey to the Stone Country*, a story also set in North Queensland and which dealt with a profound reconciliation of the past that had been effected by two friends of mine, one a Queensland Murri and the other a descendant of one of the white settlers who had dispossessed the Aborigines of their country in the 1860s. These two people were, of course, familiar with the Cullin-la-Ringo massacre, the white woman's father even having owned for a time a section of the original run on which the massacre took place. I told Anita about this web of connections and she encouraged me to write about it. Although I'm certain Anita was unaware of it, I felt that her enthusiasm was a green light to my desire to write this book. So it was in Hamburg that I first began to imaginatively piece the story together.

In Hamburg I also met and made friends with a number of German academics, most of whom were young people of my children's generation, but a few of whom, especially the professors, were of my own generation, men and women born just before the Second World War, as I was, and who had lived through it and could remember it. I was able to speak openly with the young academics about the conflict in Australia between the European settlers and the Indigenous people and its unresolved legacy of shame, guilt, denial and dispossession in our contemporary society.

In return, these young Germans were keen to talk to me about their feelings about the Nazi regime, which their grandparents and parents had lived through. For these young people, the Nazi period was obviously a source of enormous curiosity, and they were anxious to know the whole truth of their families' participation in those events. Many had never raised the issue with their own parents, who, they explained, still suffered from a terrible sense of guilt and shame by association with the horrifying deeds of their parents' generation. Those one or two who had begun to question their fathers spoke to me with emotion about the conversations they'd had. My own father fought with the King's Own Scottish Borderers in northern France against the last desperate divisions of the SS, who defended themselves to the bitter end around the city of Caen. My father was wounded physically and emotionally by those events, and our lives were changed by them forever. I felt a direct sense of association, and even of kinship, with the parents of these young people.

When I tried to talk about their fathers' involvement in the war to Germans of my own age—the sons and daughters of those who fought for the Third Reich—I found them reluctant to engage. When I pressed them, a few even began to articulate a kind of wild, nervous and historical defence of what had happened. I realised that the reactions of the two generations to the war were deeply divided, and I began to see, too, that the depth of silence in Germany about the Nazi period among my own generation was akin to the depth of our silence in Australia about the Stolen Generations.

I have listened to intelligent and well-informed Australians of great moral probity make the claim that they did not know about the Stolen Generations until the publication in April 1997 of *Bringing Them Home: Report of the National Inquiry into the Separation of Aboriginal and Torres Strait Islander Children from Their Families*. When we consider the vast army of lawyers, government officials, legislators and administrators, and the families and acquaintances of all those thousands of people involved in the active policy of stealing Aboriginal children from their parents over a period of seventy years— indeed, until well into the 1960s—it makes the claim 'I didn't know about it' implausible.

Deep silence of this kind—a feeling that we don't know about something when the evidence for it has been all around us—is a psychic and cultural phenomenon common to the experience of many individuals and countries. It is. To be in denial in this way about historical and family trauma is a well-known psychological condition among the perpetrators of the trauma and their victims. There was an incident in my own childhood about which we, as a family, never spoke, and when I tried to get my father to talk to me about it when he was an old man he wept and could not speak. So I knew about deep silence and the way we use it to cover our sins. And I knew how it can warp and disfigure lives. I knew how difficult it is for us to say, 'I knew and yet I did nothing,' and how much easier it is for us to say, 'I didn't know.'

I was sitting one afternoon reading in my vast, half-empty room in the hotel in Schlüterstrasse in Hamburg, looking out of the enormous bay window at the horse chestnut trees, which were just turning towards autumn, when I began to think about the Cullin-la-Ringo massacre and how its historical relationship to my Murri friends in Queensland was of a similar order, but a further generation removed, to the relationship of Germans of my own generation and the events of the Second World War.

I am one of those who believes the Holocaust to be unique, and that there are no comparisons to it in history. The Holocaust is not my sacred ground and I was never going to write about it. It was not the inspiration for this book, but nevertheless it always stood behind me, as it stands behind my generation and the generation of my parents, a great dark mass that will remain with us until the end. The shock of the Holocaust still poses for us the biggest question about the nature of humanity and ourselves, and we know there will never be an answer to this question that will satisfy us, except if we are prepared to concede that humanity is at heart a pack of wolves, as my friend Jacob Rosenberg said at our last meeting before he died. Jacob was a survivor of Auschwitz. There is nothing we can compare to the Holocaust that will make either moral or emotional sense to us. The Holocaust is so terrible it reaches way beyond us and within us and we will never be rid of it. We will always doubt the goodness of humanity and the worthiness of the human project because of it. When Hilary McPhee writes, referring to *Landscape of Farewell*, 'Massacre is the blockage in the Australian imagination, in our sense of ourselves in this place . . .' what I hear is, 'Massacre is the blockage in the human imagination, in our sense of ourselves in this place.'

My fiction of the retired German professor of history Max Otto writing his own fictional account of the massacre at Cullin-la-Ringo is a celebration of my real-life experience of writing my first published short story, 'Comrade Pawel'. From 1968 to 1973 I lived alone on fifteen hundred acres in the Araluen Valley in New South Wales. My closest friend at that time was Max Blatt. Max was older than me; a highly educated and deeply humane man, he was a German Jew from Upper Silesia who had barely survived torture by the Nazis.

Max used to visit me regularly at Araluen from Melbourne and we would smoke our cigarettes and sit by the open fire and talk far into the nights. At weekends friends often came down from Canberra and joined us—journalists, academics and, in those days before Whitlam's triumph, out-of-office Labor politicians. We sat around the big old table in the kitchen and drank red wine and ate salami and discussed the issues of the day and the woes of the world. After one of these evenings, during which the discussion had been about anti-Semitism, and when the guests had all driven back to Canberra, Max and I were sitting alone in front of the fire having a final cup of tea before turning in. Max had said nothing during the earlier discussion. He turned to me now and said, 'Would you like to know what anti-Semitism is?' He then told me, in a few sentences, the story of how a Polish comrade had first saved his life then turned on him for being a Jew.

Earlier that weekend Max had finished reading a draft of a novel I was writing and, on finishing it, had thrown it down on the table in disgust, saying, 'Why don't you write about something you love!' I loved Max and I recognised the enormous value in the truth of what he had said to me as a writer. That night I wrote my imaginary re-enactment of the story he had told me about the comrade who had first saved him then betrayed him. I called the story 'Comrade Pawel'. In the morning I gave it to Max to read. He read, as he always read (and as he listened to music), without saying a word and without giving away his feelings. When he finished he looked at me and I saw that he was moved. He said, 'You could have been there.' It was the moment when I first began to believe I could write and from that moment on I have always written about what I love. When Dougald says to Max Otto after he has read Max's fiction, Massacre, in *Landscape of Farewell*, 'You could have been there,' it is for me the expression of one of the most important moments in my life and is a private tribute to my friend and mentor Max Blatt.

So, even there, the connection is made. But it is a hidden connection. A connection that works in the soul and not in the lyrics of the song. It is surely the test of the authenticity of all serious literature that the one who knows intimately the subject of the work feels, as he or she reads it, that the author could have been there too.

It is a great privilege, and an even greater responsibility, to have the freedom of the artist to make it up. The result of what exactly one makes up, however, can never be gratuitous or haphazard, but must be, so I fervently believe, authentic to the moment and to the lives and experiences of the characters. The novel is not just, or merely, entertainment, but is also responsible for reflecting with accuracy the temper of the age in which it is written. If the people one writes about cannot recognise themselves in one's work, then the work fails, no matter how successful it might be commercially. All my novels have been written because I believe in the moral force of the human imagination, and am convinced that art can play its part in the conceptual work we need if we are to understand ourselves. That is what I strive to do. Whether or not I succeed is measured for me in the response to my work of those I write about.

For Australians of my generation some things are inescapable. They pervade our emotions, our attitudes and the way we experience art and life. The Holocaust is one of these things, and the confusion of childhood feelings of guilt and shame that we associate with it will never leave us. Another is the terrible price Australian Indigenous people have been required to pay for the prosperity and the opportunities enjoyed by people such as myself. As a novelist, it is not possible for me to write as if these things are not part of my life, embedded deeply in my experience and my psyche. I believe it to be at least part of the job of novelists to bear witness to the emotional and moral questions that haunt our lives, and to deal with the consequences for us of there being no resolution, nor any redemption, from questions such as the ones I have mentioned here.

So I write about what I love. But as my friend Max Blatt first taught me all those years ago with the story of his 'comrade' Pawel, human love can be a terrible thing as well as something of infinite beauty. I am not a polemicist, but write of the intimate in our lives. It would shame me to remain silent, however, about those questions that make me doubt my faith in the decency of humanity and the civilising project in which we like to believe ourselves to be involved, a belief that encourages in us the dangerous and comforting illusion that we have made moral progress, and which encourages us to believe the lie of those who say, *It can never happen again.*

2008

EXCERPT FROM

Landscape of Farewell

The touch of Dougald's hand to my shoulder startled me and I straightened and stared at him. He withdrew his hand from my sweating skin and stood looking at me. My chest heaved and the sweat cascaded down my face, the reaping hook gripped in my hand as if it were the weapon of a berserker. He held my journal and looked at me. The air thickened in my throat and a terrible prickling dryness threatened to choke me.

With a solemn and grave astonishment, he said, 'You could have been there, Max.'

Joy and relief swept through me—a little tsunami it was. And I wanted to repeat his words aloud—I *heard* them repeated aloud in my head. 'Oh, you like it then?' I said, my tone surprisingly conversational. A rush of wellbeing raced through my blood.

He stepped up to me and embraced me and held me strongly against his body, pinioning my arms to my sides. The point of the reaping hook was digging into my leg.

He released me and stepped away. 'Thank you,' he said.

I saw that he was greatly moved by what I had done for him. I wiped at the wet hairs sticking to my face and grinned at him foolishly. 'I'm glad you like it,' I said. 'So, it's okay then? That's good. I'm glad.'

'Oh yes, old mate,' he said, and he laid his open hand on the cover of my journal. 'It's all here.'

I said, 'Your approval means a great deal to me. I was afraid you might be offended by it.'

He smiled and reached out to put his hand on my shoulder and gave me a small shake, as if he forgave my foolishness and uncertainty. 'As soon as that ankle of yours is up to it, we'll take a drive down there to my country and pay the old Gnapun a visit.'

I said carefully, 'But of course he is no longer with us.'

'Gnapun's still with us, old mate.' He brandished my journal. 'His story's not over yet. We'll go up to that cave of his in the escarpment.' He was almost jubilant. Something real had happened. He had his wish. His precious story was preserved.

'Will you be able to find your way there?' I said. 'I mean, after all this time?'

He touched his chest with the tips of his fingers, just the way I had imagined Gnapun touching himself when he told the leader of the strangers his name. 'There's a map of my country in here.'

2007

Australia Today

There was a time when you needed to be a convicted felon to get a permit to enter Australia on any kind of long-term basis. Being a prison guard was another occupation that would qualify. Now that genealogy is all the rage, Australians are delighted to find a convict in their ancestral family mix, or even better an Indigenous forebear. There have been countless waves of immigration since the days of transportation, each contributing its own peculiar enrichment to what we know today as our distinctive Australian culture. As my friend Frank Budby, a Barada Elder, says whenever he hears people speak of the dispossession, 'The story's not over yet, old mate.' And of course Frank's right. The story of the making of Australia's culture is an ongoing process, each generation encountering and creating change, some of which sticks to the ribs of the country and a great deal that looks good for a minute or two then falls away.

Ridiculously, when you think of it, I've always prided myself not on being a sixth-generation Australian but on being an exemplary outsider. I've even been called an outsider by native-born white Australians: an outsider, a foreigner, a low-profile ten-pound Pom, and various other amusing and well-meant little jibes from a time now long past. The currency of Australia's contemporary culture struggles to bear these terms with any sense of authenticity. They are part of the detritus that is falling away and losing its meaning as we experience the realities of a fast-moving digital world that redesigns itself overnight. My own claim to being an exemplary outsider, which for some existential reason I thought was a wonderful thing for a writer to be, was itself knocked on the head recently when my sister sent me the results of her Ancestry.com researches. Ancestry was something I had never taken any interest in. My sister said in her letter, *This will get your interest, Al!* It did. I learned that a great-great-great-aunt of mine was married in Castlemaine in 1870 and proceeded to produce a generation of Millers. This town where I live is now crawling with Millers and Millars. So it turned out that by sneaking away from the metropolis thirteen years ago to live the perfect life of the outsider in Castlemaine I'd really only been coming home.

If we live long enough, everything we learned when we were children is reversed and there comes a time when instead of knowing everything, as our wise elders once did, we know almost nothing at all and must rely on our children for accurate information about our own society and how it works. I will make only one prediction about the future—for we all know that, no matter how tempting it is, predicting the future is a fool's game. My one prediction is that Australia tomorrow will not be the Australia of today, any more than the Australia of today is the same as that old white Australia of yesterday. If we hang on to our steady old verities we end up talking to ourselves and a few stodgy old mates just like ourselves and no one else, because everyone else has moved on. Friends visiting me from overseas often ask me if the Aborigines are ever going to make a comeback. My answer is, Go north, young woman, and see for yourself. The Aboriginal comeback is well underway and it is only a matter of a generation at most before Aborigines are in control of the north the way the Native Americans are in control of the beautiful city of Santa Fe.

The economic historians tell me we've had twenty years of a consistent increase in the net wealth of individuals in this country and that this is a record that makes us the leading country in the world for consistent net increase of wealth. Which all means, I suppose, that we are, or most of us are, worth a lot more today in real terms than we were twenty years ago. We are rich, it seems, by any world standard. Once upon a time, in fact a good deal more than twenty years ago, when we were a lot less rich than we are today, we threw open our borders to thousands of Vietnamese and Cambodian people who were seeking refuge from tyrannies. Although we were poorer in those days, we nevertheless seemed to feel we had enough to share around. And no one today, looking at the cultural enrichment that followed from this act of neighbourly largesse, would suggest we were mistaken in making these people welcome among us back then; people who have, of course, since then become 'us'. That arrival of thousands of Asian people into Australia turned out to be one of the great modern movements of immigration into this country, a movement from which they and their descendants, and this country as a whole, are still reaping the benefits. It was cultural change on a grand scale.

It was a good thing to do and we did it well back then. There wasn't a lot of opposition to it. We felt some responsibility for those people and their needs. My dear friend Jacob Rosenberg, a hero of our time and a great Australian writer, was himself, along with his darling wife, Esther, a refugee from tyranny when he first found a home and a welcome here—to have called him a foreigner would have been to insult him. Jacob always remembered the generosity of Australians, the openness and the comradely spirit of the people he met and who made him welcome. And Jacob and Esther often said they had never encountered any sign of anti-Semitism in this country. This was something that made us all feel proud to be Australians. And our pride in this, I believe, was justified. Thinking about such things, and remembering the extraordinary openness and generosity of people to me when I arrived here alone as a boy of sixteen, always made me feel that in choosing to spend my life doing my best to make a contribution to the culture of this country I had chosen a good life that was worth something. Whenever I received an award for my writing which in its citation contained the words *For an outstanding contribution to Australian cultural life* I felt confirmed in the rightness of my decision to commit my life to this ongoing story of Australia's immigrant culture, and I was happy to know myself a part of it.

When I saw Kevin Rudd on the television and heard him say, in the bitter tone he invoked on that occasion, words to the effect that refugees who sought sanctuary here by boat would never set foot on Australian soil but would be banished to a prison camp in a country that had no tradition of dealing with immigrants or refugees, and when no one resigned from the Labor Party in protest at this, I wanted to go into a state of denial. I didn't want to deal with it but wanted to go on as I had been, believing in the generosity of this rich country towards those who over the past two centuries have sought refuge here. I am still trying to go on believing in what was once our genuine acceptance of a common humanity with those in need of our protection and care, a great Australian quality if ever there was one. Surely, I tell myself, there has been a misunderstanding. Surely Australians are still the generous people I once knew. I want to believe we will turn around and admit our mistake and be big enough to offer a gracious apology and go ahead and build centres here in our own country, as we once did for migrants from the Baltic countries and other far-flung places from which they had fled cruel regimes. Surely we will find the decency to deal with the problem of refugees arriving here by boat in our own country. Surely we can't go on deciding not who comes to Australia, but who goes to Manus Island. It is a Guantanamo solution and we all know it is immoral and deeply un-Australian in its meanness. A great irony in this situation is, of course, that Afghans were some of the earliest successful settlers in this country.

But does all this really concern you and me? I mean, we're a rich country, so can't we just enjoy our good fortune and get on with our beautiful lives without castigating ourselves over the fate of the poor folk we've sent off to Manus Island and other concentration camps? I mean, clearly they made the wrong decision when they gave their money to the smugglers and stepped on board those leaky old boats. Is it our fault they did that? Why spoil such beautiful beach weather with all this soul-searching and questioning of where we stand morally today as a nation compared to where we once stood, in those good old days when we made refugees from tyranny welcome among us no matter how they got here? Or is that too much of a golden age myth? Were we really ever like that, or are we just kidding ourselves? I hope we were really like that, and I hope we can be like that again. No, I *believe* we can be again. I have to believe it. I've seen cultural change here and I'm ready for some more. I'm ready to give up a lot of things and let them slip into the past but I'm not ready yet to give up that great old idea of Australians as a humane and generous people. I've given my life and my best endeavours to the cultural realities of this country and I want to go on seeing myself as part of that story, the story Frank Budby tells us is not over yet. And, who knows, maybe one of these days some Afghan refugee will discover a great-great-great-aunt who was married here back in 1870 and who mothered a brood of little Aussies way back then. What a homecoming that would be. For all of us.

2014

The Writer's Secret

I was driving my daughter home from school one afternoon when she broke a silence that had lasted for several minutes. 'I'm good at writing stories,' she said, 'but only if someone gives me a beginning. If someone gives me a beginning I can easily write a middle and an end.' She turned to me. 'Give me a beginning, Dad, and I'll tell you a story.' I replied without a moment's hesitation, 'Better than that, darling, I'll tell you the writer's secret—then you'll be able to find your own beginnings.' When I didn't tell her at once but concentrated on my driving she demanded impatiently, 'Well, what's the secret then?' My daughter is nine, and I knew that at her age children sometimes reject angrily and out of hand anything that does not make sense to them at once. I was hesitating because I felt I'd spoken rashly and without giving enough thought to the consequences of what I was promising her. I said, 'The secret is very simple, but you may not understand it at once. Even though it's simple, not everybody understands the writer's secret straight away. It took me many years before I understood it.' She regarded me thoughtfully for some time. 'If it's so simple, why did it take you a long time to understand it?' I heard the disappointment in her voice at learning that her father was not, after all, as bright as she had thought. I fell silent, pretending I needed to give my full attention to the traffic. But I was thinking of Primo Levi's beautiful sad book, *The Periodic Table*, in which, in the section entitled 'Nitrogen', he points out to us that the most simple structures, whether in architecture or in chemistry, are also the most durable, the most stable and, to human eyes, the most beautiful. I knew that Levi's observation held true also for writing and for all the other arts. I knew that it is the artist's task, and that it is also the task of scientists and engineers, to simplify the chaos of appearances and to draw from the random impressions with which our outer and inner senses are constantly bombarded structures that will retain their form and will illustrate some underlying condition—some would say a truth—of existence. I knew that the simple and the true are sworn to a mysterious and indissoluble alliance. But I also knew that such hard-won simplicities are beyond the reach and persistence of most of us and that we must use the mask of the elaborate and hope by this means to distract our readers from our failure.

We were driving along an inner-city street that is familiar to us both—so familiar that we scarcely noticed it. The traffic was light and there were few pedestrians about. Our daily world was rushing by outside the car windows: hotels, cafes, old Victorian houses, a grid of wires above it all delivering our power and telephone services, and above the grid of wires the sky. It was a sky of an uncertain hue, neither blue nor white nor grey, neither quite clear nor exactly clouded. The day was still and humid. A sullen, muggy, reluctant day in that indeterminate season before the oppressive heat of summer at last gives way to the cool serenity of autumn. When we stopped at traffic lights my daughter turned to me and said, 'Are you going to tell me the secret or not?' The traffic lights went to green and I accelerated down the hill. Beside me my daughter stared at me, dignified and angry, waiting to hear the writer's secret, so that she would henceforth possess the whole story and not just its middle and end.

Each morning before she leaves for school she visits me in my study. She is proud of the fact that her father is a writer. Though she has never told me this, I know it to be the case, and it is on her behalf that I fear my own failure these days. We share the walls of books, the sticky tape and the paperclips and the coloured post-its and textas and marker pens, the supplies of copy paper and the small yellow Spirax notebooks and silky grey Uni-ball pens that stand in a bundle in a pewter mug on the mantelpiece. My study is also her domain. She takes what she likes from it without asking. This is our understanding. Nothing is forbidden her. She doesn't speak to me when she comes for this morning visit and I pretend that I've not noticed her and continue working at my desk. But secretly I watch her.

This morning I saw that she had been cast under a mysterious spell and could not see or hear or feel anything from the ordinary world inhabited by people like me. She moved as if she were an automaton, her arms stiff, her knees unbending, her chin held high and her gaze steady on the bookshelf directly in front of her. She stepped across the room in this manner and went up to the books until her nose touched the dark green spine of J.P. Stern's *The Heart of Europe*. She stood there, perfectly still, her arms at her sides, bewitched, waiting to be released from the spell that had been cast over her. I got up from my desk and I went over to her and cupped my hands under her elbows and I lifted her slowly—as steadily as a mechanical lift would lift her—towards the ceiling, past the leached buckram spines of *The Cambridge History of English Literature* and, without pausing, on past the gaily illustrated covers of *A Dream of Red Mansions*, higher and higher, until she was held as high as I could reach her, way above my head, her nose at last on a level with the blue sky of Patrick White's *Voss*. And that's it. I can reach no higher. My arms were trembling with the strain. 'You're getting too heavy for this,' I said and I lowered her to the carpet. She turned and lifted her face to me and we kissed. We both know that she has almost ceased to be a child.

I parked the car in front of our house and we sat looking out through the windscreen, making no attempt to get out, silent with each other and hoping for a peaceful resolution. She was waiting for me to speak. 'The writer's secret,' I said, 'is to choose just one thing from all the things you can see and to begin with that.' We looked out at our street. The parked cars along the kerb, the houses, the little gardens, the corner pub, the Housing Commission flats across the road, the motionless branches of the tall casuarinas. 'Can it be anything?' she asked uncertainly. 'The doors of the pub on the corner?' We looked across at the open doors of the pub on the corner. As if she were speaking of the entranced world of her morning elbow lift she said, 'No one's going into the pub and no one's coming out. Because they're all in the back arguing.' We sat watching the hotel doors, waiting, forgetting that we had begun a story and wondering what was to happen next. I have been reading Proust for some months and she has decided he is my favourite author, which is not so far from the truth. 'What about Proust?' she asked, to fill in time while we waited for something to happen. 'How did he begin?' I turned in my seat and looked at her. I know that no beginning is more noble than another. I know that all beginnings are the same. 'That's easy,' I said. 'Proust's beginning is famous and everyone who reads his great book remembers it. He begins, *For a long time I used to go to bed early.*' She half closed her eyes and repeated Proust's opening sentence as if she were certain it must possess some hidden magic. Then she said quietly, 'I never go to bed early unless I have to.' We looked at each other and smiled. 'That can be my beginning,' she said. Then with sudden excitement, and beginning to see beginnings everywhere, she said, 'It's easy!' She looked beyond me and pointed, 'Look! There's a fat man with no shirt coming out. He's going to sweep the footpath. He thinks it's still summer. They've told him to do it and you can see he's in a bad mood and doesn't want to do it.'

I listened to her unfolding her story, observing it in her mind at the corner pub and discovering that it does not

Alex with his daughter, Kate, 1999
(PHOTO: PONCH HAWKES)

matter where you begin, because everything is connected to everything else and you cannot speak of one thing without sooner or later speaking of another, and then another, until you arrive mysteriously back at the place from which you started out and realise that your story is finished, as surprised as if you had just read it for the first time and uncertain whether it can really be your own story or perhaps must belong to some other storyteller who has told it long ago before you chanced upon it. 'It feels real,' was the way she put it when she had found her ending and the fat man had returned inside and had closed the doors of the pub. She looked at me. 'You could write me a story that begins with, *I was driving my daughter home from school one afternoon.*' 'Yes,' I said, 'I suppose I could.' And then we got out of the car and went into our house and closed the door.

1999

Speaking Terms

I notice them when I'm going back across the island to where the ferry is waiting. We are the only ones going towards the ferry. Everyone else—a considerable crowd—is moving away from the ferry dock and fanning out over the island, moving against us. And this is what takes my attention with them, the fact that they are the only ones going in the same direction as me on this fine summer morning on the island. They walk a distance apart from each other and don't look at each other and don't speak to each other. The distance between them varies, stretching out at its furthest to around fifteen or twenty metres and coming back at its closest to around four or five metres. That's as close as they get. He's the one causing the variation. She's staying on the crown of the road, going straight down towards the ferry dock, keeping a steady pace. He strays a bit, out onto the grass verge then veering back onto the tar, looking about at whatever takes his interest. She doesn't look about. It's early and the sun is still low. It glints on his spectacles when he looks around.

On the ferry we are the only passengers. As we pull away from the dock he's leaning on the aft rail looking back at the island, his khaki rucksack on the deck beside him like a little tan dog waiting with him. Hungry. His denim jacket is dirty and frayed at the cuffs. His jeans are stained, maybe with paint or some kind of chemical substance that doesn't clean off. He leans on the rail looking back at the island and crosses one foot over the other ankle. His shoes are black and heavy and they are dull and greasy-looking. Street shoes that he's using as work boots. He's watching the in-line skaters and the families setting up picnic spots and claiming positions at the public barbeques, the children throwing balls and the older people opening up stripy canvas chairs. It's a warm Sunday in June and as the ferry moves across the open water towards downtown Toronto there's a cool breeze on deck. Even when the detail is lost in the distance the man still stands there, leaning against the rail, one foot crossed over the other, gazing back at the pleasure island. He stays there till the ferry docks.

When we came on board the woman went into the cabin and I haven't seen her since. When the ferry docks I go down to the front and she's sitting in the shade by the gates to the exit ramp, which is as far forward as a passenger is permitted to go, between her feet the plastic shopping bag. Heavy and full of stuff. Three crewmen stand talking beyond the passenger barrier in front of her. They don't look at her. As I come down the stairs from the upper deck the woman turns and looks at me. She doesn't acknowledge me in any way, but her eyes stay on me all the way down. When I reach the deck on a level with her she stands up and faces the exit ramp, her back to me, watching the three men getting things ready for the disembarkation. She is wearing a cerise headband made of some kind of silky material. It is tied like a turban or bandeau and makes her black crinkly hair stick up like an untidy rooster comb. Her yellow jacket is old and frayed and made of some light cottony or synthetic material. There is a pale stain the shape of a heart low down on the back of the jacket. Under the yellow jacket she is wearing a cerise dress in a matching silky material to the headband. The dress is coming unhemmed. Her flat shoes are heeled over to the outside. They have the same dull greasy look as the man's.

The man comes down the stairs from the upper deck and waits behind me. The woman doesn't look around for him. We make a queue, the three of us, the woman in front at the barrier, then me, then the man.

On the quay I hold back and let them go ahead of me. He is looking about again, as if he could be a tourist and has never been to the Toronto harbourfront before and is interested to get his bearings and see what goes on here. She is walking straight ahead, the heavy plastic bag hanging from her hand. They're closer now. Two or three metres apart. And keeping on a level with each other. They're not exactly sauntering, they're not aimless, they know where they're going, but they're not hurrying either. They've got time. Or maybe they're dog-tired.

I cross Queens Quay West behind them and stand watching them go on up Bay towards Union Station, see them go in under the elevated freeway, going into the neutral area between where the tourists are down at the harbourfront and where the commuters are in the business district. They're close now. Less than a metre separating them, and I see him lean in towards her. She doesn't look at him but she must be speaking to him the way he leans in towards her, stepping close beside her, his shoulder almost touching hers, catching what she's saying to him. Their shoulders touching now, bumping each other lightly as they go on. A team. A couple. Partners in life. Knowing the pace and style of the other. She never looks at him.

2008

Impressions of China

I began to write *The Ancestor Game* in the hope of coming to terms with the suicide of a friend, Lang Tzu, the fictional name of the man on whom the main character in the book is based. Lang was a fourth-generation Australian Chinese. He was an artist who had failed to achieve recognition for his work. In his mid-fifties he gave up the struggle and shot himself. Along with one or two of my fellow Australians I believed Lang Tzu was a highly talented artist and that one of the factors in his failure to achieve recognition had been the inability of Australians at that time to view the work of an ethnic Chinese as representative of Australian culture, this despite the fact that Chinese had lived in Australia in large numbers since the middle of the last century. I may be wrong—I hope not; it's always difficult to quantify these things—but my feeling is that this perception no longer holds true in Australia.

I began the book as a memorial to Lang Tzu's life and to our friendship. As I worked my way deeper into the material of the novel, this simple aim became complicated for me by questions about the nature of belonging and the meaning of the idea of home. Gradually I was drawn into an exploration of the ambiguities of colonialism and displacement, conditions which have limited and inspired the human race for centuries. The earliest poems in Old English, the works that mark the origins of English literature—*Beowulf, The Ruin, Widsith* and *The Seafarer*—all deal with journeying in distant lands, or with the presence of foreignness in one's own land. It hasn't always been as fashionable as it is today to write about life in the suburbs. I am an immigrant myself and my meditation on Lang Tzu's life soon became a kind of concealed autobiography. I was deeply intrigued by the experience of exile, by its positive aspects just as much as its negative ones. Exile as opportunity, rather than as cultural deprivation, was what interested me. And of course we don't have to leave the country of our birth to experience the condition of exile. Drusilla Modjeska's *Exiles At Home: Australian Women Writers 1925–1945* is a fine study in this condition.

After I'd been working on the book for a year I realised I would have to go to China to experience at first-hand the people and the place of Lang's origins, to breathe the air of West Lake in Hangzhou on a winter evening and to smell the smells of life in Shanghai. I knew by then that much of the book was to be set in Shanghai and Hangzhou. I travelled to China over the Christmas/New Year period of 1987–1988. It was my first visit. Through Ruth Blatt in Melbourne, and with the help of Nicholas Jose, I'd made contact with Chinese people in Shanghai and was able to travel as a Chinese for the brief period of my visit, which lasted ten days.

It was in Hangzhou, while walking among the evening crowds on the shores of West Lake, that I began to feel for the first time a confidence in my ability to write of Lang's life and his Chinese family background. I didn't take photographs or make notes. It was to be my impressions that would be important to me. I knew that.

Alex with his son, Ross, West Lake, Hangzhou, 1987

When I returned to Australia I discarded the draft of the book I'd been working on before I went to China and began again. I felt an assurance about writing of the Chinese that I could not have felt if I hadn't visited China. My visit had dispelled for me the myth of difference and given me the assurance that in writing about Chinese Australians, providing I got the facts of their history right, I would be no more limited than I would be in writing about any other Australians.

I didn't go to China expecting to become an expert on Chinese life and culture. I went to experience a little of China and the Chinese for myself, so that I would have private memories and impressions to draw on for my book. Whenever we visit a foreign country for the first time we enjoy for a brief period a kind of honeymoon, during which the depth of our ignorance seems to insulate us from danger and to imbue our surroundings with a kind of glow of infinite goodwill. It is a bit like being in love. If we stay too long, we soon begin to be worn down by the frustrations and difficulties of daily life that the locals are nearly overwhelmed by. After a few weeks or months the struggle to get a place on the overcrowded bus has ceased to be a challenge to our determination to behave just like a local and has become a daily burden. The inability of the authorities to provide adequate public transport is no longer part of the exotic spectacle but has become a source of anger and resentment and a cause for frustration and criticism. The unvarying menu in the Mongolian restaurant in Hangzhou, after we have eaten there every day for a month, has ceased to intrigue us and has begun to disgust us.

With increasing familiarity we soon lose our tolerance of difference. I don't mean fundamental difference, if there is such a thing, but petty differences. The sharpness of our curiosity has been blunted against the repeated minor frustrations of ordinary daily life. The longer we stay, the harder it is for us to experience anything outside our own immediate area of endeavour. We begin to manipulate the status quo so that arrangements will suit us better. We cease to be uncritical. We begin to limit ourselves. We define our little area of interest. We become a political being, a struggling member of the local community, a foreigner suffering all the frustrations of foreignness and determined to overcome them.

Some foreigners who stay on respond to the problem by insulating themselves from the foreignness of the place, drawing over themselves a protective carapace composed of the customs and beliefs they brought with them from the country of their origin. They live in a ghetto, whether of the mind or an actual physical community which, with the passing of time, comes less and less to reflect the cultural reality of their homeland. In some ways, of course, it's easier for migrants and long-term foreigners to live in ghettos and ethnic enclaves. In this way the problems are postponed and are bequeathed to the next generation. The ghetto people are a people lost to history, their lives are lived outside history, they are castaways on an island that has become disconnected from their own culture and from the dynamic of change and conflict within their host culture. I encountered a little ghetto of such European foreigners in Shanghai. The Chinese referred to them as Foreign Experts with just enough irony to make me immediately want to translate this as *Foreign Devils*. With the Foreign Experts I ate the worst Christmas dinner I've ever eaten anywhere. The ritual of Christmas with them was more funereal than celebratory, and I couldn't wait to make a polite excuse to escape from them back into the living world of China, on which they'd turned their backs. Another writer might have stayed and written a novel about them. There was certainly a fictional offer in the peculiar melancholy of their lives—a kind of communal *folie,* in which they had each agreed to keep silent about the death of reality. Would I notice that they were ghosts? This was their fear. They watched me closely. They knew they had ventured a long way into the labyrinth and had no hope of ever finding their way back. They could scarcely remember the brief days of the honeymoon. After a few glasses of wine their resentment at the way I was able to take my pleasure in the country they had grown to hate began to find its voice. The ghetto, wherever it is, breeds hatred. Despite legislation prohibiting their permanent residence in Australia, Lang Tzu and his forebears had never been ghetto Chinese. They had married with the Irish and the Scots and the English and had lived in the general Australian community since 1848. And so had thousands of other Australian Chinese.

It wasn't the hazardous business of staying on and becoming a long-term resident of China that interested me. What interested me was the honeymoon experience, the precious period of being insulated by my ignorance and my lack of accountability, a period during which I might hope to be a detached observer of life, a kind of carefree visiting parasite, collecting my impressions and enjoying the uncritical blindness of a lover, not the hard-boiled attitude of a spouse. It was a peculiar privilege, this period of disengagement within a culture that I knew would never require from me an atonement if I failed.

And art always fails. I already knew that. We never succeed in making the sublime incandescent object of our imaginations that beguiles us into undertaking the journey in the first place. For the novelist, the next novel may even be, in a very private way, an attempt to atone for this kind of spiritual failure of the previous novel.

The day before I was to leave China and return to Australia, a Chinese professor from the Shanghai Foreign Languages Institute where I was staying took me for a walk in Lu Shun Park. He said to me, 'Where you see only friendliness and a kind of harmless neutrality, I see deep hatreds and conflict.' He stopped and took my arm and pointed to people who were strolling about and enjoying the winter sunshine. 'Hatred and distrust are all around us,' he said. 'You can't see it in our faces. We are holding it in for the sake of peace and quiet. But make no mistake, this is a society that is deeply divided by long-standing hatreds and by the desire to avenge past wrongs. Watch us for long enough and you will see what I mean. We are just waiting for our chance. If you take home with you these honeymoon impressions of yours, this idea of a peaceful and contented people who are eager to assist each other, you will have been fooled by superficial appearances. China,' he said—and he was a man who loved his country and who had suffered much—'China cannot be at peace with herself for long.' That was in January 1988. Tiananmen Square came a year later.

This man's words entered into my work in *The Ancestor Game*, and gave to it a sense of a more vengeful side of Chinese history than the word 'honeymoon' could ever generate. It was an impression all the more insidious and intriguing for having been given to me on a sunny day among the quiet walks where lovers felt free to stroll in a park named after a poet.

It wasn't history but impressions that remained my source. When he read the book, Professor Huang Yuanshen, who was born in Hangzhou and who heads the Australian Studies Centre at the East China Normal University in Shanghai, asked me, 'How did you manage to get the smell of duck droppings in Hangzhou in 1937 exactly right? I was in Hangzhou as a child,' he said, 'and I can tell you, the smell of duck droppings was then exactly as it is in your novel.'

Impressions that hadn't seemed important at the time, and which I thought I'd forgotten, surfaced again once I was back at my desk writing the book. I wasn't proposing an historical argument. A novel, I believe, deals in the currency of the universality of human nature. Isn't that why we can still read novels about nineteenth-century Russians and French or eighteenth-century Chinese and feel able to identify our own destinies today with the destinies of the characters in those novels?

When I began writing *The Ancestor Game* I didn't start out with the idea of celebrating a rich Chinese contribution to our immigrant culture in Australia. I couldn't possibly have started out with that idea because when I began work on the book, like almost every other Australian I'd ever met, I didn't know there had been a rich and complex Chinese contribution to our immigrant culture as we know it today. Such a contribution had not been noted. It hadn't been celebrated

Alex with the poet Ouyang Yu, in Shanghai, 1988

in the literature. When I began the book I was writing about friendship. And in the end for me, whatever else it might be for others, I think *The Ancestor Game* will always be a book about my old friend Lang Tzu and my new friend Ouyang Yu. A book about friendship and home, and how those two things go together.

1995

EXCERPT FROM

The Ancestor Game

*Y*ou're Australian, Lang said, as if he were reminding me that I'd had myself tattooed while I was drunk. He blew out a cloud of smoke. He was gleeful. You told me you were an Australian. Remember? Remember that, Steven? He laughed and waved his cigarette at me. He didn't require an answer. His spiky hair shivered and sent out gleams in the firelight. His ankles were bone-white above his socks, brittle plaster-of-Paris casts. He sat cross-legged on the rug and rocked himself backwards and forwards, the wine slopping about in his glass and spilling on his old blue trousers, his left eye watering and blinking with the optimistic, greedy innocence of a child, his right eye swivelling about independently, the elder, the remote sensing organ of the lookout in the gazebo, on the alert for the approaching enemy. It steadied on me fleetingly. Would you like to see the lotus cup my grandfather gave Speiss?

It really exists then?

Of course it exists! Of course it exists! The eagerness of my interest gratified him. The lotus cup, he said. There's plenty of time. Let's have a drink first. You do want to see it?

I'd love to see it.

Good. Good. I remember everything. He drank deeply, abandoning caution, becoming master of his past again, empowered to reclaim it breath for breath and to deliver it to me, intact, its smells, its texts and textures, the precise weights and measures of things and of circumstances, the gravity and the levity of events. And to prove it, he would produce for me the celadon teacup from the Sung kilns of Fenghuang Hill, the fragile antique heirloom saved miraculously from the ruins, which Gertrude's father had held honourably in trust for him. To prove his capacity, his friendship and his largesse, to prove that it all still belonged to him, he would disclose Huang's lotus, his lien. He would produce for me not merely his mother's gold this time, but his mother herself. He would produce whatever I might desire for my concoction. Nothing was too sacred. Nothing was too precious. He was protected from his fear of saying too much, of revealing too many of his secrets, by the confessional veil of alcohol. He aspired to demonstrate abundance. Completeness. An unflawed trust that would never have permitted him to react suspiciously, as I had done earlier, to his absence from the house. He intended to prove himself to me and to rebuke me in the process for my lack of generosity of spirit. His estate was invulnerable to my incursions. It was too large and too grand to be noticeably depleted by my appetite. He would account to me for his past in its entirety. He would present me with the problem, not of what to put in but of what to leave out. He would dazzle and disorient me. He would leave me confused and uncertain.

He refilled our glasses with the heavy red cask-wine and we clinked them together. I remember everything about my childhood, he boasted. You only need the first ten years. That's all you need. The Nanking decade: 1927 to 1937. The entire period of my life in China. The worst years, the hardest years for my father and for all the Shanghai capitalists. After ten years it's too late. After a child reaches the age of ten nothing can be changed. His bleary gaze struggled to locate me in the fug of smoke and radiant heat from the fire. He reached out and clutched my sleeve. He swayed. Did he see *me*? You're my only friend, Steven, he said hopelessly and let go of my sleeve, half regretting the excess immediately.

I saw that his bravado would be easily disabled; I saw in him a kind of sorrow and a kind of love and a deep inconsolable regret, a kind of horror of what lay before him, each emotion discrete, like colours in an oily puddle, circling slowly, trapped within his eyes.

I said, And you are my only friend.

He grinned sheepishly, breaking the surface, for a split second the boy experimenting with being grown up. What do you *really* think of me? He laughed, abashed, unsteady, unable to hold to one direction.

1992

Chasing My Tale

Apart from chasing my tale I don't know what I'm doing. And I mean this in a very general way indeed. I've never been at all clear about what I'm doing. I can't be highly articulate about my writing. Andrew Riemer, the Sydney academic and critic, who is also a personal friend, told me that as a result of the publication of *The Ancestor Game* I'm now considered to be a revisionist historian by certain of his colleagues at Sydney University. When I read history at Melbourne University in the sixties with Marion Gibbs I learned, or thought I learned then, from that very great teacher that all history is revision.

So I'm not sure what being a revisionist historian means, but I do know it doesn't follow from a conscious intention of mine. My life, though I've always tried to disguise this fact, has been rather aimless. I've clung to the suggestion of a thread of sense that writing sometimes seems to offer me, perhaps the way some people cling to a religion they have never really learned to trust. Beyond this uncertain thread of sense, I don't know why I write or why I do anything else. I have, I'm afraid, a very strong affiliation with futility. Even now I feel a bit ashamed of admitting this. I look at the books I've written and, instead of drawing a satisfying theoretical position out of them, I wonder how I ever came to write them.

When I do write, however, when I'm working on a book and have reached the stage where it has fully engaged me, I feel that I don't need to worry about the problem of meaning. I feel I've left that awkward social demand behind. The business of writing fictions seems to me to be setting up barriers to intelligibility in the external sense, in the sense in which present reality is conducted, that is, and in which empires are understood to crumble and peoples to become post- or neo-colonial or some other thing.

Who has not heard writers say—*who*, if they are honest, has not themselves said at some time—such things as, 'We have written about the migrant experience. Now we have moved on from that. We have left that behind.' Or, 'The realist novel is dead. The Dickensian novel can no longer be written. The novel has become the playground of ideas.' And so on. Pronouncements about the future that are proven false the instant someone produces a book that does freshly again those very things that one has claimed have been done-with forever. When this annulment of some portentous *pronunciamento* occurs, those of us who care about the novel rejoice that once again it proves its resilience as the means for telling any kind of story about humankind we care to tax it with in any kind of voice we care to tax it with. As novelists we celebrate our liberty.

We celebrate the fact that the novel keeps on surviving in all its elaborated forms, Dickensian and realist as well as magic-realist and post-modern. Apuleius's *The Golden Ass*, which is the only Latin novel that has come down to us intact, is magic-realist. Which seems to some people a very modern thing. Apuleius's novel was written in the middle of the second century of the Christian era. Reading it we are reminded that *nothing* is new. We keep learning the same lesson over and over and forgetting it over and over: the lesson that we are a language species and that language will do and redo anything we ask of it. The lesson that language underwrites our realities. That language is the first step in the process of making the things of our imagination tangible. Nothing is finished with. Not the migrant novel or the realist novel. It has all been done before and it will all be done again, and again, so long as we go on. The human species is also a migrant species. We have always travelled. In our wanderings we are forever coming across our old tracks and speculating on the perplexing nature of the creature who must have made them. In the strange place we are stilled by the presentiment of familiarity and we know that we have been there before. Home, indeed, may be for many of us no more than this fleeting intuition. A singular truth (which we do not often acknowledge because to do so kindles in us feelings of overwhelming futility) is that there is no place left that has not been visited by us and that there is nothing to be done that has not already been done by us. Round and round the mulberry bush, that's where the novelist is going. Chasing his or her tale . . . as ever.

In our essentials, in our natures, morally and spiritually, we are today no further advanced than we were when Apuleius wrote his novel. The illusion of present reality, however, is always to insist that we are going somewhere, that there is a destination and that the day that is to follow this day will be different from this day. It is for this reason, in order to sustain our confidence in the illusion of a present reality that is taking us somewhere, that we invest our energies so heavily in innovation and change.

But really it's always questions without answers. The deeper we go into our material the more complex and irresolvable the contradictions of our material appear to us; and the more complex and irresolvable they appear, the more beautiful and alluring the material becomes for us, the more it casts its charms over us. It is not to resolve these paradoxes by making their structures of meaning intelligible that one can work as a novelist, but only to contemplate them in their irreducible splendour.

I suppose I believe a novel is like a painting or a piece of music, at least in the sense that it cannot be explained but can only be experienced. And this is one of the ways in which the concept of a work of art still remains useful to us, by enabling us to avoid (at least on the immediate level of appreciation) categories such as revisionist history and post-colonialism, categories which appear to explain things that don't require explaining on the immediate level of appreciation. To reveal these enormous wells of ignorance in ourselves. When we've completed the logical structures of our theories we have camouflaged those wells of ignorance, we haven't dealt with our ignorance or explained it, or moved on from it to a new and more enlightened place. We have cast a net of theory over our ignorance. The function of theories and ideologies, which are necessarily predicated on the insistence that we are going somewhere, that we are proceeding to the fulfilment of movements and tendencies whose ends are discernible in our present condition, is to support the necessary illusion of present reality. The art of the novel, viewed as post-colonial literatures, for example, seems to be about discourses in which power is being transferred from one cultural context to another. Viewed in this light the novels themselves seem to be about this process that is going on and that will one day, presumably, result in a fully empowered novel that is no longer post-anything but is fully present to itself and to its cultural realities. On the immediate level of appreciation, where we transcend our own individual and separate lives, where we transcend present reality, the novel is not going anywhere. It is *here* that art deals with. With us, here now. Art doesn't predict. Art isn't going anywhere. There is nowhere for it to go.

We can talk about art or we can talk about theories and ideologies. Art deals with now, theories and ideologies deal with change and the process towards something other than and different from now. The art of a thousand years ago is still dealing with now. Now is timeless. We can use art to illustrate our theories and ideologies but art is not itself an illustration of these things. Logical constructs only make it seem as though it is. Logical rigour, on which theoretical projections about the future must rely for their coherence and shape, pushes the issue of futility and meaning into the future. It postpones the problem of meaning. I'm not a philosopher but I think we can probably construct a theory out of any thought or idea, or even out of an emotion, if we are rigorous enough in our application of logic to its elaboration. Language will stand the strain. There is no doubt about that. Even this affiliation with futility could be theorised as an aspect of our age's fascination with the so-called unstructuredness of much of natural phenomena, which is a view that our new technologies of looking have revealed to us. I had dinner with James Gleick in September—it was the occasion of the Victorian Premier's Literary Awards and he and I were guests of our publisher, Penguin, at the same table. And while I was sitting there talking and listening and eating the smoked salmon and drinking the slightly too-sweet chardonnay, I thought about James Gleick's books: *Chaos* and *Genius*. And I imagined him writing another book. I could see the finished book, the single word FUTILITY in gold lettering on a white cover. The book inscribed the end of futility. The end of the struggle for meaning. We no longer needed to wonder if there was a God or not. The grand unified theory of futility: meaninglessness and faith made intelligible. I do Mr Gleick a great disservice, of course, by naming him in my fantasy. He ate his dinner in complete ignorance of my terrible thoughts.

1993

The Wine Merchant of Aarhus

The professor came to Denmark from Australia nearly thirty years ago when she was a young woman. She lived in an old railway crossing keeper's house about five miles out of the town centre. The house stood alone by the railway line in the middle of ploughed fields. It was two storeys with a steeply pitched roof in which, in the Danish style, there were also rooms. Several old apple trees survived in the neglected garden. As soon as I arrived at the house I felt there was something sad and forgotten about its situation. As if I saw at once that it did not really belong there anymore and that, in the service of efficiency, at which the Danes seemed to be very good, the railway company should have demolished the old house when the railway crossing was bridged and accommodation was no longer needed for a crossing keeper and his family. The local farmers might then have ploughed over the site where the house and its neglected garden stood and have resumed the land for their crops. Who, after all, I asked myself, would wish to live in such a place as this, isolated from neighbours, silent and alone in the middle of empty ploughed fields? Despite its picturesqueness I could see nothing to recommend the professor's house as a place to live. I imagined evenings there after long days spent alone in the study, when nothing would be more pressing than the need to get out and be among people in order to refresh one's spirits, to walk in the streets or to meet acquaintances in a cafe and drink a glass of wine. To step outside the professor's house was to enter the forlorn garden with its views of muddy fields. I was certain, moreover, that no inhabitant of this lonely gatekeeper's house could have any contact with the farmers, for their red-brick homes and cattle byres stood off on the skyline with their windowless backs to the world, as discouraging as military forts might be to the casual advances of a stranger in need of company.

We paused, the professor and I, to admire the house before going in. It's true, it was during the silvery twilight of a long northern winter evening that I arrived at the professor's house, and I suppose the darkness and the cold and the leafless apple trees made the situation seem even more gloomy to me than would have been the case if I'd arrived during the summer. But even so, what about summer evenings? Wouldn't you feel especially enticed out of the house then, to mingle with people and to eat ice creams and drink beer and to laugh, and perhaps even to fall in love? Mightn't the situation of the crossing keeper's house, I thought, be even more disheartening during the summer than during the winter? If it can still be as true for us today as it was once for Huysmans, that the beauty of a landscape resides in its melancholy, then in the rustic simplicity of its isolated setting I was prepared to believe that the professor's house was beautiful, but I was glad, nevertheless, that I was to be staying for only a few days and not, as she had, for thirty years. As we stood together in the garden, I said, 'What an incredible place! It's great! Really fantastic! Beautiful!' And when she turned to go inside I saw the smile in the professor's eyes, and that she did not believe in my enthusiasm.

As well as being an eminent scholar in the field of the new literatures in English, the professor was also the editor of an arts magazine. She had decided to publish an issue of the magazine in which my book and my visit to her university were to be celebrated. Mette Jørgensen and Lars Jensen, two of the professor's old PhD students, who had become her colleagues and were collaborating with her in the production of the journal, came back to the house with us the next day from the university to have dinner with us and to discuss what should be put into the celebratory issue of the magazine. Earlier in the day I'd gone into the town with Lars to do some sightseeing and to help with the shopping for our dinner. It was then that I met Grubert, the owner of the wine shop on Guldsmedgade—and the subject, supposedly, of this story.

It was a small family wine business. A warm brightly lit shop in the busy main street of the town. Grubert took such an obvious pleasure in helping us select the wine from his shelves that it was impossible not to feel that we were part of a privileged occasion. When the wine had been chosen he carried it to his counter and wrapped each bottle separately in tissue paper before handing it to us and receiving his payment. The practised way Grubert rolled the bottles, with a certain modest flourish, into the crinkly sheets of tissue paper, while Lars and I stood by the counter and watched him, seemed to me to be a survival from a past time. It was a gentle, unhurried and really quite complex, and even gracious, performance. It was a style that belonged in the time when the professor's house had been a railway crossing keeper's house and travellers had had to wait while the crossing keeper came out and opened the gates for them. There was the possibility in Grubert's actions that Lars and I might have been entrusted with a message for the crossing keeper who was no more.

As we walked away along the street I glanced back at Grubert in his wine shop and caught an image of him framed against the dark evening: the white sleeves of his shirt and the green of his apron in the bright shop as he rolls a bottle of wine into crisp sheets of tissue paper for an expectant customer.

'Why do you call him Grubert, and not Herr Grubert, or John Grubert?' I asked. Lars explained to me that during the past few years in Denmark the use of *Herr* had come to sound too formal and old-fashioned. 'Perhaps the rich women whose husbands own the houses overlooking the bay still call him Herr Grubert,' Lars said, 'when they telephone to order their wine. But everyone else would consider Herr an affectation these days.' 'And things haven't relaxed so far that you'd call him by his first name?' I asked. 'Grubert,' Lars said, listening to himself. 'It sounds right.'

When we'd finished the shopping Lars took me to his favourite cafe and ordered two bottles of Tuborg. We drank the beer and talked. The cafe was busy with young people drinking and smoking and talking. The beer was light and to my palate nearly tasteless. Outside it had begun to rain again. Our coats were wet from an earlier shower which we'd made no attempt to shelter from. 'We'll soon get dry again,' Lars had said, the rain shining on his face and his hair. It was pleasant in the cafe. I was curious to find out as much as I could about Denmark during my short stay. Lars had visited Australia several times and we talked about differences between Denmark and Australia. The weather mostly. I ordered the next round of Tuborg, and attempted the Danish which was unnecessary as the waiter spoke excellent English. But there is a peculiar pleasure to be had from trying out the strange sounds that make up another's language. To articulate the odd, meaningless sound and get a sensible response has the magic of incantation in it. The waiter laughed with us, sharing our pleasure, and Lars complimented me on my pronunciation. Everyone seemed to be friendly and happy. Denmark, I thought, is a friendly country. I was reminded, by this thought, however, that I was enjoying the period of amnesty from care that can be experienced whenever we are in a new country for the first time; a brief, and to the writer a precious, period during which the stranger is permitted to enjoy a kind of innocent wonder. As if it has been agreed that for a little while the stranger, like the child, will not be held accountable for the reality into which he or she has stepped. I had experienced such a period in China some years earlier and it had proved profitable to my writing. I knew that detachment was possible during this moment in between, as it were, a moment of disconnected- ness during which I would be permitted to read the social dimensions of this country as my own fiction. A moment for receiving impressions, before the imagination is closed by exact knowledge. Of course I said nothing of this to Lars, because I knew that to speak of such a thing is to destroy its power.

At the professor's house that evening after dinner, during the discussion about what to put into the celebratory issue of the arts journal, Lars suggested that a short story from me would be a good idea. 'But I've never written short stories,' I said. 'That doesn't mean you can't, though, does it?' 'Suggest something, then,' I said. 'Tell me what to write and I'll write it.' I waited while they looked at each other, puzzling over what to suggest to me. It was Mette who was first to lose patience with this procedure. 'We're not the writers,' she said. 'You should think of something yourself. That's part of being a writer, isn't it, thinking up your own stories?' 'Maybe,' I said. 'But it's nice to have things suggested sometimes.'

While we considered the problem the professor poured the last of the wine for us. One of us once again remarked on how good the wine was and the others readily agreed. The professor, however, was silent. She was thinking. 'As good as Australian wine,' Lars said, looking into his glass. The professor was gazing out the window towards the bare cold hill of dark ploughed land with the humps of the distant farmhouses on the skyline. She seemed to have forgotten us. As if, accustomed to sit here alone during the long evenings in the spell of the old house, she had fallen into an habitual reverie, sipping Grubert's good red wine and gazing out the window while the silvery light lingered and lingered on the ploughed fields, waiting interminably for the landscape to grow quite dark, and then forgetting to wait. After a while she lifted the glass to her lips and drank deeply, and she made a sound like a groan that someone might make in their sleep. Then she turned to me, her gaze direct and challenging, and she said, 'Grubert,' as if she were forming the word out of the groan. 'Lars said you liked our Grubert. So why don't you write us a story about the wine merchant of Aarhus?'

They watched me and waited. A fast train went by, making the house tremble. In the stillness after the passage of the train I recalled my image of Grubert in his shop, surrounded by his tall racks of handsome wine bottles, just like me in my study at home in Australia as I am at this very moment writing this story that is not really a story, surrounded by my tall shelves of books. 'I suppose he's the third generation of Grubert wine merchants,' I said, 'and just like his father and grandfather before him has been going to that same shop regularly at the same hour every day for thirty or forty years without a break and that the locals safely set their watches by him.' 'Good! That's our Grubert,' the professor said. 'What else?' 'Well,' I said. 'One day he takes off his green apron in the middle of the afternoon, long before the usual time, and he puts on his jacket and closes his shop and hurries down Guldsmedgade without looking either left or right and without greeting any of his numerous acquaintances as he passes.'

While I drank from my glass of Grubert's good red wine my three friends waited. And when I had drunk and remained silent Mette leaned towards me. Resting her elbows on the blond wood of the table, she examined me with her large blue eyes, a frown, which seemed to question my integrity as a storyteller, creasing the centre of her broad intelligent forehead. 'What then?' she asked. 'Where was Grubert going?'

'I don't know,' I said.

'Did he have a lover?'

'It's a sort of jest,' I said. 'Like a haiku, or a Chinese micro story. Everyone in the town knows the wine merchant has never varied his habits for forty years, then without any explanation one day he does something different, and at once there is this mystery. And all because a man has walked down a street that is as familiar to him as the thoughts in his own mind.'

Mette and Lars looked at the professor. Were they waiting for her verdict before giving their own? I wondered. 'We need something a bit longer than that,' the professor said.

'Perhaps other things will occur to me when I write it,' I said.

'I want to know why Grubert leaves his shop,' Mette insisted.

'But it's not a story about why Grubert leaves his shop,' I said. 'It's a story about your town. It's a story about Aarhus and how steady a town it is.'

'Even so,' the professor said. 'It still needs to be longer.' She pushed her empty wineglass to the middle of the table and got up and went and stood by the window with her back to us. 'You'll have to pretend to know why Grubert leaves his shop in that unexpected way,' she said, just an edge of something impatient in her voice, her interest no longer really connected to the possibilities of the story, wishing, perhaps, to think of other things. 'Make something up,' she said, standing at the window gazing out into the cold winter night across the dark ploughed fields that were no longer visible towards the farmhouses on the horizon.

'A lover,' she said eventually, when I no longer expected her to speak again of the story. 'Mette's right. A lover is a good idea.'

1993

Winter Garden, Aarhus, 1993

The Mask of Fiction

I've been asked for a memoir for this occasion yet I am uncomfortable writing directly about myself. I prefer the mask of fiction. In this preference it is self-deception I fear most, for who but the self-deceived would claim to be able to write with moral detachment about themselves? I am also cautious of the fate of W.B. Yeats, the poet, of whom Richard Ellmann wrote in *Yeats: The Man and the Masks*, 'The autobiographical muse enticed him only to betray him, abandoning him to ultimate perplexity as to the meaning of his experiences.' Memoir does not offer us a sure means for contacting the deeper dualities of the self. For this journey to the heart of darkness fiction is a more certain, if more oblique, way.

'Oh yes,' Voltaire said of Michel de Montaigne, 'he does indeed confess his faults, but only his endearing ones.' We are human and we love ourselves. When writing about ourselves the inclination for a self-portrait in an endearing light is not to be resisted. Oscar Wilde famously said of it, 'Man is least himself when he talks in his own person. Give him a mask and he will tell you the truth.' It is the mask that enables detachment from self. All fiction, after all, is self-portraiture and truth is ever an elusive tiger. It is best to take an indirect approach. The obvious is never the true goal. One needs to don a mask in order to become the other, to get behind the mirror image of self and see what is truly there. It is no wonder it was flaws that concentrated Patrick White's attention when he abandoned fiction for a moment in order to gaze directly into the glass of self-portraiture in *Flaws in the Glass*. White's determination to confess himself, to confess that his fear of the devil of vanity was going to mislead him. If the unconscious is to be our guide it can't be self-consciously so. First we must see ourselves as the other. It is by this path that fiction seeks its truth. For me it is a sacred path. For better or worse I have devoted my life to it.

I'll try to say something here about the place of my novels in my life, and to speak of their interconnectedness with each other. My writing life began in Melbourne when I was twenty-six, after I graduated in English and history from Melbourne University, having entered the university as a mature-age student. Writing became my way of locating connections in a life which up until then had been characterised by a series of disconnections. The earliest of these disconnections occurred when I was two and a half years of age and was sent to a children's home for a week while my mother went into hospital to give birth to my younger sister. The child did not know his exile was to be for a week. For the child the terrifying abandonment was forever. The experience left a mark on me that has never completely faded, and it is disconnection and detachment that have been my minor gods.

From occasional verse and entries in day books, soon after university my writing began to develop into an attempt to make sense of my worlds through reflections on my various selves and on the cultures I had lived within, and they were plural, selves, worlds and cultures. As a result of this self-absorption, this lack of external subject matter, my writing was far too introspective to appeal to either publishers or readers. I was trying to mend something in myself and looked inward in my search for the broken ends that I might fit them together. In this preoccupation with self I was mistaken, however, and it was not until I ceased writing directly about myself and began to write imaginatively of the people and the places most dear to me that my writing began to appeal to publishers and subsequently to gain me a readership. It was also with this change that writing ceased to be a kind of self-inflicted torture and I began to experience the joy of it.

The person most directly responsible for this change of direction in my writing was my friend and mentor, Max Blatt. My novel *The Ancestor Game* is dedicated to Max and his wife, Ruth, and *Prochownik's Dream* is dedicated to my wife, Stephanie, and to the memory of Max Blatt. My friendship with Max was the single most important influence on the development of my writing. To this day I write with the question before my mind: Would Max find this interesting? I ask that question of myself at this very moment. It is the challenge, the accompaniment, and the inspiration of my work. Max was

Max Blatt with Alex's first wife, Anne, Araluen, c. 1970

a richly cultivated and highly intelligent Central European, and his standards in literature were the most exacting I have met with.

I came out of the bush when I was twenty-one and went to Melbourne University when I was twenty-three and did not return to Queensland until after I had begun teaching at Holmesglen TAFE, around 1987. For more than twenty years

I thought my Queensland days would never be part of my life again. My life as a stockman was foreign to my friends and teachers at Melbourne University, and to my colleagues and acquaintances in Melbourne, who all looked towards England or Ireland or Europe for their literary antecedents and the sources of their inspiration. In writing about my early days as a stockman in Queensland I felt the inner truth of John Butler Yeats's saying that 'a work of art is the social act of a solitary [person]'.

I wasn't aware of any Australian literature being taught at Melbourne in the early sixties. There seemed to be no connection between my world of ringing in Queensland (even the term had a different meaning in Victoria) and the life of writing in Melbourne. They were mutually unvisited landscapes and were unknown to each other. There was no common language of cultural memory or association for me to deal in and I carried the precious memory of my days in Queensland with me secretly for more than twenty years. *Watching the Climbers on the Mountain* was my second attempt, after *The Tivington Nott*, to reclaim an important period of my past and to make something meaningful of it in the social context of my present.

The Tivington Nott, my first novel, was conceived initially in two parts, the first part to be set on Exmoor, where I had worked as a farmer's boy for two years, and the second part in the Gulf of Carpentaria, where I had worked as a stockman. It was to be called *Jimmy Diamond*, after a tribal Aboriginal friend of those days. Jimmy and I had worked side by side as friends just as Morris and I had worked side by side on

Exmoor. This book was going to bridge the two lives, the two worlds, and their apparently unconnected realities. My intention was to connect these experiences and hopefully to arrive at some sort of sense of wholeness about myself.

I had loved my Exmoor days and my Gulf Country days and possessed a vivid memory of them. I not only wished to celebrate them but was enticed by the fine ironies between my position on the bottom of the social scale as a labourer on Exmoor and my elevated status on the cattle station in the Gulf of Carpentaria, where I, the newcomer, was paid ten times as much as the expert Aboriginal stockmen. I understood that this social reversal expressed something of the essential reality of the deeply troubled white Australian culture in which I lived; something of the injustice and unease with which white Australians live, or which we push aside and try to forget about; migrants and invaders all, valuing the title of native born, counting our precious generations, longing for the confidence of an authenticity that can never be ours until it is bestowed on us by the first people of this land. I wanted to explore all this, to review it, to revisit it, and to examine the quality of its humanity and its inhumanity, and to see, hopefully, how it had affected me and my own humanity.

The Tivington Nott was, in its original conception, an unwieldy and far too ambitious project. When I got to the end of the Exmoor part of the book I knew the story was complete and would bear no further additions. Much of *Jimmy Diamond* had been written by then but it would never be published. The original plan had been flawed and my ambition for the book had to give way before the integrity of the story. I learned that it is the story that is master of the author, not the author who is master of the story. I learned something of the subordinate role in the making of story that is the conscious performance of the storyteller. The secret of the story is that it serves a purpose unknown to the writer, and responds to its own mysterious tides. In every story ever told it is the unconscious that has spoken. A story's power to beguile lies in what has been left unsaid. The manifest content of the story is an artful carapace for its silent meaning, that place into which the reader's imagination is enticed.

My third novel, *The Ancestor Game*, explores the ambiguous liberties bestowed on artists and writers by cultural displacement. The book began as a celebration of the life of a Chinese Australian friend who was defeated by Melbourne's racism and cultural elitism in the 1980s and who despaired and shot himself. *The Ancestor Game* was my attempt to make sense of my friend's life and death, to see his alienation from his community and culture as something of exceptional value, and to bring him back into my own life and into the lives of his other friends, those who missed him and had believed in him as fiercely as I had.

The success of *The Ancestor Game* came as a surprise and the subsequent international travel was a diversion from the steady daily task of writing. It was five years before I published my next book, *The Sitters*. I wrote *The Sitters* while I was trying to write the novel that eventually became *Conditions of Faith*. The impulse for *Conditions of Faith* came to me when my brother sent me my mother's early diaries after her death. As I read my mother's tiny girlish handwritten notes in a small pocket book I seemed to peer into the shadows of her past and to glimpse her life when she was a young woman and was not yet my mother or the wife of my father, but was looking at her own future as a place of possibility. I saw in my mother's youthful longings the same longings to escape that had preoccupied my own youth, and which had fired my decision to get away from the grey landscape of a council estate in post-war London and go to the charmed rural landscape of Exmoor.

When I left home at the age of fifteen I did not understand the depth of my mother's suffering at the loss of her oldest son. It was not until my brother told me after her death that she had always spoken of the day when I would return, and when she was dying said to him, 'Everything will be all right when Alex gets home.' In writing *Conditions of Faith* I imagined myself to be rescuing my mother's memory and giving her the independent life she had dreamed of as a young woman, whereas I may have in fact been dealing indirectly with her loss of her favoured child and how she might have come to terms with it. I knew she would not have agreed with my sense that she had been oppressed by marriage and family, and consequently the book resisted me for a long time.

It was at last in the landscape of Tunisia, in the filthy cell beneath the ruined amphitheatre of Carthage, once occupied by the grieving mother Vibia Perpetua, that I found the key to the conundrum and the story began to unfold, like a carpet suddenly unrolling ahead of me as I moved across its patterned surface in pursuit of my mother's youthful dreams. What I had found in that filthy cell in the ruins of Carthage was in fact my own story disguised by my love for my mother. I began to see this only after I had finished the book. While I wrote it I did so with my love of my mother foremost in my mind, masking the deeper impulse to tell my own story, indeed to conflate her story and my own, as if we two were one person. *Conditions of Faith* contains my own private truth of my youthful struggle to find a way to become a serious novelist from a beginning where such an ambition was laughable and unheard of. In fiction, as in the telling of our dreams, we reveal more than we imagine.

The Sitters distracted me while I was writing *Conditions of Faith*. It was partly my preoccupation with *The Sitters* that inhibited my progress with *Conditions of Faith*—our impulses are rarely the result of one simple cause, but are fibrous and collective in their force, and consequently nearly impossible to resist. Once again I failed to see what I was doing while I was doing it. I thought, with this little book, that I was writing about a working-class Australian woman who had gone from Australia to England and had become a professor and had now returned to visit her aged mother in the country (country where I'd had a farm for several years while writing my pre-novels). *The Sitters* was to offer a kind of reverse version of my own history. Except that I had *not* returned. I now know *The Sitters* wasn't about that at all but was about my relationship with my father and my lost sister. It was about the way my family, through my father's emotional and physical wounding during the war, became a distant silence for me: a painful absence that was forever present to me. That wound remained as a permanent shadow on my life.

I have a self-portrait in pastels that I did fifty years ago in which I am struggling to free myself from that shadow. It was my writing that eventually freed me. *The Sitters* is a haunted book. A book haunted by my father's wounding and by my inarticulate despair at losing him. Towards the end of the war, when my father returned wounded in mind and body, we did not know him. He was changed. *The Sitters* was my faltering approach to the loss of my beloved father, the man who had taught me to paint and to fish and to enjoy the beauties of nature and music. He had been the childhood storyteller in my life. My dad. He disappeared into the horror of war for four years and another crueller man, wearing his tortured mask, returned in his place.

It wasn't until ten years after I wrote *The Tivington Nott* that I recovered the impulse to write about the Gulf experience. *Journey to the Stone Country*, though not set in the Gulf, nevertheless embodies the spirit of that first book, but transformed and elaborated in ways I could not have foreseen or imagined. *Journey to the Stone Country* also came to me through friendships; and, once again, it was a book about people and places that are dear to me. It is a reflection of my own realities and the realities of these friends heightened, simplified and transmuted into the organic whole of story. My own displacement from one side of the world to the other, my loss of culture and home, is dealt with silently in my empathy with the displacement and dispossession experienced by the book's principal characters, black and white. It is a book about friends, people who, in their lives and experiences, connect aspects of my own past experience that had remained until then mysterious and intractable for me.

My friends Liz Hatte and Col McLennan gave me the bones of the story and blessed the project with their enthusiasm to see it come to completion. Without them that book would not have been written, and those connections would have remained unmade for me. It was when I was writing *Watching the Climbers on the Mountain*, my first published book and my first book set in Queensland, that I met Liz Hatte and began, through my friendship with her, to reconnect my Melbourne life to my Queensland past. Liz, it turned out, was born on a cattle station in the Central Highlands of Queensland and was intimately familiar with the culture of the people and the place on which I had based my novel. Meeting Liz felt like meeting a long-lost sister. As with all great friendships we each had an effect on the other's life. When Liz told me she hated teaching and wanted to be an archaeologist, I said she must risk everything for her dream and have the courage to get out of teaching and go and become an archaeologist—I knew by then that the first step in realising one's dream was to make oneself vulnerable to failure. Liz returned to Townsville not long after this and set up her business. Col and the Jangga became her most important clients (and Col her life partner).

When I visited them in Townsville, Col and I shared stories of our days as Queensland ringers. We understood each other and became friends. It was the first time I had spoken with a ringer from the old days and there was for me in my meeting with Col a poignant sense of homecoming; a return to the familiar place of my first boyhood dream. A vital connection was made for me through Col and his story between the two worlds of my early years in North Queensland and my subsequent university and writing life in Melbourne.

To encourage me, Col showed me the country of his people, the Jangga. He gave me the history of black and white betrayal that lies at the heart of this book. He also placed in my trust the spirit of Grandma Rennie, a spirit that lifts the story above the level of race conflict and endows it with the human dimensions of a love story; love for country, that is, black and white. I saw *Stone Country* as the original impulse of *Jimmy Diamond* finding its time.

It was Col who told me I would write *Stone Country* and it was Stephanie, my wife, who told me I should write *The Ancestor Game*. We do nothing alone. I hadn't seen either book coming, but once they were suggested to me I fell in love with both projects and began to understand how important they were to be for me. In writing these books I was aware that they were expressions of communal realities and longings that we share with each other, and were not simply explorations of self. They made my fragile sense of connectedness more real. When Col first took me on the journey to see his country, he introduced me to his friend and old droving and mustering partner, Frank Budby, elder of the Barada people. It soon became obvious to me that in Frank I had met a heroic and selfless man. A quiet, unassuming and deeply intelligent man, Frank rescued his people from the depredations of white culture—from alcohol, prison, drugs, despair and the dole, the terrible loss of self-esteem, the loss of aim and the will to live well—and reclaimed for them, and with them, by the force of his character and his inspired leadership, an ordered and purposeful life. It was Frank's remarkable example, and meeting the writer Anita Heiss in Hamburg, that led me to write *Landscape of Farewell*. Near Springsure (the location of my first published novel, *Watching the Climbers on the Mountain*) there is the site of the largest massacre of white people by Aborigines in Australia's history, the Cullin-la-Ringo massacre. I was haunted by local accounts of the Cullin-la-Ringo massacre, which I'd first heard when I was a stockman on a cattle station near Springsure, my first real job in Australia. I had also carried since my childhood an unexamined sense of guilt by association with the events of the Holocaust. As a primary school kid I had sat among the assembled students in the school hall while we watched in frozen silence the horrifying black-and-white films of the Allies entering the death camps of Belsen and Buchenwald. The overwhelming impression left on us young children by these nightmare images was that we (human beings) do this to each other. A sense of guilt by association was inescapable. I had never dealt with it.

In Hamburg, meeting Anita Heiss and witnessing her fiercely honest defence of her people's rights made the connection for me. I found young Germans as eager to speak with me about the unspeakable as their elders were reluctant. The elements came together for me in Hamburg, my own unvisited guilt by association for both our treatment of the Aborigines and the images of Belsen and Buchenwald, the Germans' own intractable sense of guilt by association, the silence in Australian history about the massacre at Cullin-la-Ringo, and the inspiration of Frank's heroic reclaiming of the dignity of his people. In my hotel room in Hamburg, I began with great excitement to sketch these lines of intersection and to see how they fitted together into a whole; not an Australian or a European whole, but a human whole.

As a child of nine in the assembly hall at school, watching in rigid silence while the unspeakable horrors unfolded on the screen, I saw how we humans were all touched by these evils in ways that ought to prevent us from speaking of *them* and *us*. Surely it was all *us*. All humanity. The great European civilisation and its astonishing self-assurance of superiority in the face of Indigenous cultures had been the author of the greatest evil of all time. And here were Frank Budby and his people not only recovering from that predatory civilisation but reaching out to it and teaching it something of profound significance, offering a gift from the Indigenous sensibility. It is the Aboriginal leader in *Landscape of Farewell* who gives to the European professor of history the hope of redemption from what has been the professor's crushing and intractable sense of guilt by association for the evils of his father's generation. The contemporary human, the private moral dimensions, of this situation clamoured to be explored. I was eager to contextualise historically the actions of the Aboriginal leader of the

Cullin-la-Ringo massacre, Gnapun the warrior, whose strategic intelligence and leadership had resulted in the annihilation of the strongest and most well-armed party of colonists ever to settle in the Central Highlands of Queensland. Gnapun's was a raid that resulted in no black casualties that day. His leadership and organisation were exemplary. He had never been credited. White retribution followed the massacre and continues to this day to echo in our silence, in our failure to celebrate Gnapun's heroic, indeed his Homeric, leadership.

My ninth novel, *Lovesong*, has its seed not only in my visit to Tunisia in search of *Conditions of Faith* in 1998, but also, and more deeply, in my wife's powerful desire for a second child, a child she always knew with uncanny certainty was to be a girl. In Stephanie's need, in her certainty, I saw a new level of the mystery of the impulse to motherhood and I set out to explore it. At least I *think* that is what I did. It may well be that I am still too close to this book to know yet what it was really about.

Autumn Laing, the tenth novel, has its origins in the same period of my life as my first, *The Tivington Nott*. My association with Sidney Nolan's work began when I was a boy working on Exmoor. An Australian came to live near the farm and he and I became friends; he is memorialised as the stranger who owns the black entire Kabara in *The Tivington Nott*. We talked of what we hoped for from life. I told him I dreamed of going to the frontiers of civilisation. He gave me a book illustrated with hauntingly suggestive black-and-white photographs of the Australian outback. The photographs enthralled me and I longed to go and find the Australian outback for myself.

Many years later, in 1961, the year before I went to Melbourne University, I bought the first monograph to be published on Nolan and sent it to my father as a Christmas present. In the first few pages of *The Ancestor Game* I refer to the gift of this book and how I came to get it back without it having ever been opened. My father was a lover of the faded watercolour landscapes of Cotman and Crome and viewed my gift of Nolan's bleak modernism as a provocation.

After the English edition of *The Tivington Nott* was imported into Australia (I had failed to find an Australian publisher for the book), I received a letter from an old friend of Sidney Nolan's, the poet Barrett Reid, who was then living at Heide, the house which had stood at the centre of Australia's modernist art movement and where Nolan had found his muse and his sustenance for the practice of his art in the person of Sunday Reed, a woman deeply loved and respected by Barrett. Barrie's letter praised *The Tivington Nott* and asked me who I was and why no one in Melbourne had heard of me. When he and Paul Carter awarded *The Tivington Nott* the Braille Book of the Year Award in 1990 (five years after I had written it), the three of us met and became friends. Sid Nolan, his art and life, and the life of Heide, when John and Sunday Reed made it the centre of our new art, were often the subject of conversation with Barrie. Barrie pointed out to me that it was most likely that the book given to me by the Australian on Exmoor had been illustrated by Nolan's photographs of the outback. For me, as you can imagine, this was a magical connection. *Autumn Laing* fulfils a lifelong preoccupation with Sidney Nolan and his life and work.

The idea for *Autumn Laing* in its present form came to me in London. Autumn Laing (the woman) sprang into my head fully formed. She sprang, however, not from nowhere, but from the springboard of my previous work on this book and from my decades-long preoccupation with certain tides in the life of Sidney Nolan, tides towards which I had always felt a deep sympathy and curiosity. I recognised in Autumn's voice a prompt of my imagination. It was a precious gift from my unconscious, the writer's source. It was in her voice (within her mask) that I wrote the book. It felt right for me to do so. My wife has since pointed out to me that this book is as much about a certain period in my own life as it is about either Nolan or his muse.

In writing my novels I have learned that the writer is not master of the story but that the story is master of the writer. I have learned that it is the writer who serves the story, not the other way around. As early as my failed original plan for *The Tivington Nott* I learned that fiction won't be squeezed and warped into self-conscious symmetries of organisation without losing its spirit. Fiction, I believe, obeys deeper and more hidden laws than plotted narratives. Despite the contemporary desire to exchange the word *story* for *narrative*, mere narrative is not story. Story obeys mysterious laws embedded in the human unconscious and is made available to us only through the prompts of our imagination. To trust these prompts is not as straightforward as it might seem. The novel as a form of storytelling may die, but we will always find ways of telling our stories. No one speaks of the death of story.

As I said, I don't like writing directly about myself. Truth evades us by means not perceived by us. Truth is not a given but requires a continuous effort to be won. We are fools if we think we are masters of the truth (as I once foolishly assumed I was master of the story). We stumble towards our truths and our stories with uncertainty. Finding truth is like understanding ourselves. It is a view through the window of a moving train. Next time we look the landscape has changed. It is never finished. Never done with. Never completed. Death finishes it. Truth, like understanding, changes with our days. The impulse towards it, however, I believe remains constant in us. Our desire for it. Our desire to *be* true. The urge we have to touch it and to claim it for ourselves. To know in our hearts that we have not fooled ourselves but have truly understood.

It is I, not my readers, who must be beguiled by the mask for it to be an effective means of achieving detachment from the mirror image of self. The mask, as both metaphor and reality, was well known by the classical dramatists to reveal more than it conceals. No matter how artful the mask, the goal of all storytelling is, finally, to account for one's own story. To the interviewer's question, 'Is it autobiographical?' the honest answer must be, 'Inevitably.' Writing is a joy. When I'm not writing I feel unplugged. Powerless. Disconnected from myself. When I am writing I enjoy a mysterious illusion of invincibility and connectedness. Life without writing is not only no fun for me, it is also life without meaning.

2012

EXCERPT FROM

Conditions of Faith

She did not resist but let him lead her deep into the vault until they reached a small open space at the far end of the racks. A pile of loose wheaten straw and a pitchfork rested against the wall. It was a kind of encampment. There was a three-legged stool and a small haversack. A priest's square biretta rested on the haversack. Beside it was a black stove. The window of the stove glowed red and there was a smell of kerosene. A smoky hurricane lantern hung from an iron hook in the wall, shedding a poor light over the scene.

They stood together in this small open space, their hands clasped, their shoulders touching lightly. She could hear his breathing. He reached and felt about in the straw on the rack in front of them and drew out a large pink-and-yellow peach.

'You must close your eyes,' he told her, and he held the peach behind his back.

'Why?'

'It's the rule. Just close your eyes. It won't work if your eyes are open. Close them!' he insisted.

She closed her eyes.

He held the peach under her nose. As she breathed, he breathed. 'There!' he said, exhaling his breath and gazing at her.

She opened her eyes. 'I saw an orchard in the sunlight.'

They looked at each other.

She swallowed nervously and would have taken her hand from his but he tightened his grip. He touched the peach to her other hand. 'It's for you. It is yours.'

She accepted the peach from him. Something gracious and solemn in the exchange surprising them, impressing them, and rendering them mute. In the surrounding darkness, the deeper shadows of his eyes, the sharp gleam of reflected light within his pupils.

He asked softly, 'Do you know how we ripen the fruit as it is needed?'

'How?' she asked, the firm globe of the fragrant peach enclosed in the palm of her hand between them. 'Tell me.'

'To ripen, their skins must touch. We lay each piece of fruit on the straw singly or they would all ripen together.' He reached into the straw on the rack and removed another peach and he took the peach from her hand and set the two peaches together, their rosy skins touching. 'Now they will ripen each other.'

'Is this really true?' she asked, a little breathless, a little childlike, gazing at the two peaches as if she expected them to ripen magically before her eyes.

'It's true. Fruit kept singly for too long rots before it ripens.'

'I must get back,' she said, but she did not withdraw her hand from his.

'Who is waiting for you?' He looked into her eyes.

She hesitated. 'I'm with a party of tourists. They must think by now that I'm lost. They'll be looking for me.'

'But you *are* lost. You said, I lost my way.' He waited. 'You came here as if you knew the lamp had been lit for you.'

She withdrew her hand from his. 'I must get back to my group.' Her voice was unsteady.

'You're not with a group,' he said, a touch of fierceness in his voice.

'Yes, I am.' His smell was close and warm in the chill air.

'You're alone. I can tell.'

'I came with a party of Germans. That's the truth,' she whispered helplessly.

'You came in search of something. You persisted until you reached this place. You must have climbed the barrier. Why?'

'I don't know.'

'*I* know!'

'It's no good,' she said hopelessly. 'I must get back!' He was looking up into her face, his neck thick and powerfully muscled. She reached and with the tips of her fingers she touched the vein in his neck and felt his heartbeat surge beneath her fingers.

2000

The Inspiration Behind *Lovesong*

My daughter was visiting us in the country. We were sitting by the fire reading. I was reading Edward Said's *Musical Elaborations*, the series of three lectures on a musical theme that Said had given at the University of California in 1989. I was close to the end of the third and last lecture, 'Melody, Solitude, and Affirmation', when I read the following: 'And that memory led me back to Louis Malle's film *Les Amants*, constructed around the relatively innocuous tale of a nameless unknown man happening on a lonely wife (Jeanne Moreau) in the country, and then becoming her lover for a time before he moves on.' When I read this I put the book aside and said to my daughter, 'I think I'll write a simple love story.' My daughter, who was eighteen at the time, answered at once, 'Love's not simple, Dad. You should know that.' The young are wise. I *did* know it. Love, or at least sensual love, is surely the most complicated and hazardous of our states of mind.

What I imagined, when I laid Said's little book aside and looked into the flames of the fire, was a man driving along the old gravel road to Lower Araluen, where I once had a farm. The man, who was in a sense the nameless unknown man of Said's memory of the Louis Malle film, and in another sense was of course myself, was returning to the farm which had once been my own. He was returning after an absence of many years. He was coming back out of curiosity, just to see the old place again. When he came to the farm, the old house below the road and just above the creek flat, he pulled up and sat looking down at the place that had once been his home. A woman was working in a well-tended vegetable garden at the back of the house. He sat watching her for a while, then decided he would go down and make himself known to her.

Before sending the nameless unknown stranger down to the nameless unknown woman in the garden, I began to wonder where the man was returning from. As the author of this love story, I believed I should know. Who was this man? He could not be me. But perhaps he could continue to have something of my background. During the seventies I had lived for a year in Paris. So why couldn't he be an Australian who had gone overseas and, instead of living in London, had lived in Paris? What, I asked myself, might have kept this man in Paris for so long? Was it love? Was he returning to his old home after the breakup of a marriage?

I sold my farm in the Araluen Valley when I went to live in Paris, invited to go by a woman friend who, when she visited me at Araluen, had seen how jaded I was by my lonely life on the farm. After I'd been living in Paris for a year, I decided I liked it so much I would come home to Australia, sell my house in Melbourne and move back to Paris permanently. When I got home, however, I met a young woman and we fell in love, and instead of selling my house I lived in it with the young woman, who soon became my wife and, eventually, the mother of our children. In a sense I gave John Patterner the reverse of my own story. His story is why he stayed, and the life he lived there with his wife, when, like me, he had not intended to stay.

I used to visit a cafe in Paris called Chez Max. I visited it regularly. It was my place for coffee and to eat my evening meal. It was run by a North African, a Pied-Noir, and many of his clients were North Africans, but it was not exclusively North African and always had a good mixture of people. I liked the easygoing atmosphere and the *padron* made me welcome. Also the other clients were not French and spoke French little better than I did. We got along. We were outsiders in Paris. Chez Max, of course, became, with a little twist here and there, the model for Chez Dom in this story—the book that became my complicated love story, as my daughter had predicted.

I had visited Tunisia some years before while researching my novel *Conditions of Faith* and had made Tunisian friends. The country and its people have stayed with me and have become part of the vocabulary of my imagination. Tunisia and its people fit easily for me into the Paris I know. When I think of my Paris days I think also of my days in El Djem and Sidi Bou Said and the people I knew there. Perhaps one day I shall return to the farm at Lower Araluen and let the unknown and unnamed strangers meet at last. But that's another story!

2009

EXCERPT FROM

Lovesong

As I stood there enjoying the pastry smells and the friend-liness of the place, I felt as if I'd stepped into a generous little haven of old-fashioned goodwill. This, I decided, was due to the family that was running the shop, something to do with the sane modesty of their contentment, but more than anything it was due to the manner and style of the woman.

When my turn came to be served I asked her for half a dozen sesame biscuits. I watched her select the biscuits with the crocodile tongs. Separately and without hurry, she placed each biscuit in the paper bag in her other hand, her grave manner implying that this simple act of serving me deserved all her care. She was in her early forties, perhaps forty-three or -four. She was dark and very beautiful, North African probably. But what impressed me even more than her physical beauty was her self-possession. I was reminded of the refined courtesy once regularly encountered among the Spanish, particularly among the Madrileños, a reserved respect that speaks of a belief in the dignity of humanity; a quality rarely encountered in Madrid these days, and then only among the elderly. It was this woman's fine sense of courtesy to which the customers in her shop were responding. When she handed me the bag of sesame biscuits I thanked her and she smiled. Before she turned away I saw a sadness in the depths of her dark brown eyes, a hint of some ancient buried sorrow there. And on my way home I began to wonder about her story.

2009

How I Came to Write *Autumn Laing*

My first encounter with the work of Sidney Nolan was when I was a boy of fifteen and was working as a labourer on an Exmoor farm. An Australian gave me a book on the outback. The book was illustrated with black-and-white photographs of a vast silent land that was mysterious to me and which compelled my imagination. Although I didn't know it at the time, the haunting photographs in the book were the work of the Australian artist Sidney Nolan. I came to Australia on my own at the age of sixteen in search of Sidney Nolan's outback. It was the most important decision I have ever made. I still revisit Central and North Queensland and have many friends there. That strange and beautiful country photographed with the imagination of Nolan has been a deep and lasting influence on my life as a writer.

My second encounter with the work of Nolan was in 1961, when Thames and Hudson published the first major monograph on the Australian artist's work. Though I had very little money at the time—I was earning a living in Melbourne cleaning cars while studying at night for my university entrance exams—I thought this expensive book so important that I bought a copy and sent it to my father as a Christmas present. Nolan's art, it seemed to me, would reveal to my father more about Australia than my letters ever could. It was through my father's encouragement that I had first developed what proved to be a lifelong interest in art. He wanted me to be an artist. I did the next best thing and became a writer.

When I was writing my third novel, *The Ancestor Game*, in the late eighties—it was published in 1992—I quoted from Colin MacInnes's essay from the Nolan monograph: *Australia is an Asiatic island that Europeans inhabited by accident . . . Everything about Australia is bizarre.* I read until I lost interest in the writer's insistence on a uniquely eccentric nature for Australia and for the 'kingly race' of Europeans who inhabited the continent. These were views of Australia current among the intelligentsia of the time when the book was published, at the beginning of the sixties. They were views that *The Ancestor Game* challenges and which a subsequent generation of Australians has discarded. By the early nineties, Nolan, and our interpretation of his work, however, remained important in what we might call the process of Australian cultural history making. Cultural change is continuous and is generational. Each generation rewrites history for itself, but while historical texts become outmoded in this process, the art and literature of the nation continues to be the stuff of reinterpretation. Culturally we are not yet done with Nolan and his art any more than we are done with the poetry of Judith Wright or the novels of Patrick White. Nolan's art is as much a part of Australian history as the defeat at Gallipoli, and we will surely continue to reinterpret its significance for us till the cows come home.

Barrett Reid at the launch of
The Ancestor Game, *Melbourne, 1992*

When my first novel, *The Tivington Nott*, was distributed in Australia—I'd been unable to find a publisher for it here—Sidney Nolan's old friend the poet Barrett Reid wrote to tell me he thought highly of the book and that he wished to meet me. Barrie, as his friends knew him, lived at Heide, the home of the Reeds, where Nolan's art had found its first and most important champion in Sunday Reed. When I told Barrie about the inspiration of the book given me by the Australian in Somerset all those years ago, it was Barrie who told me it was Nolan's photos I'd been looking at. On more than one occasion during the years of our friendship Barrie suggested to me that I write a novel based on Nolan's life. The project did not greatly appeal to me at the time and I did nothing about it. But it was Barrett Reid who sowed the seeds of the idea with me.

Barrie revealed Nolan's art to me in a way I could not have done for myself and he educated me about its sources and the life of art Nolan had lived at Heide in his early years as an artist. Barrie remained a dedicated friend and champion of Sunday Reed to the end of his life.

In *Autumn Laing*, the resident poet laureate of the group of artists whose work is favoured at Old Farm is Barnaby. Like Barrie, Barnaby was born and raised on a cattle station in the Central Highlands of Queensland (where I had also worked as a boy). Barnaby is my private homage to a dear friend who is no longer with us. The connection of Nolan and the Queensland cattle station that I made through my friendship with Barrett Reid was a compelling one that was rich in those emotions that make us feel we not only belong to a certain place but that we are in some sense fated to belong to it. Sooner or later I knew I would attempt to write about Nolan. What I have written in *Autumn Laing* is not, however, what I expected to write. Novels are a kind of dream for the novelist. Although they are most often based on observations of reality, the writer is not in control and must follow the compelling prompts of imagination. For me it has never been possible to plot or plan a novel beyond a few very basic elements. The story reveals itself to me as I proceed with a book and is nearly always a surprise. This book, *Autumn Laing*, was no exception.

I first wrote what is now chapter two, Autumn's (realist) portrait of the artist's first wife, Edith. After writing this chapter I had to leave the book while I spent a month on tour in the UK with my previous novel, *Lovesong*. At the end of the tour (the end of September 2010) I was sitting on a bench in Holland Park watching squirrels and remembering my boyhood in London's parks when the idea for the present form of the book suddenly occurred to me. I hadn't given the book a thought for a month. As I was sitting there that lovely September afternoon, watching the squirrels diving about among the ivy, I suddenly heard the voice of Autumn Laing. 'They are all dead,' she said, 'and I am old and skeleton-gaunt . . .' It was a realisation. The realisation that the character I had originally based on Sunday Reed, Nolan's muse and lover and his greatest supporter during his early years, might have lived on until the age of eighty-six, alone, deserted and with a deep sense of having been betrayed. The woman whose voice I heard that day was no longer the Sunday Reed of history but was my own fiction, a prompt from my imagination, a fiction of how such a person *might have become* had she lived another ten years and had she decided to tell her story, telling it at a time of her life when she had nothing left to lose. Autumn has nothing left to lose but everything to gain morally by telling her story. She quotes Tennyson, '*Let me shrive me clean and die.* None of us,' she says, 'willingly dies unclean. Religious or not, to seek confession and absolution is surely an essential moral imperative of the human conscience, isn't it? To absolve means to set free, and that is what we yearn for, freedom. Young or old, it's what we dream of and fight for. We never really know what we mean by it.' And so she tells the story of their youthful passions, their betrayals and their terrible judgments. What is youth for, she says, but to commit the great follies? And they do.

When I got home to Castlemaine from London in early October I wrote for ten hours a day six days a week for five months in the voice that I had heard in Holland Park—the voice of Autumn Laing. It is the longest novel I've ever written and the quickest. I loved every minute of it and was sorry when she finally left me. I don't think I will ever find anyone like her again. She is confident, well informed, passionate, cultivated and very down to earth. She is, in some ways, the personification of a certain type of cultivated Australian woman. She couldn't possibly be English or French. Like Sunday, Autumn's commitment was always to Australia and to our art. She was never tempted to live in England or Europe. In her person, my own early life as a stockman in North Queensland is connected to my life as a writer in Melbourne, just as these aspects of my own life were connected for me by my friendship with Barrie Reid, a faithful friend of Sunday Reed until the end, and a faithful admirer and interpreter of the art of his old friend Nolan. It is the experience of the artist and of Autumn in this book while they are visiting Barnaby's parents' cattle station in North Queensland that changes them both forever.

Autumn Laing is a story about the intimate lives of passionate, ambitious and gifted people, it is a story about their loves, their hates and their betrayals, but it is also a story about Australian art and culture and some of the questions and problems Australian art and culture have had to confront and which they continue to confront today. The inspiration for this story may have originated in the model of the relationship of Sidney Nolan and Sunday Reed, but Autumn Laing and Pat Donlon are my own fictional inventions. They are the products of my own dreaming, the presences of my own haunting and my own experience. Anyone looking in this book for the real Sunday Reed or Sidney Nolan will be looking in the wrong place and they will not find them. *Autumn Laing* is not biography or cultural history, and makes no claim to any such thing. It is fiction. My own fiction, and that is the only sensible claim to be made for it. And there is nothing novel in having based these characters on real people. All my major characters in all my novels have been based on real people. I've had only one objection, and that was from the original of the Cap in *Lovesong*. He is the only one to have disliked his fictional representation.

But why fiction? Why *not* cultural history or biography? My only answer can be that my interest is in the currency of the intimate lives of 'us', and neither the historian nor the biographer can safely deal in such a currency. Private intimacy is of necessity a language requiring something more than textual and eyewitness sources. One has to make it up. And this is what I most enjoy doing—dwelling among the liberties of the imaginative arena of make-believe. Writing novels. Doing fiction. Making it up. The inner life is where my interest lies and for this I have to pretend to understand, to empathise to the best of my abilities, with my characters. Our motives may remain opaque to us even in our most lucid moments; confused, changeable, impenetrable, and interesting only when complex and irreducible. And what interests me is motivation, shadows forever shifting their ground in the partly conscious spaces from where our hopes and fears for ourselves arise, and for those we love and cherish—and equally our hatreds for those we love and our wish at times to see them destroyed. Without this enduring interest there can be no energy for the work, no inspiration to visit the tangled webs of the interior life. Vivid moments of destructive hatred that we reserve for our intimates. Dangerous moments when we are not ourselves. Absurd and irrational behaviours driven by the almost hallu-cinatory power of lust. Or when we are too much ourselves. It is these private shadow grounds of contradiction and elaboration beyond fact and outward appearance that interest me. Fiction is the only mode with which we can approach this ground in others. As with all modes of writing, we are at liberty to do it well—in which case our readers are convinced and willingly enter into the illusion with us—or to do it badly—in which case they are repelled and abandon us.

2011

EXCERPT FROM

Autumn Laing

We search among the jumble of discarded things, disclosing the layers of the years. Most of it was junk—transistors, toasters, old blankets, yellowed pillows, a rat's nest or two. I wondered which of us had thought to store bundles of newspapers tied neatly with butcher's twine? His drawings were not there. I felt betrayed and was convinced someone had visited the loft and stolen them. Something else was there, however. Something I had never expected to see again. Stony handed me Edith's modest oil of their white cottage and the embroidered field, as if he knew this was what I had really been looking for—had I only known it myself. I had long ago forgotten that Edith insisted Arthur take the picture with him the day of our abortive picnic.

Propped there on the floor of the loft with my back supported by the bundles of newspapers, my purple shanks stuck out in front of me, I held Edith's picture across my legs and looked at it. I saw at once that for a young woman of twenty-one it represented an extraordinary level of skill. It is on the kitchen table in front of me now, a pile of books behind it, facing the veranda so that it catches the light. She solved her problem of the oxalis with simplicity and wit, the golden yellow of that wild weed an ironic reference to Monet's cardinal fields of immemorial poppies. Everything I see in this good light confirms my first impression that Edith's embroidered hill is a first-rate work. To have been guilty of stealing her husband and destroying her little family was crime enough, but it is clear to me now that I also destroyed her chance of establishing herself as one of the very few truly gifted Australian women artists of her time. And for this surely there can be no redemption.

2011

Meanjin

Eighteen months after writing the story about Max Blatt's betrayal by his comrade during the Nazi onslaught on Poland, I sold the farm at Araluen and went to live in Paris. When I returned to Melbourne a year later I decided to submit the story for publication under the ironic title 'Comrade Pawel'. The only literary journal I had even the vaguest connection to at the time was *Meanjin Quarterly*. I hadn't published anything in it but Clem Christesen, the founding editor, had encouraged me to write poetry when I was a student at Melbourne University. The other prominent literary journals of the time were *Overland*, *The Bulletin* and *Quadrant*, but as I'd had no connection with their editors I decided to submit the piece to *Meanjin*.

A week after sending 'Comrade Pawel' to Christesen I had a phone call from the biographer Jim Davidson. Jim told me he was the newly appointed editor of *Meanjin* and was eager to publish 'Comrade Pawel'. When he asked to speak to Alex Miller, I said, 'You're speaking to him.' Jim then said, 'Well it's probably your father I want to speak to.' I said my father was dead and that I was the author of the story. He was surprised. The piece seemed to have been written, he said, by someone whose first language wasn't English; it read almost as if it were a translation. I told him the 'voice' I'd adopted for the piece was that of the German Polish friend who had told me the story as an illustration of the culturally embedded nature of anti-Semitism in Poland when he was a young man.

Jim and I met for lunch in a Carlton pub across the road from Melbourne University to discuss publication of my story and his vision for revitalising the journal, which he did with great success for the next eight years. We became friends and remain firm friends to this day. The publication of 'Comrade Pawel' in Jim's first issue of *Meanjin*, No. 1, 1975, signalled my beginning as a published writer. To see my work in print alongside such Australian literary luminaries of the time as Jennifer Strauss, Michael Wilding, Humphrey McQueen and Frank Moorhouse was gratifying, but it was also challenging and rather disturbing in a way I hadn't foreseen. Reading my story in its final printed form in the smart journal, I was no longer able to smugly celebrate its brilliance. Instead, I found myself highly critical of it. All writers will be familiar with this response to their work once it is fixed in a published form. It was my first lesson that nothing we write is ever finished and that our works are not tailor-made suits, stitched to perfection for a particular occasion, but are imperfect experiments abandoned and left to survive as best they can on their own.

2015

Comrade Pawel

We had dug in before Warsaw. The series of trenches was perhaps sixteen or twenty miles long, running roughly north–south in a more or less even curve. Every few hundred yards or so there were gaps at which the troops of cavalry were stationed. To our front, towards the west, stretched a plain without a single feature to interrupt the distant skyline. It was the end of summer and I remember that it rained almost every day. After the rain a mist would rise off the plain, and for an hour or two the skyline would be obscured.

It was quiet there, very quiet, and although rumours and counter-rumours circulated among us constantly, they did so without causing us any real alarm. They were a kind of necessary entertainment for us, and they passed among us, were embellished according to our peculiar needs, and passed on. We became attuned to the subtlest nuance of meaning— the exact nervous pitch as it were—of these rumours, and maintaining our 'ear' for them soon became our principal preoccupation. You see, although we began there as individual men, each with his own ideas, it was not long before we lost this very personal sense of separateness and became—to use a metaphor—somewhat like a shoal of fish that swerves or dives or is still according to a common sense.

Towards the end of the third week, and apropos of nothing, Pawel, my usually taciturn companion, said, 'Ah, you see? So there you are!' and he smiled ironically.

'Whatever are you talking about?' I asked him, for his sudden remark seemed to me quite without point.

'The hawk,' he replied drily. 'Don't you see that it's gone?' And he spat contemptuously onto the parapet of earth.

I was startled, and I carefully searched the sky in all directions. But the hawk, which every day hunted about the plain and whose horizon of course lay beyond ours, had indeed departed. But whatever it was that the keen-eyed bird had seen was still hidden from us, for the plain was as silent and empty as ever.

I turned to Pawel and laughed—not of course because I was amused, but because I was afraid. 'Really, Pawel,' I said scornfully, 'you're a proper yokel. What old woman's superstition will you come out with next? Now tell me,' I went on, in a condescending tone and as if I were speaking to a child, 'what do you suppose that bird knows about war?'

Pawel shrugged; he knew nothing of war himself. 'The bird knew when it was time to run,' he said, again without in the least attempting to conceal the contempt he felt for my inability to comprehend the obvious. He actually looked at me then and grinned in a peculiarly malicious way. 'And you, my friend,' he said, poking me in the chest with his finger and leaning close to me so that I smelled his stale breath, 'will learn something of running when our time comes.'

Pawel was an illiterate peasant. I, on the other hand, was an educated young man of the new generation, so naturally I pretended to be unimpressed by his foreboding. Even so, I secretly watched the sky in the hope that the hawk would reappear. Nor did I feel sufficiently confident to go on teasing Pawel about it at that moment.

That night I woke up and lay still, watching the broken clouds above me and listening. I felt that something had woken me, though what it was I couldn't tell. Off to the south of the line I could hear the quiet clink of hobble chains, and a little behind us and to the north a group of officers were drinking in the back of a truck. The officers' laughter was coming in uncertain gusts, like fitful wind before a change in the weather. There was nothing in all this to alarm me, yet I continued to feel uneasy and could not get back to sleep.

I wrapped myself more tightly in my blanket and tried hard to think of something pleasant, for I'd often found this to be an effective cure for insomnia. But as I turned over, searching for a more comfortable position on the lumpy earth, I noticed with a start that Pawel was sitting up. His knees were drawn up tight against his chest and he appeared to be listening.

'Pawel!' I whispered urgently, not wishing to disturb the other sleepers who lay all around us in the trench. 'What's up? What do you hear?'

It was as if he had not heard me, and for a moment he did not respond. Then, slowly, he turned his face towards me and just looked. I could see his white teeth in the starlight, but the expression in his eyes was hidden by the brim of a woollen cap that he wore. At last, and in a tone of voice which implied that I really was a bit of a fool to ask such a question, he said, 'I would like to smoke a cigar, eh?'

'Oh would you really!' I replied sarcastically and, reassured, I turned over and faced the other way. I knew how Pawel was tortured by a craving for tobacco, but I had no sympathy for his suffering. I must add, however, that Pawel was a man who could keep his troubles to himself, and he never pestered people with complaints. So it was rather a surprise to me when a moment later he whispered, 'Janek! Are you awake?'

'Yes,' I replied quickly, again alarmed, for my nerves were very much on edge. 'What's up?'

He sighed deeply. 'I can smell their Havanas, eh Janek?' he said, as if it were the most solemn disclosure of which his soul was capable.

'Damn your triviality!' I whispered fiercely at him, thoroughly angered by the fright he'd given me, and feeling immeasurably superior to this man who had permitted himself to become so slavishly dependent on such an irrelevant thing as tobacco (how truly young I was then!). 'Listen here, Pawel,' I said, almost gritting my teeth, 'why don't you have the guts to go and ask them for one if you're so unhappy?'

He didn't reply, just hugged his knees closer to his chest, like a man who is very hungry.

I think I must have felt that he despised me. 'All right, if you're too cowardly,' I said scathingly, 'I'll go and ask them for you.'

He stared at me and said nothing. I think my challenge had really surprised him. Certainly it had surprised me. I mean, when I spoke I did so without being thoroughly prepared, if you see what I mean, to go through with it. I was thoroughly dismayed therefore when I saw that Pawel had taken my words seriously. I wanted to say, Now look here, Pawel, we're comrades after all you know, and you can't really expect me . . . and so on. But, and here I must explain my peculiar position, I was a Communist, and Pawel knew it. I was, despite my youth—though in some ways no doubt because of it—the Secretary of a certain province. And ever since the first day I had met Pawel, there in the front line, I had been at great pains to convince his simple intellect that the salvation of mankind depended entirely on the Party. Not only this, I had I believe bragged a good deal about the courage, among a host of other things, that being a member of the Party enabled one to possess. Courage, I had carefully explained to him, was not, as he and the rest of his untutored fellows believed, simply a matter of dashing blindly into the most dangerous situation without fear, it was, I insisted, the ability to overcome fear by considering consciously the principle behind one's action.

Oh yes, there is little doubt that I had managed to say a great many interesting and very intellectual things to Pawel about courage. And there is even less doubt that the net result of all this had been to convince Pawel that I had not the least idea of what I was talking about. He, on the other hand, had never said a word about courage. And now that I had rashly stated that I would go and ask the officers for a cigar he just sat and silently stared at me. And I, nonplussed as I was at finding myself in such an awkward situation, just sat and stared back at him.

The silence between us dragged on for several minutes and finally became too much for me. 'Well,' I said angrily, 'why don't you say something?'

He certainly took his time about replying, and indeed I was almost on the point of cursing him, when finally he said, with a sense of immense gratitude in his voice, 'Thank you.'

'I see,' I said icily, meaning by this, So you are going to insist, are you? You are going to let me risk my life for a stupid cigar, is that it? What kind of man are you then, if you will permit a comrade to risk his life because he was rash enough to offer you a smoke? Are you a typical example of our common people? Are you—I asked myself, though of course I said none of this aloud—are you worth it? And so I went on for quite some time, sitting there mumbling to myself and trying to outface him—to beg from him, if you like, a reprieve. But his silence was much stronger than mine. It was simpler. For him, if I did not go then I was a coward and there was an end of it.

I believe in the end I said something like, 'Yes, well, I see that you are quite immovable,' and at once began making a great show of discarding my blanket which, until that moment, I had kept securely wrapped around me. But Pawel did not say a word either to encourage or to discourage me. He just sat and watched me and waited to see what I would do.

Of course it was strictly forbidden for us to leave our sectors. In the strained atmosphere of our long vigil, during which nervous guards mistook their own shadows for a sinister prelude to the expected attack, it was undoubtedly an almost suicidal act to get out of the trench and start walking about. And this was especially true at night, when spies and deserters were known to make their moves. And these must have been desperate men, for as everyone knew they were shot without ceremony. Despite this there were a great many desertions from among our ranks, and some even got clean away, though to what ultimate refuge I could not say. Most, however, were caught. I had myself, only a few days earlier, been detailed to assist with the burial of one of these unfortunate men from our own sector. So, you see, for the sake of a cigar I had placed myself in a rather bizarre position—though it is true to say that really the escapade had reached a point where considerably more than a cigar was actually at stake for me. But, never mind, it was not that but the grotesquely ridiculous nature of my position if I were caught that struck me at the time. Who, except perhaps someone as unbalanced as myself, would believe me if I said that it was not my intention to desert, but that I was simply on my way to get a cigar? And from whom? From officers who neither knew nor cared to know whether the men under their command even got enough to eat, let alone smoked expensive cigars.

As I carefully and very slowly folded my blanket, watched all the while by the silent Pawel, it is no exaggeration to say that I felt like weeping and begging him to let me off. And why I did not do so remains a mystery to me to this day. At last I was ready and there was nothing else for it but to climb out of the trench. I found it a dreadful struggle to get up onto that low earth parapet, over which in the normal course of my duties I would leap easily. And the more careful I was to proceed silently the more noise I seemed to make—and still that cunning peasant watched my struggles without uttering a sound.

At last I was out of the trench, sprawled on my belly on the muddy ground, and awaiting with terror the inevitable bullet. It is difficult to say how long I lay like that, but I felt dreadfully short of breath, and I think it must have been for some time. From where I lay I could clearly see the truck in which the officers were having their party, for the canvas had been carelessly fastened and a warm shaft of light struck outwards into the dark. I must say that I cannot express to you how difficult it was for me to stand up. I can only say that if you have ever been forced to jump from a great height then you will know something of my feeling at that moment. My desire to crawl back into the shelter of the trench was so powerful that when instead I suddenly stood up, indeed leapt to my feet, I felt as though I had cunningly tricked myself, and I even wanted to laugh.

Standing there on the plain, alone under the faint star-light, I experienced a dizzy exultation, and so great was my irrationality that I actually felt safer than I had when I'd been lying in the mud. And instead of sneaking fearfully forward, inch by inch, I stepped out boldly, and with almost a feeling of arrogance, towards the truck. I might say honestly that I did not want my courage to go unnoticed and I dare say I could have walked to Warsaw in such a mood—or so I felt during the thirty-metre walk to the truck. On reaching the truck without being challenged, however, my careless optimism subsided as quickly as it had arisen, and gave way again to a painful uncertainty. The officers were making a great deal of noise, shouting and laughing and forgetting their worries with the help of vodka, and I could scarcely bring myself to imagine the kind of reception they would give me. Timidly I raised my hand and shook the canvas backdrop so that the metal rings clattered noisily against the wood. The noise inside the truck stopped as if it had been switched off, and for a moment the night around me was still. Then, very slowly, the canvas was pulled back an inch or two and the startled face of Captain Sienko peered cautiously at me. No more than a foot separated us and for a moment we stared uncertainly into each other's eyes. When at last he recognised me, a bemused rage overcame his features and he violently wrenched the canvas aside, so that I stood in the full glare of the pressure lamp.

'Why it's that fucking little red Jew!' he shouted, and so relieved were the other officers to discover how groundless their fear had been that they too began immediately shouting abuse and threats at me—all, that is, except the colonel. He just regarded me with a peculiarly malevolent stare, as if I were a cockroach that had dropped from the roof.

'Get him in here,' the colonel said quietly—and such is the nature of real authority that no amount of noise will drown it out.

Captain Sienko not only heard the colonel's order above the din but immediately put it into effect. He reached down and, grabbing the front of my blouse with both his huge hands, he hauled me bodily over the tailgate of the truck and set me down in front of him. I stood there and immediately the rest of the crew quietened down and waited to see what would be done. The captain appeared to me to be very drunk, for he swayed about as if he could hardly contain his impulse to murder me.

Without so much as glancing at me, the colonel addressed himself quietly to Sienko. 'What does he want?' he asked, and it seemed to me that he was very much enjoying the spectacle of the captain attempting to keep his rage under control. And perhaps it was the colonel's sinister enjoyment that gave me courage then—heaven knows, my position was desperate enough—for invariably in such circumstances one notices little things that might be to one's advantage. But whatever it was, I drew myself up, stared Sienko squarely in the eye and, with the arrogance of an assumed equality, said, 'Could one of you gentlemen spare me a cigar?'

At this the officers' hilarity burst out like a firework display, though not Sienko's of course. For their laughter was as much directed at him as it was at me. He screamed at me, almost choking with bile, 'I'll shoot your fucking balls off first, you pismired little yid!' and with that he drew out his revolver and rammed it against my crotch. I have no doubt that he would have carried out his threat there and then and without any hesitation if the colonel had not said in a tone of voice that would have befitted the atmosphere of a drawing room, 'Put away your gun, Captain, and give the young man one of your cigars.'

There was a stunned silence. All eyes, including my own, were focused on the captain's face. Like an enraged bull that has received an electric shock and does not know which way to turn in order to crush its adversary, Captain Sienko shivered and rocked his head from side to side. The colonel did not repeat his order, but waited silently in the expectation of being obeyed, no doubt revelling in the exercise of such refined cruelty. After what seemed to me to be at least an hour of agonised suspense, during which the point of the revolver remained pressed against my body, Captain Sienko at last, slowly, and with the greatest reluctance and disgust, sheathed his revolver and handed me a cigar.

As I took the cigar from him our eyes met, and I knew in that instant and for a certainty that, as soon as he could arrange it, this man would have me killed. Undoubtedly the colonel knew it also, but for him my fate was a matter of the utmost indifference.

I got back to my sector and slid into the trench beside Pawel. My teeth were chattering and I was shivering violently with the effect of delayed shock. I was quite sure I had just accomplished the stupidest and the last thing of my life—but fate, as you see, was not to let me off so lightly. Pawel, who still sat with his knees drawn up and his back against the earth, did not turn to look at me as I wrapped myself in my blanket beside him. I took his silence for the usual stoic indifference that was so characteristic of him, and in that moment I hated him for it, and determined that he would beg me for the cigar before I was finished with him. I am quite certain now that I was wrong in my interpretation of Pawel's silence on that occasion, and that it was not indifference but a surfeit of feeling which prevented him from speaking. Had I handed him the cigar without a word, I am quite certain now that he would have generously given me his friendship in return, for he perceived in my action none of the complexity and self-interest that I have attributed to it, but saw in it rather the simple action of a sincere comrade. For him, in that moment of my return with the cigar, I suspect that I was the hero I had so often claimed to be. But I had determined in my heart to humiliate him, to demand from him what he would freely have given.

When I had recovered a little, and Pawel had still not acknowledged my presence, I began to toy with the cigar as if I were considering what I should do with it. I rolled it between my palms as I have seen smokers do, and I sniffed it and altogether did my utmost to tease the poor fellow out of his wits. At last my game proved too much for him, and he turned and looked at me. Then, very quietly, and as if he had been dealing with any common dealer in the marketplace, he said, 'How much?'

I pretended not to have understood him, and turned towards him with an air of surprise, as if I had until that moment been unaware of his presence. 'What did you say, Pawel? How much? How much what?'

There was a sort of grim inevitability, a, to me, frighteningly self-conscious offer of surrender in his voice when, after a considerable pause, he said, 'How much do I have to pay you for the cigar?'

'Pay me?' I laughed with feigned incredulity and thrust the object at him. 'Here, take it! Whatever made you think I wanted payment for it?'

He took the cigar and gazed at it, nodding his head and saying nothing.

Fearing suddenly that I had dangerously overplayed my hand—as indeed turned out to be the case—I said, with an effort at cheerfulness, 'Come on, Pawel, light it up.'

Ignoring me and with much care, as if it were his most precious possession, as I suppose apart from his life it was, he hid the cigar away inside his blouse—such was his self-control! Then he turned to me. 'By my true mother,' he swore solemnly, 'I shall pay you, Janek, everything that I owe you.' And with that dreadful promise he turned away from me and lay down.

I did not sleep again that night. I sat hunched in my blanket in that damp and chilly trench and contemplated the inevitability of my imminent death. Gone was all my anxiety about the coming attack, my fear of enemy bullets, thoughts of my membership in the greatest movement in human history; all this dissolved in the face of the certainty that for personal reasons two men would soon seek to kill me. Why didn't I run away, take to my heels and risk being shot as a deserter? I didn't think of it, it's as simple as that. Does a rabbit struggle when the jaws of the hound are on its throat?

The morning brought with it a partial and very welcome distraction. As it turned out I had not been the only one to have been awakened by something mysterious during the night, and at breakfast the whole regiment was astir with speculation. Pawel offered no opinion on the matter. Understandably I watched him that day with a special interest, and was deeply impressed by the way he remained unaffected by the general mood of instability. It was as if he already possessed a secret certainty and was sure of how to act in the face of it. I looked again for a sign of the hawk, but it did not reappear.

By the early afternoon it was possible to feel a continuous tremor running through the ground. I am certain that not one man among us had any doubt as to what this phenomenon signified, yet everyone went on acting as though its cause were a mystery, and as the tremor increased so the theories grew increasingly fanciful.

Towards mid-afternoon the cavalry mounts began to grow restive, so much so in fact that their attendants soon had their hands more than full coping with them. Some foolish officer decided that what was needed was for some of the infantry occupying the trenches closest to the troop to come in and assist with quieting the frightened beasts. Naturally enough such inexperienced handling, by men who were themselves nervous and overwrought, only resulted in the horses becoming even more disturbed.

Pawel, who was himself a horseman, was for once noticeably affected, and indeed thoroughly disgusted by the scene of confusion that was rapidly developing. But for all his cursing and pleading, our lieutenant wouldn't permit him to go to the picket lines. Pawel even raised his fist and threatened to slit the lieutenant's throat, but the officer just laughed and told him to calm down and to stay at his post. But the confusion grew, and with it the noise. It was soon impossible to converse in a normal tone, if one wished to be heard one had to shout and it seemed that all at once every man of us wished to be heard above the others. Some took advantage of the situation, and there was a good deal of nervous hilarity and abuse. And when the order came to stand-to it had to be repeated several times and accompanied by threats before it had the least effect. It was quite late in the afternoon before some semblance of discipline had been restored to the lines by the officers, but even so the atmosphere was more like that of a country wedding than a front line.

Then, quite suddenly, the mood of everyone took a different and rather more sombre turn. A low rumbling, rather like a distant goods train passing slowly over a trestle bridge, became faintly audible in the west. Gradually this noise increased, and, as it did so, the noise of shouting began to subside. At first in ones and twos, but soon in large groups, and finally in a body, the men turned and silently watched the horizon. It was, as I mentioned earlier, late summer, and as the sun was about to set it was impossible to see anything clearly for the glare. When finally the sun did sink below a ridge of cloud which hung over the horizon, the stupefying scale of the German attack was revealed to us at once. The horizon, from one end to the other and without a single break, was entirely obscured by a line of tanks which were thundering towards us under full power and with an irresistible momentum. No man, however pessimistic his soul, could have foreseen this. Shocked and dumb, we stood like corn in the path of the mower.

And so we may have continued to stand, until we were cut down, had we not been alerted to a new circumstance by the sound of motors revving wildly close at our backs. On turning around I saw our lieutenant running towards the truck where I had got the cigar. He was shouting something and waving his cap. But he was ignored, and the truck turned in a tight circle and accelerated away rapidly in the direction of the Warsaw road. The hasty retreat of the colonel pulled the plug and drew after it the flood. Bedlam ensued, and men, trucks, motorcycles and horses converged in a panic-stricken mob onto the road and streamed away through the deepening dusk towards Warsaw.

Pawel touched me on the shoulder, his beautiful white teeth gleaming as he bent close to my ear and shouted, 'Now, Janek!' I stared at him and he smiled slowly, then shouted, 'Now, Janek, you will learn how to run!' He unclipped his bayonet and leapt nimbly out of the trench. His rifle he left lying in the mud, the bayonet he rammed firmly into his belt.

'Pawel!' I yelled, senselessly—it was like shouting into the teeth of a storm. He paused and looked down at me, his lean frame poised for flight. Then the first salvo of shells shrieked over our heads and detonated beyond the lines among the retreating mob on the road. Pawel turned and began to run.

Someone trod on my hand and I was knocked violently aside. Grovelling about in the bottom of the trench I was gripped by panic and I struck out, slipping and stumbling as I clawed my way onto the parapet and, hurling my rifle aside as if it had been a drowning companion, I sprinted after Pawel's retreating figure. I shall never forget how I thrust myself through the press of men and called on God to keep Pawel in my sight. But no, I did not choose to follow Pawel, it was he who chose to lead me!

Pawel's pace was steady, almost unhurried, a regular clip-clip of his heels going up and down. So naturally I soon caught up with him, for my pace was headlong. If I had not indeed checked my pace abruptly I would have crashed into him. As soon as he reached the road he dropped lightly into the drainage ditch which ran along just off the verge. The ground was muddy and uneven in the ditch, with pools and rivulets of water to further impede our progress. But the congestion was a great deal less than it was on the road, and in addition to this the parapet provided us with an excellent shelter from the lethal shrapnel with which the air was now filled.

Also, it is worth adding, even had I wished to I could not have passed Pawel without first knocking him out of the way. Those on the road above us were fairly flying along, overtaking us with ease and, it seemed to me, leaving us in the rear. In my panic I urged Pawel, with all the force in my lungs, to go faster. He may as well have not heard me for all the difference it made to him. Clip-clip, clip-clip, went his heels and he may have been running for the exercise of it to see him.

It was at this point, being forced to content myself with the unhurried regularity of Pawel's pace, that I began to overcome my panic and to perceive the sound common sense behind his attitude. I settled in a pace behind him and it was not long before I noticed that the crowd of figures on the road had started to thin out. The strain of their initial sprint must have begun to quickly tell on them. Also I was further encouraged after a time to notice that the shells were now exploding more often to our rear. Unlike me, Pawel looked neither to his left nor to his right, but kept on, his heels going like clockwork and his arms held up and swinging like a real runner. It occurred to me that perhaps the whole front had not broken before the onslaught of the tanks, and that perhaps only our sector had bolted in panic, the rest remaining behind to engage in a hopeless struggle. But I had no thought of turning back. It was too late for that, and I stayed in close behind Pawel, who ran not as a man who is running away from something in fear of his life, but as a man who has a destination to reach. Also, I must say, that despite my strong initial sense of being led by him, he ran as though he were alone. It was impossible to say whether or not he knew that I was close behind him, for if he knew he gave no sign. So, copying his style as well as

I could and disciplining my breathing to the regular rhythm of his pace, I followed.

We ran on into the deepening night, leaving the roar of the battle further and further behind us, and any straggler who was still on the road above us we overtook with ease. It was a great reassurance for me to feel the firm thump of my boots and the energetic drive of my legs carrying me along. I was his shadow. Clip-clip, clip-clip, went our heels, spattering the mud effortlessly aside. And while I was still fresh then and able to view the situation with a little clarity it seemed to me almost beautiful, this running not like a scared rabbit ahead of the dogs but running with control and rhythm, driven on by a purpose not by fear.

It is easy enough for a man in the last decade of his life to become intoxicated with memories of his youth, and not difficult at all for him to create a legend for himself. You must understand that such beauty as there was that night was brief.

Without the slightest change of pace or of direction we ran on, our boots thudding in unison like the steady beat of a pump, and an hour or more or less passed. By now I was seriously feeling the strain. After sitting in a trench for three weeks without drill or other exercise my muscles were slack and my wind, despite my attempts to control my breathing, was shallow and erratic. A pain which had begun in my knees was rapidly extending upward into my thighs and making each stride an effort. Somewhere far in the rear I thought I heard the sound of a motorbike and this put thoughts of calling Pawel to rest quite out of my mind. And Pawel? Well he just kept on running. A metronome could not have maintained a more imperturbable measure.

My chest and thighs felt red-hot, and at every breath and every step the pain increased, and I was soon calling on unimagined reserves to measure stride for stride with Pawel. And minute by minute it began to seem to me that he was going faster and faster. The mud itself seemed to congeal and grope at my boots, as if it had a conscious design against me, and all this time Pawel moved seemingly with the ease of a phantom. Once I slipped and almost fell. So close was I to Pawel that my outstretched hand touched his heel, and that accidental, minute event was enough to keep me going. Though it was almost certainly too dark for me to see his boots, my imagination was enough, and I believed that I could see his heels flicking back at me with each stride. Undoubtedly I could hear the thud and splash of his boots but it was not that, it was the imagined sight of them which mesmerised me and kept me compulsively attached to him from then on.

And so we ran, measuring stride for stride until the lapse of time ceased to have any meaning for me. The moon rose and I saw then how the distance between Pawel and I would increase perceptibly the moment I permitted my concentration to falter. That is when I began seriously to fight in order to retain my clarity. So long as I held doggedly to the unwavering and rhythmical flick of Pawel's heels I could keep up, but the moment I permitted fatigue to blur my vision I would begin dropping behind. Though it was impossible that any man should have been unaffected by the strain, Pawel ran, or seemed to me to run, as though his energy and spirit were without limit.

My goal, which was simply to keep up with him, began to seem to me hopelessly unattainable. I prayed that his stride would break, that he would trip or stumble or change his pace, but he ran relentlessly on like a machine. All I prayed for was a sign from him that he too was suffering, that the strain was also becoming intolerable for him, that he was human flesh like me. But I received no sign and the race continued with the hypnotic insistence of a nightmare. The end lay in the vague moonlit spaces ahead of me, where I would at last drop, and where Pawel would run on, his emphatic strides carrying him into another world that lay somewhere beyond my endurance.

I ran, and I entered at last into a final strange dimension of exhaustion in which weird and fantastic images leapt into my mind, dazzling and bewildering me as if a flashbulb were being repeatedly exploded in my face. I scarcely knew whether it was the moon I saw or Pawel's heels, and the struggle for clarity—to keep before my mind some sense of the real—became harder minute by minute. Impressions of huge birds sailing and looping around my head distracted me, and I shied wildly as grotesque and threatening shapes leapt at me from the passing shadows. I would shake my head and thrust myself forward through the illusions and for an instant I would regain touch with those relentless heels.

But increasingly the illusory became more seductive as the pain of my reality increased. I gave in for brief moments without really meaning to, then came to with a start, terrified for an instant that I had actually ceased running. In the end it was only my pain which told me whether I was still running or had finally given in. If I could feel pain then I knew that I was still in the race, but the moment a warm feeling of effortless wellbeing began to spread through my consciousness, I knew that I had at once to renew the struggle without a second's delay. To renew the struggle at each lapse I had forcibly to smash my way through this mental barrier, I had to cry out in my mind that to give in would mean death. But no sooner had I broken through the numbness to a sight of Pawel's heels than I was again assailed by unbearable pain, and the question arose once more . . . Why not death? Because, I cried in my mind. Because . . . because Pawel! And so it assumed the metre of a chant, an echo and reinforcement of the physical rhythm, and I could not relinquish my hold, I refused to die, and the wind roared in my lungs and I was shackled to the mud and I tore my feet from the earth with my teeth and I ran and ran and ran in pursuit of the unreachable Pawel. And like a phantom of my mind Pawel ran on ahead . . .

He must have hit the wooden footbridge a split second ahead of me and I must have crashed into him, for I came to my senses with a feeling that I was suffocating beneath a great weight. I hadn't the strength to push his body off me, and lay there half deliriously aware that there was nothing to be done about it. I think I passed out a couple of times before at last beginning to regain a real sense of my surroundings.

With an effort I struggled out from beneath Pawel and rolled him onto his back. On all fours and shivering like a wet dog I gazed down into his face. His mouth was wide open and he was making a loud snoring noise. The blow had smashed out most of his teeth and blood from a large wound on his forehead was welling blackly across his face. I sat back on my heels and closed my eyes.

As I sat there slowly recovering I became aware of the distant sound of gunfire. Another sound, intermittent and closer than the guns, began after a time to intrude on my consciousness. I listened, then crawled up onto the bank with difficulty, and gazed back the way we had come. The skyline was lit by a continuous series of flashes, and from my new elevation the sound of gunfire was much louder. About a mile down the road a powerful light swept the fields on either side; slowly it traversed, probing this way and that and occasionally coming to rest briefly, then moving on again. About twenty yards off to my left, and no doubt served by the bridge that had proved our downfall, there was a barn. I slid into the ditch and began alternately hauling and pushing Pawel up the bank. It took all my remaining strength, but with frequent rests I at last managed to drag Pawel into the barn and out of the moonlight. Then I lay back on the straw and gave myself up to exhaustion.

I opened my eyes and saw him. Pawel was kneeling at my feet and swaying slowly from side to side. He was a ghastly sight. His toothless mouth, through which he breathed noisily and with difficulty, gaped blackly, and without his cap his shaven head and deep-set eyes gave him a cadaverous appearance. In his right hand, with the point lightly touching the open palm of his left, he held his bayonet. His gaze was fixed steadily on my face. We confronted each other thus for a full minute before I managed to speak.

'So,' I said, and my voice was like a dry whisper in the straw, 'you are going to kill me, Pawel.'

He gave no sign that he had heard me, but went on rocking slowly from side to side, and I realised that he was working himself up to the point where suddenly he would plunge the bayonet into my chest. My body contracted involuntarily beneath the threat, my muscles cringing away from the steel shaft in his hands.

Suddenly the roar of a machine-gun shattered the silence and, as Pawel's lifeless body fell—it seemed with an infinite leisure—I glimpsed the silhouettes of two German soldiers in the doorway of the barn.

1975

The Story's Not Over Yet

This lecture was given in honour of my late friend
Frank Budby, elder of the Barada Barna people

To stick only to the facts seemed to deny the fictional
paradox of truthfulness.

Drusilla Modjeska, Poppy

I'm a novelist, not a critic, but something I've noticed and think
worth remarking on is that the most vigorous development in
Australia's cultural landscape in the last twenty years has been
the emergence into the mainstream, and onto the international
stage, of Aboriginal art, music and literature. This seems to
me to be a reflection of what is happening in contemporary
Australian society generally. Not politically, to be sure, and
not quickly enough for people who are understandably frus-
trated by the slowness of cultural change, but it does seem
nevertheless to be a reflection of what is happening within
contemporary Aboriginal culture and to the wider underlying

cultural realities among the general Australian population. The Aboriginal voice in art, music and literature is now heard from centre stage rather than from the wings. For the first time since the arrival of Europeans in this country, in fact, the idea that artistic inspiration runs from its origins in Europe to Australia no longer holds true. And this is not a matter of the empire writing back, but on the contrary is the origination of new formal artistic inspirations from within Australia's own Indigenous culture finding a central place here and being widely celebrated in Europe, America and Asia.

I say twenty years, because as well as cultural change generally it's particularly the novel I want to talk about and it is roughly twenty years since Kim Scott's first novel *True Country* was published by Fremantle Press in 1993. It was recognised by a number of critics as marking the debut of a powerful new voice among Australian novelists not only in its subject matter but also in its style and tone. The reviewer in the *Australian Book Review* rightly said the 'novel marks an impressive debut and a challenging direction for Aboriginal writing'. With hindsight we might now amend this to say that *True Country* marked a challenging direction for Australian writing generally. Since then Scott has won this country's most coveted literary prize, the Miles Franklin Award, twice, the first time in 2000 for his second novel, *Benang: From the Heart*, and the second time in 2011 for his third novel, *That Deadman Dance*. It is an astonishing record. With his first three novels Kim Scott has established himself nationally and internationally as one of this country's, and the world's, most innovative novelists writing in the English language.

Even more challenging, arguably, than Scott's is the work of Alexis Wright. Wright's monumental second novel, *Carpentaria*, was published by Giramondo in 2006 and won the Miles Franklin Award the following year. Her third novel, *The Swan Book*, published by Giramondo in 2013, is just as uncompromising in its challenge to the traditional form of the novel as is *Carpentaria*. While the source of Wright's vision arises principally, though not exclusively, from her confident sense of her place within the contemporary forms of Indigenous and European cultures and language uses, she sees that to adhere to any one culture or tradition is too questionable a proposition to be embraced in the twenty-first century. Belonging and home are not what Wright seeks to establish. When you read Wright you are aware of reading a new literature that is not striving to make itself new in the traditional European modernist sense, but which is of itself authentically new. If I were a critic, which I'm not, I suspect I would be examining here the complex new ways in which Wright perceives cultural decline and revitalisation. The re-emphasis of what might be called an Australian tradition is not Wright's concern. For Wright, something that might once have stood for an Australian tradition is far too simplistic and, indeed, manifestly outpaced by events, to hold her attention. She is a writer of the world. While her centre is Australia, it is crisis and ambiguity, what might be called the whirlwind of diffuse cultural collision in our world today, that offer the widest focus of Wright's vast imaginative energies. The result is a revitalisation of the novel form itself.

Benang: From the Heart, *That Deadman Dance*, *Carpentaria* and *The Swan Book* have radically reinscribed not only the cultural sources of the Australian novel's energies but its form in a way that no non-Aboriginal novelist has done, except possibly Patrick White. These four novels, and they are all large major works in the widest sense, represent by far the most challenging, vigorous and innovative development in the Australian novel that has ever occurred and take it beyond the traditional European confines of the novel form as that form was theoretically developed in the Hungarian Marxist philosopher Georg Lukács's *The Theory of the Novel*, which was written during the First World War. I'm not a great fan of Lukács, but he said some beautiful things. Lukács, like Milan Kundera fifty years after him, in his persuasive and influential 1986 *The Art of the Novel*, was writing about the European novel. For Kundera, the European novel had its origin in the early seventeenth century with Cervantes's *Don Quixote*, which was published when its author was nearly sixty. Lukács, like Kundera and the Russian philosopher and literary critic Mikhail Bakhtin, was also examining the European novel as essentially the form of long prose fiction that replaced the epic, which they too saw as having its origins in the classical world. I want to make the point that the novel is a universal form which has belonged and continues to belong to all literate cultures.

One of the greatest strengths of the novel form has been its durability and its adoption by and adaption to all literate cultures. The Greek 'novels' of Achilles Tatius, Chariton, Heliodorus, Longus and Xenophon, with the exception of Chariton, were all written during or after the second century AD. There was a continuous tradition of prose fiction among the Greeks long before Europe possessed a literate culture. Chinese and Japanese novels also existed at a highly developed stage well over a thousand years ago.

I don't wish to suggest that Kim Scott and Alexis Wright are concerned with the same subject matter, or that their style and approach are closely related. But I do wish to make the point that they are not alone but are eminently successful representatives of a wide and growing movement among Aboriginal writers and intellectuals that is in the process of shaping and inscribing a deep shift in Australia's culture. An interesting feature of their success, especially overseas, is that their international reception seems to have largely bypassed the context of this nation and its institutions, including the discipline of Australian literature. These writers, like the Indigenous visual artists before them, have gone straight from the regional to the international. Many of these writers and intellectuals have written richly perceptive accounts of this change. (For one such view I would recommend Tony Birch's keynote address to the Edinburgh World Writers' Conference in 2013.) It is worth noting that Sally Morgan's *My Place*, which was published in 1987, is, according to the AustLit database, by far the most translated example of Australian literature, both in terms of range of languages and numbers of translations. Whether in art or literature, the Aboriginal perspective is proving to be the most interesting for the rest of the world. It is new, fresh, exciting and challenging, and in both art and literature, the Aboriginal practice is freer from, and less self-conscious of, the weight of the European tradition.

In Australia, and no doubt in many other countries as well, we have been through a cultural change in our approach to education and to our sense of belonging in the world in the generation since Kundera's and the three generations since Lukács's and Bakhtin's works were published. Today education in Australia, and elsewhere in what we fondly call the West, seeks to avoid a Eurocentric point of view and to be inclusive of the sensitivities of a multicultural student body. Our sense of the history and imaginative origins of our literary and artistic forms has extended beyond Europe to include, for example, the earliest extant Chinese and Japanese novels. Though even today what is called World Literature—for example, in the works of academics such as David Damrosch and Pascale Casanova—is usually Euro- or US-centric.

We have no difficulty reading Murasaki Shikibu's eleventh-century work *The Tale of Genji* as a novel. In Murasaki's rich evocations of the intimate lives of people living a thousand years ago, we are able to enjoy the sense of being in a novel written six hundred years before the birth of Kundera's European novel. The form of the novel is not so radically changed today from these early appearances that we can't at once recognise *The Tale of Genji* or *Chin P'ing Mei* or *A Dream of Red Mansions* as novels. We read these books indeed as if they were modern novels, and are enthralled by the same spirit of the human story. To be sure, James Joyce did blow up the firework factory going on for a hundred years ago now, but when the stars had settled it was clear that what he had done was to have written novels, two of them so extraordinary as to leave many of us dizzy and bedazzled for years afterwards, but novels all the same. The form endured and was enriched by Joyce, not destroyed by him. After Joyce writers could do anything they felt like doing and call the result a novel, just as after Duchamp's urinal, art was whatever you said was art.

Writing and reading novels and history—and sometimes it's hard to know which of these I'm doing at any given moment—has provided me with the greatest satisfactions and frustrations of my life. When I was a boy growing up in London it wasn't a novelist, however, but an astronomer who first inspired me with the idea of the limitlessness of the human imagination. In 1950, at the age of fourteen, I listened with rapt attention to Fred Hoyle's series of lectures 'The Nature of the Universe' on the BBC and was thrilled to learn that the universe wasn't a static reality but was still in the process of creation and would go on being created forever. (Hoyle wasn't the originator of the notion of an ever-expanding universe—that honour belongs, I believe, to the little known Dutch astronomer Willem de Sitter, who had trouble convincing Einstein to accept the theory—but Hoyle explained it in language that every schoolboy and schoolgirl could understand.) It was the most liberating idea I had ever heard. From then on the notion of the fundamental necessity for change, the limitlessness of the human imagination and of the ongoing process of creation became for me, and for many of my generation, a keystone of my beliefs, and I found it natural to reject ideas of stasis and completion in every dimension of human life and the natural world as being an outmoded, conservative way of thinking.

In 1953, at the age of sixteen, driven by a youthful desire for adventure, I left England and came to Australia on my own to work as a stockman on cattle stations in the Central Highlands of Queensland and later in Alexis Wright's Gulf of Carpentaria. In the Gulf I worked with the legendary tribal Aboriginal stockmen on Augustus Downs Station on the Leichhardt River. These black stockmen became my friends and made me welcome in their country. They had no birth certificates, could not travel without a permit to do so from the police, were not able to get a permit from the police. And they were not paid anything for their work. Their pay was supposed to be held in trust for them. They never saw it. They were not citizens of Australia and were not counted in the census and did not have the right to vote. In other words, they lacked the basic human rights and the respect that we expect to be accorded to all human beings in this world. You can imagine, therefore, what a joy it is for me today to see Aboriginal novelists and intellectuals leading the way in a major cultural shift in this country.

Frank Budby, the friend in whose honour this lecture is delivered, sadly passed away on the morning of 6 April this year. I had hoped Frank would be here with us today and that this event would give his spirits a lift. I was greatly honoured by his trust and the gift of his friendship and I shall never forget him. When he first stayed with us when we were living in Port Melbourne I was astonished to learn it was the first white man's house he had ever been a guest in. Frank was one of those legendary stockmen who inspired me in my early youth in Australia. Later in his life he reinvented himself, as many of us did. Frank became a leader of his people, and in establishing Woora Consulting to protect and manage his people's cultural heritage he formed the business basis for the salvation of his people from prison and violence and drugs and all the other curses that had been laid upon them. His family and the Barada Barna elders asked me to read the eulogy at his funeral in Mackay on Monday, 14 April. Frank was one of the finest and wisest men I have ever met. No one who met Frank was ever unaffected by him but took away with them from the meeting the conviction that they had met a leader of true wisdom and generosity of mind. Memorably, one time when he was our guest at Castlemaine, we had some visitors for dinner to meet him and one of them lamented the dispossession of Aboriginal country. Frank's quiet response to this was, 'The story's not over yet.' Nothing could be truer than this observation, which immediately put me in mind of Fred Hoyle's expanding universe. For the story of Aboriginal recovery of country and culture during the past twenty years owes everything to unsung leaders of Frank's capacity. He is a hero of his people and to everyone who met him and it is my hope to continue to honour him in my own work. The story of Aboriginal recovery of country and culture will continue and will go from strength to strength so long as there are leaders and visionaries of Frank Budby's kind to show all of us the way. Frank owed his success not to welfare but to his own intelligence, personal courage and initiative.

It is due to Indigenous leaders of Frank's rare energies, unselfish commitment and abilities that the Aboriginal story in much of Australia has been one of new confidence and increasing power over the past twenty years, especially in the north. Without Woora Consulting the historic and cultural legacy of the Barada Barna people would have been neglected or even destroyed by the encroachment of mining and other industrial developments. The success of Woora Consulting has meant that many of the children of the current generation have been able to attend private schools and to qualify for university in increasing numbers. The old poverty cycle in which Frank's people were still caught when he began his work of recovery has been broken.

I was fortunate to come of age in Australia at a time and in a place where Aborigines were not viewed as a dying race, as they were in the cities of the south in the fifties, but were abundant in number and were at the very centre of the work I was taking part in. By the early sixties I had left the bush and had become a student reading history and English at Melbourne University. It was a time of great social change. What Hoyle's lectures had done for me, and for many others of my generation, was to liberate our young minds from the static and conservative views of our elders. He liberated us from the idea that the job had been done and that reality was known and measurable and was subject to unchanging laws and that we might become part of that continuing tradition. Well, we didn't. Ten years after Hoyle's lectures, by the time we were in our twenties and I was at uni, we had become the generation of the counterculture, and the social revolution of the sixties was well underway. The serious fight to end capital punishment and to bring racism and sexism to an end had begun in earnest and was no longer the province of a few far-seeing dedicated souls. We may not have understood it in quite this way at the time, but to have heard Hoyle in 1950 was to have heard the voice of a prophet of a new freedom. Possibilities, it seemed, were limitless and were naturally so. It was prohibitions and rules that were limiting and were against the natural order, and so they had to go. And of course many of them did go. Conservatives, whose voices we are hearing again today, say far too many of the old rules were discarded and ought to be reinstated. Hearing those conservative voices repeating their old mantras of stasis and withdrawal today I am reminded that what we used to call the good fight, like the universe itself and the recovery of Aborigines from the dispossession, is never a done deal but must go on being fought with vigilance and energy from one generation to the next. The bad old days of a conservative social order can be reimposed, step by stealthy step, and they will be if the present generation is not vigilant.

My very dear friend the philosopher Raimond Gaita asked me some years ago if I would like to join him in a discussion at the Sydney Writers' Festival on the subject of the relations of philosophy and fiction. I agreed at once, as I have always thought of the novel and philosophy as siblings, just as history and the novel are siblings. As the biographer of Rosa Luxemburg, J.P. Nettl, says in his introduction to that book, 'Every history is a matter of selection and emphasis.' No less is true of the novel. Interestingly Lukács's *The Theory of the Novel* (1971) is subtitled *A Historico-Philosophical Essay*, thus bringing together in the one work the three cultural sibling forms of history, philosophy and literature. There is a persistent edge of rivalry between these three forms in their claims to cultural territory and truth, to be sure, but there is also a wide area of shared ground that is not in dispute but is complementary. History is often inspired by literature and without history there would be no novels. Philosophy and the serious novel often work the same moral ground. The serious novel is always, indeed, an ethical text, and is aware of the effects on individual human beings of ideologies. Without history, without a consciousness of the story of the formation and reformation of the social order, the serious novel, among much else that is essential to a civilised perception of the human project, would not exist. As the great European thinker Hannah Arendt said in 1955, 'No philosophy, no analysis, no aphorism, be it ever so profound, can compare in intensity and richness of meaning with a properly narrated story.' The three siblings thrive with and depend upon each other for their vitality and authenticity as cultural documents. Lenin insisted he had learned more about France from reading the novels of Balzac than he ever had from reading the histories, which was really a compliment as much to historians of the day as it was to Balzac. Balzac, after all, had read widely in the history of pre- and post-Napoleonic France. Indeed his first title for his cycle *La Comédie humaine* was *A Study of [Social] Mores*. Balzac was actively involved in the politics of his day and possessed a keen understanding of the distinctions between the Crown and the revolutionists and the historical origins of the views of each side. History and the serious novel are close cousins. There is, however, something the serious novel does that history doesn't do, just as there are things history does that the novel doesn't do. By serious novel I mean the novel the reader can trust for an accurate portrayal of the intimate lives and social realities of individuals at a given moment in time, be it contemporary or historical. The vast area of our private and interior lives that is subject to the ambiguities of the human heart is the true, indeed the unique, home of the so-called realist novel. In the experimental novel this centrality of human intimacy is given over to a concern with style and form. The serious novel is the novel in which the author does not shape the truth of his or her story to meet the expectations of the market, but holds to the truth of the story despite the fact that it might be unpalatable to the market.

The novel endures in all literate cultures because its subject is our story, the intimate lives of us. In a serious novel the intimate lives of the characters are set within an authentic cultural and historical moment. Tolstoy's and Balzac's characters carry their social realities and their sense of history and culture with them, but remain identifiable for us today as individuals nevertheless; people just like us, caring, hating, loving, suffering and dying, traitorous or heroic, they are as human as we are and elicit our empathy. And it doesn't matter if we are of one gender and they are of another, or we are of their time and place or of another time and place. We care for the characters in the novel and often identify their fate with our own.

During our discussion about philosophy and fiction at the Sydney Writers' Festival, Rai came up with the phrase *the limitations of fiction*. We didn't explore what these limitations might be and I don't recall Rai elaborating on what he might have meant by the phrase, nor did I ask him what he meant by it. We left it hanging suggestively between us, as one often does in a real conversation. The phrase has stayed with me and has continued to hang about in my thoughts ever since. The limitations of fiction are, of course, the same as the limitations of philosophy. Or, for that matter, the limitations of scientific thought—remember Einstein's initial reluctance to accept de Sitter's theory of an expanding universe—or the limitations of historiography. The limitations of all human intellectual endeavour are determined by the limitations of the human imagination. In order for us to be able to measure the limitations of the human imagination so that we can come to know its limits, however—as Einstein wished to measure the limitations of the static universe before he was interrupted by de Sitter—we would need to propose a static model for the human imagination. We would need to adopt a position outside the imagination from which to gain a detached view of it as a whole measurable and complete entity. In order to do this we would need to employ our imagination. It doesn't immediately follow from what I've just said that the human imagination itself, like the universe, is still expanding, but I believe this to be the case. And my belief is not unrelated to the early influence of Hoyle; a conviction formed in youth, in other words, that we can't measure the extent of our possibilities before they are fully realised.

The epic, the novel, the poem, the scientific treatise, the work of history, the work of biography and so on, just like the universe, are no longer viewed by us as finished static forms but are—or in the case of the epic and the sagas have been—transitory conceptions along the way of an ever-changing universe of human culture and ideas. This is not to suggest a qualitative progress of human culture and ideas. Change, not progress, is what I'm asserting. The universe and the whole of nature and humankind, as Einstein was required to accept, is an unfinished work. This surely includes the human imagination. As Frank said, 'The story's not over yet.' I believe he was right. Cultural formations change from day to day like cloud formations. The limitations of these changes are not known to us. We are ourselves performers within the dynamic of the process, and are performed upon by these forces as much as we ourselves are the creators of the forces. This is the territory of Alexis Wright. We are culture's offspring as much as we are her maker. We are embedded in culture and often find it difficult to see or to accept the way our culture changes around us, often creating in us a sense that we are strangers to ourselves. Rai and I were for a moment silenced, I think, by the phrase he had come up with, the limitations of fiction. It was as if he had struck a bell that sounded into the deeps of our ignorance.

Soon after I began to read history and English at Melbourne University in 1962, having conceived what then seemed to me to be the nearly impossible ambition of becoming a serious novelist, it was my great good fortune to meet and win the friendship of Max Blatt. I soon began to bring to our regular conversations in his home my first impressions of modern European history and the work of the poets and novelists as they were taught at Melbourne. I thought I was studying two separate disciplines, but Max soon showed me that literature and ideology are not separable. I've seen it recorded somewhere that Max was born in 1907, the same year as my father. He was a Central European intellectual who, like the hero of his youth, Rosa Luxemburg, grew up in Poland as a Jew speaking German at home. He was gentlemanly and formal in his manner, slight in his appearance, and often seemed frail. In fact he was not frail but was physically robust. He once helped me rebuild a fence that a flood had carried away and he wielded a heavy fencing bar for hours in the muggy heat apparently without becoming fatigued. Max had been a member of ORG Neu Beginnen (New Beginning) in the 1930s, a German Socialist intellectual group committed to resisting the Nazis. The fight, as he saw it, was of course primarily to save his people, but it was also a fight to save the human project of civilisation itself. As for Arthur Koestler and Ignazio Silone and other novelists and intellectuals of his time, the reality of Communism had shown itself to be as brutal and authoritarian as Fascism. During one of our long talks about European history and politics and novel-writing in the sitting room of his house in Caulfield, which Max and his wife, Ruth, shared with the Viennese pianist Robert Kohner and his wife, Peta, Max stood up and went to the bookshelf at the side of the fireplace, took down a book with a red cover and handed it to me. 'This will make my intellectual journey clearer to you,' he said.

Ruth and Max Blatt

The book Max gave me that evening was *The God that Failed: Six Studies in Communism* (1950). The first three contributors are all ex-Communists and novelists who were once deeply committed to the ideals and aims of the Communist International. The other three—André Gide, Louis Fischer and the English poet Stephen Spender—were either briefly members of the party or were at one time deeply sympathetic to its aims. All of them, except the journalist Louis Fischer, also wrote novels. They were people intent on bringing about cultural change of a heroic order against the forces of evil. I don't remember what my reaction to the book was at the time except that, having read it, I was left with a persisting sense of its importance and it has remained on my shelves ever since. Max also gave me at that time Thomas Mann's *Doctor Faustus* and Nikos Kazantzakis's *The Last Temptation*. It was clear to me that these novels represented Max's idea of the serious novel. I still have them. It wasn't until I recently decided to write an autobiographical work in order to further explore my friendship with Max Blatt, and hopefully to celebrate something of his life and his enduring influence on my writing, that I took down *The God that Failed* and reread it.

Almost at once I was reminded of Max's conviction that the novelist carries a responsibility to his or her culture and society to seek after the truth of our individual and social existence and to offer critical insight into the moral and ideological dimensions of our lives, and does not owe his or her allegiance to the forces of the marketplace. Max's idea of the seriousness of the task of the novelist met in me one of my deepest longings and his influence was profound and remains with me to this day. Without his influence I would not have been the novelist I have been. He set the bar high and I have never reached it, but I have aimed for it. Max was convinced that, in order to be properly equipped for his or her task, the novelist must know history, not only to have a sense of the origins of culture but also in order to be in a position to question history's assumptions and conclusions and the claims of politicians. Rereading *The God that Failed* I wondered why so many of these committed intellectuals, all of whom had also been activists—even Gide, momentarily—had chosen also to write novels. The answer to this was in Max's conviction, a conviction of his youth, that the novelist's work must be a reliable guide to society. By this he meant that we must be able to trust the work of the novelist just as we expect to trust the work of the historian or the biographer. He didn't say we had to agree with any of them, only that we must be able to trust them. To differ with works and with the opinions of friends without arousing enmity is one of the great gifts of what I think of as true friendship, and is also necessary if productive conversations are to take place between disciplines and individuals. This was one of the wonderful conditions of my friendship with Max Blatt. We disagreed often but always respected each other. Such respect is the medium through which we are enabled to learn from each other, rather than simply try to convince the other of the rightness of our own position.

The vital connection for me with the idea of the reliability of the novel and of the influence not only of *The God that Failed* but of Max Blatt's idea of what it meant to be a novelist became clearer to me once again the moment I reread, after fifty years, this beautiful passage in Ignazio Silone's untitled essay:

> As for the difficulties and imperfections of self-expression with which I sometimes have to wrestle, they arise, not from lack of observation of the rules of good writing, but rather from a conscience which, while struggling to heal certain hidden and perhaps incurable wounds, continues obstinately to demand that its integrity be respected. For to be sincere is obviously not enough, if one wants to be truthful.

Silone and Max belonged to the same scattered diaspora of non-aligned ex-Communists. These idealists wrote novels because they believed the form of the novel was a noble thing and could be trusted.

How do we begin to measure the reliability of a novel? One way, and I believe it is a good way, is whether the people the novel claims to be about recognise themselves in it. If a writer from another country comes to Australia and writes about us and our times, we expect to be able to recognise ourselves and our environment in the work. We might not agree with or like the work, but we should be able to see that its portrait of us is authentic. When the authenticity of our work is celebrated by those we have written about, we know we have been trustworthy at least to that extent. This is one measure of our seriousness. Just as there are no absolute objective values by which to measure the universe, because it is constantly in motion, so there are no absolute objective values by which we can measure the trustworthiness of history or the novel or of biography. But there are a number of soundings we can make, a number of tests we can apply that are not entirely subjective. But we can't be either proscriptive or prescriptive about these. For in the end, as Silone rightly says, 'Anyone who has reflected seriously about himself or others knows how profoundly secret are certain decisions and how mysterious and unaccountable are certain vocations.'

As a boy of fourteen I trusted Fred Hoyle. That trust was important. I've published eleven of the fourteen novels I've written. The greatest satisfaction for me has been when those whom I have written about have celebrated the novels in which they appear, or when intellectuals and readers in the country whose society and history has come under examination in my work, such as China, Tunisia, France, the country of the Jangga and the Barada Barna or the suburbs of Melbourne, have celebrated the work. This has been poignantly true for me with *Journey to the Stone Country* and *Landscape of Farewell*, which are both books written about dearly loved friends that would not have been published if these friends had not approved of them at the manuscript stage. It is also true in a national sense with the celebration in China of my novel *The Ancestor Game*. The writer can strive to maintain a level of authenticity for their work, but in the end they can't be the judge of whether what they have done can be trusted or not, any more than a historian can be the judge of the trustworthiness of his or her work. Despite his enormous ambition to get it right, the critical and popular fate of Manning Clark's passionately debated six-volume *History of Australia* is a devastating example of history needing to be written again by the generation that follows.

Historiography, however, which we've only come to know in its secular form since the mid-nineteenth century, shares with the exact sciences today a quality not shared with the novel. The novel, and art generally—and this is also true of philosophy—does not progress or get better but merely changes. Historiography, however, has become more reliable with new methodologies and new systems for retrieving and examining the record in greater objective detail than was once possible. History is objectively more reliable today than it was, for example, when I was at university in the sixties. The novel, on the other hand, in common with all the arts, changes its content, its style and its focus and the cultural sources of its inspiration, but it does not become more reliable. We don't get better at novel-writing. The arts don't progress in quality, but move with their times and reflect cultural change, as in the case of Kim Scott and Alexis Wright. We are not more reliable as novelists today than we were in Tolstoy's or George Eliot's time. We are merely different. And, in fact, not all that different, despite the cry to make it new.

I've had great joy from writing novels. But now I need to obey the rule of the necessity for change and have taken on a new challenge. This need to take a critical look at what I've been doing with my life possibly has something to do with Socrates's remark that an unexamined life has not been worth living. I have begun to write what I hope can become a celebration

Frank Budby

of the tragic beauty of Max Blatt's life and of our friendship. The ocean of my ignorance, I soon found, is far deeper and broader than the island of my knowing. In reflecting on my own history I am aware of the paradox that I am going into a largely unknown landscape along a road I have never travelled before. It has also become clear to me that recollection is itself fiction. It was Derrida who warned us to be aware that the scandalous infidelity of memory makes no distinction between fact and fiction but endorses both equally as unlimited categories of the human imagination. In making these remarks about cultural change and the novel I'm happy to give the last word to a beautiful phrase of that much-maligned thinker Georg Lukács: '. . . everything that falls from our weary and despairing hands must always be incomplete'. It is a sentiment both the astronomer Fred Hoyle and the cultural leader Frank Budby agreed with.

2014

Prophets of the Imagination

In the beginning was space, this mysterious, intellec-
tually incomprehensible invention.

Max Beckmann

'. . . we like to be among strangers.' She looked out the
window. 'To be anonymous is what we most want, not to
be known. Secretly we want to be solitary. We can't stand
having people know who we are. It terrifies us.' She turned
from contemplating the street. 'I love feeling lost and alone
in the city. The city is our natural place. We need it. I fear
more than anything being lost and alone in the bush. Out
there we're confronted with ourselves. In the bush there's
no escape from who we are or from each other. We pretend
to love the wilderness, but we hate the thought of it really.'

So says Marina Golding, a contemporary non-Indigenous
Melbourne artist and one of the principal characters in my

265

new novel, *Prochownik's Dream*. In real life Marina is intense, honest, a gifted artist and an intellectual. The evidence for the truth of Marina's opinion is overwhelming. Australia is the most urbanised country in the world, and except for a handful of notable tourist destinations the hinterland of the continent remains unvisited and unknown to most people who live here.

The idea of the outback has been largely replaced for this generation of educated Australians by the less specifically Australian and more global idea of wilderness. In the old view of the hinterland as outback it was the survival of the human individual that was challenged. But in landscape as wilderness this perception has been reversed, and it is the landscape itself that is seen to be fragile and at risk from human intervention. The landscape itself, the space that is being referred to, has not changed. Whether we find ourselves in the outback or in the wilderness these days depends on our style of thinking. But undoubtedly for the great majority of Australians, for those millions who live and work in the great coastal cities such as Sydney and Melbourne, the outback is little more than a marketing term of the travel industry.

It was unequivocally the Australian outback in its former sense, however, that notion of a vast frontier hinterland where a heroic striving of the human spirit was required from the individual, that took me to Australia from England half a century ago. I was sixteen when I set out alone from a farm in the West Country of England to travel to the Australian outback. I did not think of myself then as a migrant but as an adventurer. In my heart I knew myself to be on a quest.

My decision to go to Australia was not governed by the desire to better myself. I was not going to the land of opportunity. The usual reasons in those days why people of my kind went from England to Australia did not interest me. The benefits I hoped for from my journey to the outback were not tangible. I went because I longed to find a culture in which the values of the fabled heroic age of my own ancestors still possessed some currency. The Australian outback seemed to me to be the one place left in the world where I might fulfil this romantic dream of my youth. My good friend, the biographer Hazel Rowley, said to me when she first heard my story: 'You seem to be tremendously haunted by landscape. Space,' she said, 'is clearly tremendously important for you.'

When I set out on my journey, my knowledge of the Australian outback was limited to one small black-and-white photograph that I had seen by the light of an oil lamp in the kitchen of the Exmoor farm labourer with whom I lived. One of the photographs in the book, the details of which have remained vivid to me, was of a group of stockmen lounging in the shade of a low verandah and gazing out at the landscape. Except for the silhouette of a dead tree in the middle distance, the flat landscape the stockmen are contemplating is featureless space. It is as if they are waiting for a sign or a sound, a signal of some kind that will relieve the tension of their expectation.

When I got off the boat in Sydney I walked north along the highway carrying my suitcase. A truck driver took me to Queensland and got me a job with a mate of his at Gympie. Although there were stockmen and cattle among the dairy cows, the lush coastal district was not the outback. So the Gympie farmer, who wished to help me in my quest, introduced me to another mate at the Australian Estates office in town and they found a job for me as a stockman on a cattle station in the Central Highlands of Queensland. 'That's the outback, mate,' they assured me confidently. But in the Central Highlands there were mountains and flowing rivers and well-grassed forests of great ironbarks, and there were frosts in the morning and wildflowers and ferns and towering escarpments and ravines that glowed with an ochre light in the setting sun. And when I mentioned the outback the locals shook their heads and pointed to the west and the north and told me, 'This is not the outback, mate. She's way out there.' I was beginning to learn that the outback was not so much an actual place as an idea in people's minds. I stayed in the Central Highlands for two years. They were generous, kindly, emotional people and their country was spectacular and exotic. But I still dreamed of the stockmen in the photograph and the austere solitude of their heroic persistence in that remote, expectant landscape of the outback. And I knew that sooner or later I would be resuming my journey. In my dream the stockmen still lounged on the verandah, gazing at the empty horizon, waiting for a sign. Their appeal for me was irresistible. They had already become the tragic heroes of my own personal mythmaking.

The station owner for whom I worked on the Central Highlands cattle station understood my yearning and he contacted his old mate, the manager of a vast cattle run on the Leichhardt River in the remote Gulf of Carpentaria. 'That's the fair dinkum outback, Alex,' he assured me. 'You won't see any fences up there.' So I said goodbye to this family who had treated me like a son and I took the train east from Springsure to Rockhampton on the coast—the beef cattle capital of Australia, where the train still steamed down the main street—and from Rockhampton I took another train north along the coast to Townsville. From Townsville a slow train carried me west at last across the mysterious landscape of the anthill plains to Cloncurry, the last town on the line. I had come a long way from the farm on Exmoor. But had I reached the outback?

In the dusty main street of Cloncurry I caught a ride with the mail coach and rode the load the three hundred miles north through the bulldust to Augustus Downs Station. There was no road and for the most part the driver picked his way along the dry bed of the Leichhardt River. At the station the manager drove me thirty miles or more out to the ringers' camp and left me there. The camp was on a bare claypan in the lancewood scrub on the bank of a long waterhole. A settlement consisting of a canvas fly and various items of kitchen equipment. I thought the place deserted until I found a man sleeping under a mosquito net on a bunk in the shade of the fly, a radio faintly playing country and western music close beside his ear. I did not disturb him but hung about until evening was coming on.

Thirty horsemen rode into the camp, appearing out of the long shadows of the timber and forming a semi-circle around me almost before I had detected their approach. I stood alone out in the clearing, and they looked down at me from the backs of their horses as if I were a curiosity. They wore wide-brimmed hats and spurs, their long hair flowing around their shoulders and their clothes and horses powdered with dust. No one spoke. I recognised them at once as belonging to the same caste as those stockmen on the verandah in Nolan's photograph. These were the legendary stockmen of the great northern cattle runs, men of the local Aboriginal tribe still dwelling in their own country.

Once again I stayed two years, living and working with these men in their tribal country. Then, to satisfy another urge, I left the Gulf and went south to Melbourne and enrolled at the university. I believed I had known the heroic comradeship of the outback with these black Queensland ringers during those two seasons in the cattle camps, and I cherished the memory as something to be understood by only a few. Forty years later I visited a friend in Townsville, Liz Hatte, and met her partner, Col McLennan. Col might have been one of the Queensland ringers I had known forty years earlier. He was a Jangga elder now, a consultant on the culture and lore of his clan. We reminisced about the old days of the great itinerant cattle camps that had roamed the vast grasslands out west in the days before the granting of equal pay.[1] Col said to me, 'You'll write a book about all this one day, old mate.' I said I had no plan to do that, but he seemed to know better, and a year later when I told him I was going to write the book he had spoken of, he offered to show me his country.

So began for me the journey that became my novel, *Journey to the Stone Country*. Col and I camped in a stand of silver wattle and poison bendee out in the Jangga heartland south of Mount Coolon, country as uninhabited and remote as any outback place of the imagination could ever be. And in the morning we walked into the scrub. The country was flat, the scrub open and easy of access. To the European eye the scene was not picturesque but was undifferentiated and monotonous. There were no dramatic features for the tourist camera to focus on. This was not the outback of the travel brochures but was a desolate place. The wind was cold and the scrubs untracked and silent. I wondered where Col was leading me but I had learned to wait for the story to unfold and so I did not ask him.

We had been walking through the scrub for maybe an hour when Col squatted and rolled a cigarette. When he had taken a drag on the cigarette he pointed, his hand going out

Liz Hatte and Col McLennan, Bowen River

in the characteristic gesture I had grown used to reading—a smoothing and moulding of the landscape with his spread fingers and open palm, almost a caress or benediction. 'He would have had a good view back to the river from here, old mate,' he observed quietly, as if our thoughts were the same. He did not say who he was referring to. 'He'd catch a nice little breeze up here. See anyone who was coming up from the river.' We had, I realised, stopped on a low rise. It was not enough of a rise for me to have noticed it as we walked through the bush. To me it seemed we had stopped at random. Nowhere in particular. There was in this place for me no sense of having arrived at a destination but only of having stopped.

As we squatted there, close to the earth, however, I began to notice certain things. The stony ground was different. Col leaned and loosed from its embedded cast in the earth a fist-sized lump of quartzite. He examined the stone, fitting it to his hand, then he handed it to me without a word. He selected from the ground at his feet several splinters of quartzite. 'You could fit these flakes back on to that core again if you had the patience,' he said. We were at the work site of one of his stone tool–making ancestors. During the next half-hour or so Col's quiet observations gradually brought the space around us into being and it soon became for me as likely a destination as any I have ever known; a good place to work, a place favoured by Col's practical-minded ancestor, the Jangga toolmaker, and I understood that this desolate wilderness was not the outback for Col but was his homeland. I understood that it possessed a beauty for him that was not picturesque but was in his mind and in his dreams. I learned that this was the country of his Old People and for him they still dwelled there, as they always have and always shall. And I began to understand that the European had never truly dispossessed this Jangga of his land, and that culturally, historically and spiritually he was still richly in possession of it. A thousand years, after all, is a long time in the wandering steps of European history, but is little more than a flicker in the vast hinterland of the Australian Indigenous reality.

When I was back in Melbourne writing the book Col had predicted I would write, I thought how the outback had always remained for me an elusive destination, a place of the mind rather than a particular geographical location, somewhere 'out there', further than any of us had ever been. And it was then that I began to think of the outback as an Australian embodiment of an idea that has existed in the European cultural memory since the time of the northern tribal migrations, since before the time of the heroic histories of settlement and colonisation that produced the great literature of the Icelandic Sagas. For certainly the outback was an idea of the Australian landscape that was without meaning for Col and for his ancestors. For Col the vast stony hinterland of unvisited endless scrubs was homeland. And it is of home that Aboriginal songs sing, but the earliest poems in Old English sing of journeying in distant lands. The poetic and literary culture of the English, since the beginning, since even before the English permanently colonised Britain, has had to do with the wanderer in strange lands. Home, in the literature of the English, like the outback, has been an ideal rather than a real place. Home and the woman and the hearth represent the place the wandering English poet leaves behind, as in the Old English poem *The Seafarer.*

> For the harp he has no heart, nor for having of the rings,
> Nor in woman is his weal; in the world he's no delight,
> Nor in anything whatever save the tossing o'er the waves!
> O for ever he has longing who is urged towards the sea.

In the fifty years since I saw my first photograph of the Australian outback, those stockmen lounging on the verandah have not moved. Unlike me they dwell in a place beyond the reach of time, a place of the imagination and of romance and myth. A place, like the abode of the Old English seafarer, beyond the reach of homeland. One stockman squats on his heels, his broad-brimmed hat tipped back and the silhouette of his spurs, another leans against the near verandah post, and a third sits on a bench against the wall, craned forward, forearms on his knees, gazing steadily from the shade of the verandah towards the flat horizon separating the broad expanse of earth from sky. No sound or sign has broken the rapt contemplation of those stockmen. Nothing has come into view over that distant horizon to break the stillness of their eternal vigil, and for me the mystery of their faith remains intact. It is an ancient European faith, a faith in the heroic potential of the human spirit. More than all the great paintings and sculptures in all the museums I have visited around the world, the image of those stockmen in that photograph represents for me the deepest longings of the human heart, and those silent figures are still the tragic prophets of my imagination. In them my being is inextricably both European and Australian. Col and I are different but we are friends and we share our love for the haunted landscape that for some will always be the outback, a place of heroic memory, and for others will always be homeland.

When Col first came to stay with me in Melbourne I showed him an ancient cylcon, a carved ritual stone, I had found eroding out of the bank of a creek thirty years ago. I confessed to feeling a little guilty at keeping it in my possession. But as to possession he gently corrected me. 'It hasn't come to any harm with you during these past thirty years,' he said easily. And with that characteristic sideways fling of his hand he added, 'She's on her way home, old mate.' He was content for me to be the keeper of the stone for as long as it needed my protection. It was a sentiment that moved me greatly. For me that stone was a precious memento from my days in the outback, for Col it was a sacred object of the ancestral household.

And of course the book that Col had accurately predicted I would write was *Journey to the Stone Country*. Hazel tells me it is a book about 'transcendence, the past, landscape and quest'. For it is not a story about Queensland ringers and the old cattle camps, after all, but is a contemporary story of Col himself and his partner, Liz Hatte. *Journey to the Stone Country* is a fiction, but like all fictions it carries its author's truth as well as the realities of its characters. It is a fiction based on facts, a story that is partly my own and partly Col's and Liz's. And I am thankful they find in it a story that celebrates the spirit of the Jangga and the country they both love. But it is also a story that has been owned and celebrated by Frank Budby, portrayed as Dougald Gnapun, and his son Graham, portrayed as the silent Arner. While I was writing the book I often wondered at Arner's role and what he might say if he were ever to speak the thoughts that were in his mind. A reader told me Arner is the silent witness. And I believe there is some truth in that. For in Arner there is surely something of the tragic beauty of his people, something that is perhaps too large and too encompassing for the sly intelligence of our slippery English tongue. The poets tell us we are a language species, but in the dignity of his silence Arner defies that perception. English has not colonised him. In him something stronger than the imperialism of the language has resisted and he has kept his silence. And with it he has kept his strength. But Arner's is a tragic strength. Like Samson he is not invulnerable to betrayal by the Philistines.

Alex (right) with Frank Budby at Nebo, 2009

His father, Frank Budby, tells me Graham cherishes the book and his role in it, but it was only long after I had written the story that I began to see how central to its theme his character was. We never know what we have written, after all, until our readers tell us to look again. Frank tells me that his son has found his dignity in the book. And I think of the books in which I first found my own dignity.

2004

---

1 While only mentioned here as a footnote, the granting of equal pay to Aboriginal stockmen is a big story in its own right. The cattle companies refused to pay their Aboriginal stockmen a fair wage and instead drove them off their country, thus bringing about the destruction of their culture. It is one of the major tragedies in the history of Indigenous and European relations in Australia.

EXCERPT FROM

Journey to the Stone Country

Annabelle and Arner fetched the swags and gear from the Pajero and the truck while Bo lit the fire. Annabelle wrapped potatoes in foil and set them in the heart of the fire. They sat around looking into the blaze, waiting for the potatoes, Bo smoking and no one in a mood to talk, the wind shaking the timbers of the old kitchen and snatching at loosened pieces of roof-iron. When they could smell the potatoes baking and judged them to be nearly done, Bo spread the coals and barbecued the meat. She and Bo sat close, cross-legged on the swag, Arner seated on a plastic crate, eating their dinner from blue enamel plates. The wind slamming the door back and forth against the lintel and no one getting up to fix it.

When Annabelle and Arner had cleaned the dishes, Arner said goodnight and took the flashlight and went out to his truck. A moment later his music started up, the thumping of the bass a drumbeat against the wind in the night, like the ritual accompaniment of a soul possessed. Annabelle wondered

Col McLennan with Alex on the occasion of the recognition of the Jangga people's native title rights, October 2012

at his emotions, visiting for the first time the heartland of his father's forebears. Or was he untouched by it? To have asked him directly, it seemed to her however, would have been to ignore Bo's unspoken rule. Would have been to be insensitive to his preferred style and have risked setting a distance between them. It was not a matter of understanding, but of enduring. She resolved to wait for the story to unfold, as Grandma Rennie would have advised her to do. *You'll know where you're going when you get there.* It was Grandma Rennie, after all, who had brought them here together this night. Without her there would have been no return. For none of them, not even for Bo himself.

2002

Sweet Water

The Proposed Damming of the Urannah Valley

When the Birriguba people of North Queensland successfully acquired the 162,304-acre Urannah Station on 1 April 1998 through a grant from the Indigenous Land Corporation, they rejoiced in the belief that they were at last returning to a place from which they would be able to revive their culture and their language. Urannah is a pristine valley in the old heart of Birriguba country. There they would re-establish the strength of their shattered ties to their land and reacquire a full sense of their dignity. The Birriguba elders believed that at Urannah they could begin to come to terms with the social problems confronting their people while the cattle station would provide them with an economic base from which to move forward into a more secure future and out of the landscape of ruins that had been theirs ever since the arrival of Europeans.

A little over five years later the elders are divided, their dreams have unravelled, and the intact flora and fauna of the valley is threatened with permanent extinction. Urged by the Bowen Shire Council, who are supported by a group of Birriguba elders, a proposal is under consideration by the Queensland state government to dam the Urannah Valley. Those elders who support the building of the dam do so in the hope that the Birriguba will receive a half-share in the sale of the water. Elders opposed to the dam, however, argue the dam will be run by the state government in alliance with private enterprise and that the interests of the Birriguba will be swept aside and forgotten as they always have been in the past. The water from the dam, it is claimed, is required for the growing city of Bowen and for crop irrigation in the Collinsville area downstream on the Broken River. There is also little doubt that with a state election due before next May, Premier Beattie will be tempted to make the building of the dam an election promise in order to assure a secure water supply to the powerful mining interests in the massive Bowen Basin coalmines. Frank Budby, one of the Birriguba elders opposed to the damming of Urannah, and a man exhausted by the long struggle to regain dignity and independence for his people, said to me, 'Words can never explain how important this place is to us.'

Scarcely anyone outside North Queensland has heard of the Urannah Valley. But then to be unheard of is in the nature of pristine wilderness. How many Australians had heard of the Franklin before we were called upon to save it? And to our credit we did save it. Australians saved the Franklin because they were certain its loss would impoverish our landscape and our culture. Will the loss of the Urannah Valley entail a similar impoverishment? Will its loss affect the moral and spiritual quality of our lives as inhabitants of this country? Or will it be enough for us that this beautiful valley continues to exist in its pristine state only in a novel and has no other reality? We all know without any doubt that it would be a poorer world if Mount Everest ceased to have a physical reality and was a cultural memory only. But what about our own place?

The valley of Urannah Creek is an aspect of the landscape in my novel *Journey to the Stone Country*. In reality, as well as in my story, Bo Rennie's sweet water of the Ranna is to be sacrificed to the so-called needs of progress. This is not simply a problem for North Queensland. For it is the powerhouses of the economies of demand generated by the great cities like Brisbane, Sydney and Melbourne that make developments such as the damming of the Urannah Valley feasible projects. Growth, we are told every day of our lives, is the sacred key to our wellbeing in this modern economy.

The Birriguba lived in the Urannah Valley since the beginning of time. And the European settlers—Victorians, for the most part, who overlanded their cattle and their pianos and their libraries of books—trod lightly on that country when they came. Consequently, today the flora and fauna of this astonishingly beautiful place are as intact as they were in 1863 when the last of the Birriguba were either murdered or driven out and were replaced with cattle. According to Frank Budby, 'The Urannah Valley is the place where the last of our people lived in a fully tribal state.'

Bo Rennie, a fictionalised elder of the Birriguba in *Journey to the Stone Country*, is re-entering the valley with his partner,

Annabelle Beck, after an absence of more than twenty years. It is a view of the valley I was privileged to see during my researches for the novel:

It was late afternoon going into evening by the time they came off the spur. Bo pulled up in a tall stand of untracked grass and they sat looking at a dark bank of lofty trees along the river ahead of them. Ancient forest gums and casuarinas, here and there a red bottlebrush blossom low down among the blue shadows around the bases of the trees, the glint of running water between the foliage, a dense traffic of insects and birds back and forth through the failing sunbeams. The charmed coolness of evening in the perfumed air of the valley.

Bo said, 'Smell that sweet water!' He pointed. 'The old Bigges causeway's in over there.'

Annabelle leaned close to see along his pointing hand.

'To the left of that sheoak,' he said. 'See up in that high fork? That's where the Bigges anchored their steel ropes when they was setting them stones in. The last time I seen that tree me and Dougald was tailing a mob of bally Herefords out of this valley. I sat here rolling a smoke, my horse snatching at this sugargrass, and I looked back at them trees. I can smell that mob of cattle coming out of the water now, their backs all steaming and them bellowing at each other for comfort.'

Behind them the sun was topping the high ranges, the distant stony ridges of Furious and the Hearn's Zigzag. He looked at Annabelle. 'The Ranna valley,' he said.

'It's beautiful.'

'Take a photo.'

'No,' she said. 'It won't come out in a photo. Not in one I'd take anyway. I wonder how old those trees are? I've never seen such big casuarinas.'

'Them trees have always been here,' Bo said, offhand, as if the ancient trees were not subject to the years as man is and their ages could not therefore be calculated by such a measure . . . He engaged the gears and they moved off across the flat towards the trees, easing their way through the tall grass and keeping an eye out for old flood debris. They crossed the river at the Bigges causeway, the water running clear and deep over the black stones, and they rode on up the bank onto a wide plain of silver grass, isolated crow ash pines casting long shadows in the late sun. Far over to the east the grasslands edged the ironbark forest at the base of the ranges, foothills rising in tiers towards the far-off rockwall of the escarpment, standing tall and cold and hard in the splendour of the evening light. A purple shadow across the deep of the sky.

'She'll be a cold night,' Bo said.

Annabelle pointed. 'Look!' she said excitedly. 'There's the homestead!'

'That's her.'

A pale cluster of buildings out ahead of them on the plain, catching the evening light like a village set along the dorsal of a low rise back from the treeline of the river. Bo was silent, gazing at the old Ranna Station homestead for the first time since he was a young man . . . 'Yeah,' he said. 'There she is. I can just about see smoke coming out of that kitchen chimney.'

'It looks inhabited.' She turned to him. 'Has there really been no one down here for twenty years? You expect to hear dogs barking.'

'If the Bigges was here there'd be white-faced cattle all over this pasture. I don't like to see good pasture empty of beasts.'

'That's just what my dad would have said.'

'It don't seem right. All this feed falling down onto itself and not a track through it.'

They drove on slowly towards the station buildings through the strangely trackless grass, silent with each other. Bo drew up at the main house. The old homestead sat solid and unmarked, apparently still intact within its perimeter of fence and wildgrown European shrubs and trees. Some of the less substantial outbuildings were in a state of partial collapse. One structure engulfed entirely, its timbers and ripple-iron ridden flat by a giant bougainvillea, the violet blossoms glowing and intense in the failing light.

As Milan Kundera says in his Jerusalem address of 1985, 'The novel is the imaginary paradise of individuals. It is the territory where no one possesses the truth . . . but where everyone has the right to be understood.' The novel is always about the intimate lives of individuals. About us. And if it is any good and is doing its job, as well as entertaining us the novel also says something about the moral and spiritual worth of the lives of its characters. In other words, it explores the relationship of its characters not only to each other but also to the values of the culture they inhabit. 'Every novel,' Kundera tells us, 'offers some answer to the question: What is human existence, and wherein does its poetry lie?' There are three principal characters in *Journey to the Stone Country*: Annabelle Beck, Bo Rennie and the landscape of the Jangga homeland, the Urannah Valley. These are not simply fictions, they are not only imaginative inventions. I didn't make them up. Each of them has its counterpart in our reality. The real Annabelle and Bo live in Townsville and the real landscape of the Jangga homeland is in North Queensland.

An assumption driving the great diaspora of European culture for at least the past five hundred years has been that the acquisition of land and knowledge is a sacred duty. Colonialism and European culture are not separable but are aspects of the same urgent meditation. We will not be in a post-colonial age until we are in a post-European age. The great German philosopher Edmund Husserl identified *the passion to know* as the central axiom of the European identity. There were a couple of politicians recently recommending something they called *the knowledge nation*, as if they had discovered a new challenge for us to meet. But really they were reiterating the age old colonial mantra of Western culture: *know it all, own it all, consume it all*. That the acquisition of knowledge is really a project of ownership is not a new idea. Adrian Desmond and James Moore in their great 1991 biography of Charles Darwin remind us of it: 'Even this project [insect collecting] had its imperial ramifications. Naming is possessing, said the old insect specialist William Kirby. Science was a sort of metaphoric appropriation.'

Despite the disclaimer of something we like to call *pure* research, the problem with the passion to know is that the freedom of scientific inquiry is conflated with the right not only to know everything but also the right to own everything and to put it to use in the service of our own wellbeing. No knowledge is out of bounds to the European mind. There are no limits on scientific inquiry. For scientific inquiry no aspect of existence is secret or sacred. The whole of created nature is its subject. On a practical day-to-day level, this is often interpreted to mean that the natural features of our landscape can be utilised to supply the growing needs of our cities: in other words, landscape as natural resource.

The vast and ever-growing bodies of our cities represent an exemplary paradigm of the vast and ever-growing body of our knowledge. In this project we ignore our past and drive confidently towards a future in which everything is to be known and everything is to be consumed. We have abandoned our past in favour of a dream of the future. Tomorrow, not yesterday, is where our hopes reside: with the manipulation of the genetic codes of being, with designer offspring, designer parents, the 'cure' for ageing, the 'cure', indeed, for nature itself. We are engaged on a cultural project in which we define human existence as something that is in need of a cure and we retain a deeply ambivalent love/hate tension with the land we occupy—both our resource and victim, the ancient dark of our spiritual wellbeing:

> . . . that first morning they walked down the rise to the river Indian file, Bo in the lead trampling a track through the ribbon grass, Annabelle and Trace staying close behind him for fear of brown snakes. The air was filled with a moving tide of living creatures. Grasshoppers, beetles, clouds of small chocolate moths flickered in the sunlight around them. Arner was back some way wearing shorts and thongs and seemingly untroubled by the possibility of venomous serpents in the grass. After a hundred metres they came out of the tall grass onto a cropped greensward of soft ankle-high couch grass, black wattles standing like park trees. Closer to the river the shade of the old casuarinas and bluegums, a coolness in the sweet air, brightly coloured butterflies and birds feeding on the insects and nectar among the drooping foliage and blossoms. The warm air vibrating with the shrilling of millions of insects.
>
> Annabelle and Trace came up and stood beside Bo on the smooth benchrock at the edge of an open stretch of sunlit water. They stood gazing on the scene at their feet, the flow of the river green and clear in its depths, the water golden and rippling with sunlight where it slipped over the shallow bottom sands.

I believe there are profound moral and spiritual consequences for us in pursuing knowledge at all costs. One enormous impoverishment that European culture has suffered because of the unbridled passion to know is a loss of the idea of the sacred. This loss is experienced by growing numbers of people as a deepening divide between themselves and their sense of belonging. It is surely a paradox at the heart of our European culture that each technological advance in the race to possess the future brings with it this sense of failed private experience.

The fate of the Urannah Valley is not a simple matter of European interests versus Indigenous interests. The fate of the Urannah is not a nineteenth- or even a twentieth-century colonial issue of black versus white possession or ownership. It is a contemporary question involving a complex cultural mix of the interests of innumerable groups and sub-groups in our entire society.

I believe that the preservation of the Urannah Valley is as important to our sense of who we are as Australians and as citizens of the world as the fate of the Franklin or the physical existence of Mount Everest. The complexity of interests competing in the determination of the Urannah's fate, the fact that no simple line can be drawn between Indigenous and non-Indigenous interests in this conflict, is emblematic of where Australian culture has shifted in its struggle to move beyond a colonial mindset of exploitation and ownership. In this conflict it is not a question simply of reconciliation, important as that is, but is the far more difficult question of the acknowledgment of difference: difference between cultures, between two dreamings, the European dreaming discarding the past and struggling to possess the future, the Indigenous dreaming the struggle of remaining morally true to the ongoing ancestral project, a project that is inseparable from the sacred moral duty to care for the land.

Some critics assure us that our novels are irrelevant in discussions of the important issues facing our society. I don't share that view. As well as entertaining us, our novels have always explored the individual's relationship to the great moral questions of the day. Not answers, but an awareness of the questions we need to face. Something, dare I say it, such as an image of the Urannah Valley out there in our landscape, intact as yet and just as filled with mystery as the deepest and most hidden part of the great Amazonian forest. A fragile and precious reality of ours that we are about to destroy in order to provide water for coalmines and crop irrigation. As a wilderness, Urannah has nothing to do with the knowledge nation or productivity outcomes, but is something that calls to the ineffable and the inexplicable in our souls. If we Australians cannot find a way to preserve the Urannah Valley as a place sacred to both Indigenous and European dreaming alike, then we will soon join those civilisations that failed. Two hundred years, after all, is little more than a moment in time when it is held against the measure of forty thousand years.

Let's hope we yet learn from the great Indigenous cultures of this country that not everything is to be consumed but that some things are to be cherished and preserved. And if we do learn this, we may yet come to see that we are also embedded within the story of our own past, the story of our ancestors, the story of our old people, and that there is an ongoing moral obligation for us in this sacred association that will eventually make the land our own; an association that has something to do with our worth as human beings. For it is ourselves, after all, who are the figures in this landscape and it is for us to decide whether it is to be a landscape of ruins or the paradise of our dreams.

Annabelle observed the two young people gathering firewood together, their graceful forms moving among the drooping foliage of the trees, back and forth between shadows and sunbeams, their voices sudden and brief, a quick uncertain laugh then silence, and she thought how easy it was for them, their existence uncluttered and without ambivalence. Out in the sunlight beyond them, Mathew Hearn's mare trailed her rains and lipped the sweet green couch grass. At the crack of a stick she raised her head and gazed into the shadows at the young man and the girl, her ears working. They came back with armfuls of kindling and firewood and chose for their hearth a natural hollow in the rock. They crouched together to set their fire, he sitting back on his heels when they had arranged the sticks and watching while Trace bent low and touched the flame to the silky grass heads. Together they watched the curl of blue smoke rise through the sticks and ascend into the trees, the smell of burning gumleaves suddenly in the still air. A yellow flame leaping up through the laid sticks. 'It's going!' Trace exclaimed with delight. 'I lit it!' The young man and woman looked at each other and laughed. And in their laughter it seemed to Annabelle it was to be enough for them that they had struck this fire, and for the moment they would ask for no more, but would be content. As if they could believe their actions served some more worthy power than their own desires.

So Trace Gnapun, a modern young woman and a Jangga, and Mathew Hearn, the son of a white settler, build their fire together in their doomed paradise and fall in love with each other as young people will. Such optimism of the young and the will to build our dreams together, not the knowledge nation, is the hope of our civilisation.

2004

The Black Mirror

To understand art, we must know artists.

Rilke

He moved about in front of the chair, perhaps two metres from me, nervously adjusting the set of the canvas on the easel, then the position of his stool. Every few moments he looked up at me. His look disconcerted me, for it was not the look of the friend I knew, but was the look of a man who examines an object. He had invited me to sit for him and I had been flattered that such a great artist as he, an artist whose work I had long admired and had considered among the greatest of all our artists, should wish to paint my portrait. When he had adjusted the easel, the canvas and the stool to his satisfaction, he examined me in silence, searching my features, as if he searched a landscape for some familiar feature; then, suddenly, evidently locating the feature he searched for, he began to paint. I remained still, as I had been instructed, my hands folded on my knees, my gaze focused on the reverse of the canvas—a vacancy in which no likeness was ever going to appear.

But it was more than flattery. To be admitted to his studio, to see him engaged in the privacy of his endeavour, to watch his eyes and his hands at work—to be a part of this—that is what interested me. When we took a break from the sittings, I wondered if he would show me his drawings. Would I be permitted to open the drawers of the great plan press that stood against the wall under the window and browse through the archives of his art, the small and the intimate drawings and gouaches, the ideas that had flooded through his hands and his mind for years, the unfinished sketches that had never blossomed into major works but had remained secret and alive and alone, perhaps even forgotten? It was all there, in the ordered clutter of his studio. Years, decades, of labour, the accumulation of a lifetime of dedication to his art, his search for something.

On the aeroplane flying back to Australia from New York, I slept through the long leg from Los Angeles to Sydney and woke with the story written in my head. I had dreamed the solution to my novel, *The Sitters*. It was the artist in his studio and he was painting a portrait of his lost sister. While he painted he talked with himself. His sister was not in front of him, as I had been in front of my artist friend, not in the flesh, for she was dead long ago, but she was there in his mind's eye. He struggled to remember her onto his canvas. The struggle was great. To paint the portrait of an absent loved one. Like Giacometti, he failed many times to reach the modelled illusion he strove for and, like Giacometti, he scraped back his painting to the canvas and began again many times. But he did not begin again each time from the place from which he had begun before. Each time he began, he did so from a more elaborated familiarity with the problem confronting him, and each of his new beginnings was based upon a more highly achieved failure than the previous failure—each time he built his new illusion on the black mirror of his memory it more closely resembled the thing he was looking for.

Rick Amor in 1997 with his portrait of Alex

The painting he produced, however, was not of his sister but concerned his lover, for that was the direction in which his memory had taken him. It was a painting not so much finished as abandoned. He left it there, leaning against the wall, where it would confront him with the mystery of his work, the mystery of his failure. It contained no likeness of his lover, but only her bed, the door to her room open, the light from the window driving shadows and presences from the room until it seemed her figure had only that moment departed from it. It was a portrait of absence and longing, and there was no likeness in it but the one he recollected each time he looked on that scene of lost intimacy.

When Rick Amor—the real artist, my friend and not my fiction—finished the portrait of me, he invited me to look at it for the first time. He had not let me see it while it was in progress. We stood side by side looking at the sombre likeness of me gazing back at us from within that black mirror of his art, and I began to consider the story that I would dream a year later on the plane home from America, the idea for it seeded in that moment of uncertain recognition in his studio.

2006

EXCERPT FROM

Prochownik's Dream

He set up *The Other Family* and mixed a glaze and, within a few minutes of beginning work, Teresa and the rest of the world had gone out of his mind—the rest of the world, that is, except for Marina, with whom every now and then he enjoyed a brief imaginary exchange; the perfect companion of his solitary hours. He worked without a break through what was left of the night and on through the dawn and into the day, until the naked male figure stood boldly to the left of the principal group in the big painting, poised side on to the viewer. It was a figure that was strangely familiar to Toni, one which in some essential way represented himself, even though its features—or such of them as could be made out, for it stood within a puzzling array of shadows—were those of an old man. As he stood in front of the painting, seeing the figure with a feeling of surprise, he had little recollection of the hours he had spent painting it. He felt that he had at last taken root in his own work, and the possibilities for his art seemed to him to be endless. With the inclusion of himself, he had stepped through a doorway and the field of his future endeavour lay open to him.

2005

A Circle of Kindred Spirits

I'd rather not be doing this. It feels strange and unreal for me to be standing here about to give something called the Hazel Rowley Memorial Lecture. Hazel should be here with us herself at this festival talking about her latest book, *Franklin and Eleanor*, which was brought out in an Australian edition by Hazel's great supporter, Louise Adler, in 2011 and is still fresh in all our minds. That Hazel is not here in person is a tragedy. It is also such a recent tragedy for her friends and family that her absence still seems puzzling and unreal and has not yet become an accepted fact of reality. Perhaps it never will. Hazel was so powerfully alive until almost the last days of her life it is not possible to imagine her dead. I've titled this talk A Circle of Kindred Spirits. It's a quote from Marguerite Yourcenar's reflections on the composition of her masterpiece, *Memoirs of Hadrian*, the most impressive melding of biography and fiction I know, and one of the greatest portraits of a man I have ever read.

I've had a great admiration for biographers at least since the time I met John La Nauze, which was in 1963. I make that half a century. La Nauze was one of my tutors at Melbourne University in the early sixties in a subject which honours history students were required to take and which was titled The Theory and Method of History. It was one of the most interesting subjects on the curriculum and proposed a comparison of historical treatments at different periods of the same historical subject. The conquest of Mexico and Peru was at the centre of this study, but the work of E.H. Carr, and particularly his book *What is History?*, was also critical to the ideas we were asked to ponder. The subject, I believe, was essentially designed to rid us of any residual naivety about history writing that we might have had and to alert us to the fact that there can be no such thing as objective history. It may just as well have been designed to enlighten us about the impossibility of something we might have imagined to be objective biography.

At the time I had the very great privilege of knowing him— and I doubt I would have made much of an impression on him, as I wasn't a student who ever had much to say—John La Nauze was writing his ground-breaking two-volume biography of Australia's second prime minister, Alfred Deakin. One morning La Nauze came into the tutorial room, sat in his usual place, and laid his head on his folded arms on the table in front of him. It was Monday morning. I was sitting immediately to his left and I remember thinking he was probably suffering from a hangover as vicious as the one I was suffering from myself and I felt sorry for him and thought him brave to have made it in to work. After a minute or two he raised his head and looked me directly in the eye, as if he had read my thoughts, and said, 'Whatever you do, never take on the writing of a major work of biography.' He then went on to tell us what an octopus his own subject, Deakin, had become for him. It was consuming his whole existence and he had no way of escaping its clutches. I think he called it an octopus. It was too late, he was in the tank with the creature and had to wrestle it to death or fail.

The sense of the immense load of work that is required from anyone taking on the job of writing a biography of a major public figure has stayed with me. I never read La Nauze's book on Deakin—the idea of it seemed too heavy—but despite his weariness with the demands of it that particular Monday morning it must have turned out to be a beauty, because Allan Martin, the biographer of Robert Menzies, whose two-volume biography I have read and who knew what he was talking about, said that La Nauze's *Deakin*, which appeared in 1965, 'established a standard of excellence in Australian political biography not subsequently matched'. I was relieved to read Martin's words, and felt glad La Nauze had beaten his octopus. And I took his advice to heart. The idea of writing a biography scared me, and I have stayed well away from attempting it, though I have a number of friends who have succeeded emin-ently as biographers. Hazel Rowley was foremost among them.

She was a very special friend and a greatly admired writer and scholar who often complained bitterly to me from La Nauze's Monday morning position, but who also, like John La Nauze, was sufficiently passionate about and committed to her subjects to go on wrestling the beasts and to finish her work at a level of excellence that is bewilderingly fine and for which it is difficult to find comparisons. Reading biography remains one of my favourite things to do. I'm presently reading Josyane Savigneau's biography of the French novelist Marguerite Yourcenar, and it is enriching my life, just as Yourcenar's own work has done. Indeed, Yourcenar's masterpiece, *Memoirs of Hadrian*, is surely the most inspired and perfect blending of the three arts of biography, memoir and the novel. I can say, and often do, with serious and genuine gratitude, thank god for biographers.

On Friday, 8 August 2003, at a little after noon, I was having lunch with the eminent Melbourne editor and writer Hilary McPhee in Mario's cafe on Brunswick Street in Carlton. Predictably, I suppose, among the things we talked about were books that we admired. We weren't talking about the latest books or even books that had been published recently. We were talking about books which had left a deep impression and which had remained with us over the years. Hilary told me that, in her opinion, one of the great Australian books was Hazel Rowley's biography of the novelist Christina Stead. It had been published by William Heinemann in 1993 to rave reviews. Had I read it?

No, I hadn't, I was ashamed to admit. Straight after lunch I walked down to the Brunswick Street Bookstore and asked for a copy of Rowley's biography of Stead. I was told it was out of print. So I walked on a bit further to the Grubb Street second-hand bookshop. I found a copy on the shelves in pristine condition and bought it for twenty-five dollars. Hazel's first book, *Christina Stead*, was published by William Heinemann in 1993, ten years before my conversation with Hilary and twenty years before now. Twenty years? Is it a long time? It depends. I was in a restaurant in Norwich last year having dinner with a bunch of writers. We were attending a conference and festival at East Anglia University. Michael Ondaatje arrived late and stood at the door looking around the restaurant. Michael and I became friends in 1993 and had not seen each other since except for a brief stay I made in Toronto. He spied me sitting in the far corner from the door and came over and grasped me in his bear hug and kissed me firmly on the cheek, his own bristly cheek reminding me of my father's kiss. When we drew away, I said: It's twenty years, Michael! As if I'd said, It's a lifetime. He replied at once with great force and emotion. Twenty years is nothing, Alex! It was a poetic claim and its truth struck me to the heart. So twenty years then, this year, since Hazel's first great book, *Christina Stead*, came out to rave reviews with William Heinemann Australia. For those readers whom that book impressed, twenty years is no time at all. Great books, like great friends, leave an impression that refuses to fade with the passing of time. Michael was right.

I took Hazel's *Stead* home with me, from Grubb Street that day ten years ago, Hilary's warmth of feeling for the book still fresh with me, and I read it at once. Later on in the year, around late November (I've no diary entry for the exact date) Jason Steger, the literary editor of the *Age* asked me for my list of the books I'd most enjoyed reading in 2003. I was grateful Jason didn't object when I asked if I could write about one out-of-print book. Here's what I wrote. It appeared in the *Age* on 13 December 2003 (I've kept a copy of it pasted inside my copy of Hazel's book):

> Hazel Rowley's 1993 biography of the Australian novelist Christina Stead is for me one of the great literary biographies of all time and must be counted among Australia's intellectual treasures. I read it the first time with greedy, engrossed application and a fiercely selfish need to be left alone with it. It is written with an enormous scholarly sweep and the dramatic drive of a novel. Hazel's *Christina Stead* is as central to the richness of our literary life as David Marr's great biography of Patrick White. In both cases subject and biographer are ideally matched—indeed almost dangerously so in Rowley's case, for there is a sense here that the biographer finds something central to her own life in the life of her subject and shares with her subject something of the same vulnerabilities. Get it from your library if you can't get it in a bookshop. For, ridiculously, sadly, it's out of print. Our gutted literary culture.

Louise Adler, bless her heart, has since then of course brought this splendid book back into print, a publishing act of faith that thrilled and delighted Hazel and lifted her morale and energies at a time when she was feeling particularly beleaguered.

I had never met Hazel when I wrote that piece for the *Age* and had no expectation of ever meeting her. I knew by then that she lived in New York and spent as much time as she possibly could in Paris. A friend of Hazel's sent her a copy of what I'd written and Hazel wrote me a letter via my publisher. I wrote back by email. And so began an email correspondence that over the years until her death must have run into many thousands. *You are my hero*, Hazel said in her letter. *I thought I was forgotten.* It wasn't a bad start to what became the most magically trusting epistolary friendship I've ever had, or am ever likely to have. For nearly eight years we wrote to each other almost every day. Nothing was too private or too sensitive for us. No momentary rage too fearful not to be included in the moment of its white heat. We excluded nothing. We felt safe with each other.

It is not necessary, and can be, I believe, damaging, to try to understand love—indeed, understanding is, in my opinion, a vastly overrated thing when it comes to our motives and emotions and to art and life generally. Although we had never met, Hazel and I trusted each other completely and wrote to each other with a freedom and energy I'd never experienced before in writing letters—emails were our letters, of course. Email, after all, has made the quill redundant. We didn't write scrappy little grabs just because we were using this instantaneous medium, but respected both the language and each other and wrote decently, with thought, with reflection, and with enormous enthusiasm about everything that deeply and shallowly concerned us. I've included an exchange between us that took place very close to the time of Hazel's death. We knew nothing about death at that stage. Death was far off. Hazel and I had often spoken of how she would survive me by many years. I was supposed to go first, indeed long before her.

Sent: Friday, February 11, 2011 7:42 PM

Dearest Haze,

Here you are again! Boldly centerfolded in the *Age* two weeks in a row. This time it's you more than the book. My god, if this book doesn't sell bucket loads here it won't be for lack of backing from Louise and Jason Steger. I don't think I've seen Carey get this much *Age* space two weeks in a row—and I have gone nowhere near it.

Congratulations! This must surely make up a bit for the down shit you've been experiencing over there. You come out of it boldly and vigorously and as one of us who has made it strongly into the front rank in New York. I hope you are thoroughly pleased and your morale has received a jolt upward. And a great photo. The one of you striding through the park that you sent me.

Your appearance at the Wheeler will be packed.

I have to make a pie for Rick and Meg Amor for lunch. But I couldn't wait to tell you this great news.

Enjoy!

Love and hugs,

Alecko

Hazel responded the following morning, Saturday, 12 February:

Alecko,

I love your enthusiastic emails. I got one from Louise Adler this morning too. She's ecstatic! I can't get on to the damn thing online. Don't know why not. Glad you told me which photo it is. Louise just said it was a lovely photo. (Yeah, carefully culled.) I DID see the review in today's *Australian*, which is muddleheaded, but very positive. It's wonderful for me, this reception, you're so right. It means so much to me. The shit here has been heartbreaking. So this is just fucking wonderful. I told you, didn't I, that I am thinking of coming back to Australia in three years or so. It has suddenly become an immensely appealing thought.

Everyone I know and their dog is coming to the Wheeler Centre! I tell them that you and I are having dinner together.

Amazing really. It all seems quite unreal.

I'm off this weekend to the Hudson Valley to give a talk at a little place called Kinderhook, staying the night at a friend's up there. Old house etc. Should be great fun. Snow on the ground.

Good Lord. I leave in two weeks, you know. I have to start getting out some summer clothes. I'm as white as hell, of course. And thin.

This business has done nothing for my appetite.

Must get on with things. Hope you're still writing in white heat. Thanks so much for the beautiful message.

Much love,

Hazel

Hazel's sense of home was about as conflicted and elaborate as my own. She loved to remind me that she was born in England, was spiritually at home only in Paris, and was just as uncertain of finding herself at home in Australia as

I was at the idea of ever finding myself at home in England. Something of this was recorded in her books. Her biographical notes were different for each book and for each edition of each book. She never quite settled on which country was her home country—perhaps because none really was. There were also political reasons for these variations in her biographical notes. For *Richard Wright*, her truly great biography of the African American novelist whose work seems to be little known here, she and her publishers considered it politic to leave out any reference to her English origins or to refer in any direct way to the fact that she was a white Australian, and instead to emphasise her American connections, which were considerable. No author photo was included with this book for the same reason. 'How in hell did you happen?' the Chicago sociologist Robert Park once asked Richard Wright. This is quoted in the blurb of Hazel's biography of Wright. Robert Park might as well have asked this question of Hazel Rowley, and of many writers who often appear among us, arriving from the most unlikely origins, and going they know not where. The first subject of Hazel's work, Christina Stead, like Hazel herself, was only truly at home within the borders of her work; for the rest she was an uncertain nomad. Hazel might have been writing of herself when she says in *Christina Stead*:

> In her autobiographical piece 'Another View of the Homestead', which told of her four-month return to Australia in 1969, Stead played down the 'going home' aspect and portrayed herself—in strikingly Nietzschean terms—as a

wanderer. She was enthusiastic about being 'a temporary citizen of a flying village with fiery windows, creaking and crashing across the star-splattered dark'. She made clear that 'home', for a traveller like herself, was only ever a temporary arrangement.

After her return to Australia, Stead never wrote again, only letters to friends, but continued to hope, Hazel tells us in this moving passage in her book, that she was not finished with writing yet. In writing about Stead, Hazel was writing about a kindred spirit.

In my faulty memory—and whose memory isn't at fault?—Hazel and I met only once. When I made this claim recently, Hazel's oldest and closest friend, Lyn Buchanan, reminded me that I had met Hazel on another occasion. Lyn was right; there had been one other occasion. But still my obstinate memory makes its claim that we met only once. I suppose it's more literary, more to the story's liking, to have it this way, more easily part of the fictional narrative of my life that I like to cherish. I once wrote a piece in which I claimed to favour the mask of fiction as a vehicle for my truths over the bare-faced facts of memoir. Once again, it is Marguerite Yourcenar who has the beautifully simple insight to accompany this idea when she says 'eventually the mask becomes the real face'.

The meeting with Hazel I like to refer to in my memory as the only one that ever took place was at the Sydney Writers' Festival a few years ago. We had lunch together at a table by the water in the sun with Drusilla Modjeska and Rai Gaita, both much-loved friends. We were to meet again at the Wheeler Centre, where I was going to chair a celebration of her wonderful books. We were to have dinner together afterwards. We both said we must keep it to just the two of us for this dinner, as it might be our only chance to ever sit together, tête-à-tête, and talk our beloved talk. We never had that dinner. Hazel died on the 1st of March. I still struggle to believe she is dead and is not somewhere between New York and Paris, the eternal wanderer. Her silence makes no sense. So I have returned to her books and I find her in them.

When our friendship began in 2003 Hazel had published two grand and very powerful biographies. The second, *Richard Wright: The Life and Times*, was published in 2001 by Henry Holt. The appearance of this book was overshadowed by the events of 9/11. The two African American critics who reviewed the book were exuberant in their enthusiasm for it, though it remains little known here in Australia. When I hear Australians lamenting the intellectual insularity of the Americans and the French I think of this and of how unconscious we can be of our own insularity.

When I met her, Hazel was working in a new direction. She had swerved away from the traditional form of the great scholarly biography and taken a new path. She was writing about a great relationship rather than a great individual; *Tête-à-Tête: Simone de Beauvoir and Jean-Paul Sartre* was a study of the relationship of these two giants of French culture and literature. In the book Hazel stares squarely into the private lives of this legendary couple, and she does so without making any moral judgments on their behaviour. Like all the great writers, Hazel leaves moral judgment to her readers. The book was published in the USA by HarperCollins in 2005. Hazel posted me a copy on publication, inscribing it: *For Alex, far away soulmate, with love, Hazel Oct 2005*. She included with the book a postcard. I still have it. It is a picture of the terrace of a Paris cafe, two vacant chairs and a little round table. We are not sitting there together talking the talk. But we might have been. And perhaps we were in spirit.

Tête-à-Tête is not a study of the thought or the writings of Beauvoir and Sartre but a ground-breaking excursion into the formidably difficult business of making a portrait of greatness and genius linked to the intimate lives of her subjects. Hazel understood that this was the challenge of this book and it is why she considered it an advance on her previous work. The intimate lives of their subjects are not easy for biographers and historians to get at convincingly. But in *Tête-à-Tête* Hazel gets there with the narrative power of a novelist. This is not a book that can be described by the usual conventions of biography. As Barbara Ehrenreich said of it, '*Tête-à-Tête* has just about everything: sex, philosophy, politics, and the world's most unconventional love story. Hard as I tried, I could not put it down.'

Like most writers, when Hazel had finished a book, she struggled with the business of settling on a subject for her next. The worst time, in many ways, for any writer is just after a book has been finished. You have lost your anchor. Almost lost your job. You may easily lose your faith altogether in the entire process of writing. Who, after all, needs another book? Haven't we got enough yet? You've been made redundant until and unless you settle firmly on a new subject for your next book and get going with it. With *Tête-à-Tête* Hazel had succeeded in finding her way through the conventional expectations of publishers and readers of biography and had elaborated, with intelligence and imagination, a new sub-genre of that grand species. How to continue after doing something like that was the big question facing her. The subjects that Hazel took on, from the beginning with Christina Stead, were all of the first order of importance to the cultural record. She didn't go for little-known or unknown people. Nor did the existence of several, or even a hundred, previous books about her subject daunt her. She wrote about her subjects because she had fallen in love with something about them and their lives. And in the end she didn't write unless she believed she had something new to say about them.

With *Tête-à-Tête* Hazel had found a new way of approaching her already world-famous subjects, and with her new way she had found a new readership. It wasn't a form she was going to give up easily. *Franklin and Eleanor: An Extraordinary Marriage*, continued along the path she had set out for herself. In October 2010, when Farrar, Straus and Giroux published *Franklin and Eleanor* in the USA, Hazel posted me a copy with the dedication: *For Alecko, my inbox mate and inspiration, with love, Hazel, New York Oct 7, 2010.* I'd become Alecko by then and she had become Azelle. She couldn't wait to enjoy the enthusiastic reception that was waiting for her and her book here in Melbourne. She had a bit of a fever but couldn't bear the thought that if she went to see her doctor he would tell her she couldn't fly. So she didn't go to see her doctor. She was fifty-nine and scared as hell, not of dying, but of growing old. I used to tell her it was great fun, being old—so far. Her tragic death in mid-flight affected a great many people. For me it is an enormous personal loss. But we are here this evening not to lament her loss, but to celebrate her, her courage, her success and her wonderful contribution to our cultural life, and to commemorate these things with our words, our thoughts, and with the award of the Hazel Rowley Fellowship. It is the love for Hazel of her sister Della that has brought this award into being. It is a wonderful thing to have done.

With the biographer of great figures in our culture, women and men, more so than with the novelist, there is formed, in Mme Yourcenar's words, 'a circle of kindred spirits, moved by the same interests and sympathies, or concerned with the same problems'. Hazel was of that circle of kindred spirits in the arenas of the lives of her subjects, all people who had drawn to themselves and their work over the decades a vast circle of devoted scholars and readers. Rereading her books these last few weeks I have known myself to be in the presence of Hazel's great humanity. My love for her is undiminished. Friendship is for life. Her great books are for life. To read a great book a second time, just as to listen to a great piece of music for the hundredth time, is to be in the presence of a new creation.

2013

Sophie's Choice

I've been greatly affected by the book *Romulus, My Father*, and by my friendship with Raimond Gaita, in ways I will probably never adequately express. Both have been late gifts in my life. The impression of the book which has persisted with me most strongly is of Rai's mother's unhappy life and her tragic death, when her beginnings had seemed to me to have been so promising. Indeed the influence of *Romulus* and of my deepening friendship with Rai continue to play an evolving and increasingly important part in my life.

After revisiting Rai's childhood home, Frogmore, recently with Rai and Col McLennan, a Murri friend from Queensland, to whom Rai was showing his country, I wrote to Rai in an email:

> It was very moving walking behind you across the wheat field
> coming down from the abandoned house yesterday evening.
> I had a deeper sense of the tragic beauty of that landscape
> and your childhood as a part of it than I've ever had before.

And I thought to myself how wonderful it is that you've made
sense of that past of your parents and your father's friends
and given it a real presence. I think it is a truly heroic thing
you have done, and I mean this in the old sense of the way
in which shiftless peoples and tribes founded their stories of
their own pasts in order to cherish their forebears and celebrate their lives and deeds, and by doing so gave a deeper
meaning to their own existence in the present. The creation
of story. It is magical and beautiful. And to think of you as a
young boy writing that story of the struggle between good
and evil in the guise of your hero Elvis. It is as if you were
announcing your own future—the old people, and I mean our
own old people of the North, would have said the gods gave
you the gift of the story. And none of this would have been so
if you had flinched from the whole truth of your family's history
at Frogmore, terrible and frightening though so much of that
history was. I have never before understood quite so clearly
as I did yesterday evening why you had to reveal all the
deeply private pain of that time. But that is what all the great
foundation stories do. They tell of the irredeemable tragedy
as well as the triumph of life. And that is what makes them
great, and gives to them the lasting significance they have for
all of us.

When Rai told me he had titled his essay on his mother
(published in the collection *After Romulus*) 'An Unassuageable
Longing'—Helen Garner's expression for her sense of Rai's
emotional state as a result of the loss of the nourishment

of his mother's love at an early age—I thought of Emily Dickinson's image: 'The craving is upon the child like a claw it cannot remove.'

This paper is a personal reflection on Rai and our friendship, and it also looks at the effect on me of *Romulus* and of Rai's essay on his mother. I've titled it *Sophie's Choice* because it is in the circumstances of their beginnings that friendships, and indeed all our relationships, establish the enduring qualities of their character. It is in the inception of relationships that we most often experience the earliest nurturing of something enduring within ourselves, something which forms a deep connection that remains with us—the deepest of all these emotional beginnings for us is, of course, in our mothering. To find a friend is often to find something in oneself that one was not fully conscious of before, something which the friendship brings more fully into the light—something that is the result of the nurturing acknowledgment of the other.

If it had not been for Sophie Halakas I might never have met Rai and my life would have been the poorer for that. Rai's influence on me has been immense. Sometime—I'm not good with dates—after my wife Stephanie and I moved to Castlemaine ten years ago, Sophie Halakas, the owner of our local fruit shop and the matriarch of her large Greek Australian family, asked me if I had met Raimond Gaita. I told her I had read his books and that I greatly admired his work, but I hadn't met him. In admitting this to Sophie I felt as if I were admitting a fault. 'You should give him a call,' she said with a quiet insistence that confirmed my sense of being in the wrong for not having met Rai already. 'You are both writers,' she said, 'and you would like each other.'

Sophie spoke to me, a stranger, with more than a hint of reprimand that day, in a tone that implied, *This situation is not as it should be and we had better set it to rights as soon as possible.* Charles Dickens would have put her in a novel. You can't know Sophie for long—a day or two at most—before also knowing she is actively concerned about the moral quality of the community she lives in, and has every intention of seeing to it that her community reflects her own sense of what is right. In this, as in a number of other ways—though with a very different delivery and style—Sophie holds a number of values in common with Rai. As I left her shop that day, with my bag of beans and potatoes, I said to myself, Well, I'd better get in touch with Rai Gaita before I go in there again.

When it came to making the call, however, I was shy about picking up the phone and out of the blue ringing the author of such imposing masterpieces as *Romulus, My Father, The Philosopher's Dog, A Common Humanity* and the intimidatingly dense and scholarly work *Good and Evil.* Why would this writer and thinker, who I also knew to be the Professor of Moral Philosophy at London University, and whose essays and public statements had given him a commanding presence in the intellectual life of Australia, want to hear from me? Surely he would already be far too busy with the pressing demands of a richly elaborate international private and public life? How should I seem to casually break in on this? Would I say, 'Hi, Rai. Sophie from the fruit shop told me to call you'?

I am a coward about these things so I avoided the fruit shop for as long as I could. But we needed fruit and vegetables, and eventually I could avoid it no longer and I went in. Sophie, who was not always there, was at the counter that day. She greeted me as I came through the door. 'Hello, Alex,' she said. 'We haven't seen you for a while.' Her gaze followed me around the shop and when I arrived at the counter with my basket of vegetables, she weighed and packed my things in silence. Only when I'd paid and she was handing me my change did she at last look directly into my eyes. 'So,' she said. 'Did you get in touch with Rai Gaita?'

'No,' I said. 'I'm sorry. I'll call him today. I promise.'

'Good,' she said. 'I think you should.'

After this encounter I was more intimidated by the thought of fronting Sophie again than I was by the thought of calling Rai, so I phoned him. He said that for some time Sophie had been urging him to call me. We arranged to meet for a coffee. I can't remember what we talked about at our first meeting, but on my way home I wondered why I'd thought Rai Gaita would not be as his books are. What had made me think that the man who had written about Jack the cockatoo and Gypsy the dog would be a haughty and difficult highbrow and not the warm, humane, caring person he is in his books? A man, that is, motivated by a modest but passionate determination, not so very different from Sophie Halakas's, to see to it that, in so far as he is able to influence these things, the community he lives in is a decent one; is a community, in other words, in which people and animals, and indeed all things, are respected simply for what they are and *because* they are, because they share with us our being-in-this-world. Rai Gaita, I realised after our first meeting in the cafe, was a practical philosopher for whom the congested moral qualities of the life we live from day to day provide the principal focus and ground not only of his thinking but of his actions. As I walked home from the cafe I knew that I had met a man who was not only a very great writer (something I had already discovered for myself) but who was also a great human being.

I'm not a Christian, and dislike all varieties of proselytising religion, but I'd be a fool to imagine that my thought has not been influenced by the imprint left on me and on the culture I inhabit by two thousand years of Christianity; by the shaping conviction, that is, that the struggle between good and evil is the principal moral focus of human society and the rule of the good the measure of its moral health. Though Rai would almost certainly not express it as I do here, from my reading of his books and essays I knew him to have spent his most serious intellectual energies in dealing head on, as it were, with this subject, and I knew that his judgments on questions of good and evil would always be nuanced and complex. I did not expect my own judgments to be as keen as his, even though as a novelist I'd been concerned my entire writing life with the intricate dilemmas of private and social morality. Would our views on these things be at odds? I wondered. I had liked Rai at once and was anxious to discover that we shared some deep common ground so that our friendship might flourish. I was, of course, looking in the wrong place.

After my meeting with Rai I couldn't wait to go into the fruit shop again. But Sophie was too quick for me. Before I could deliver my punchline, she said, 'Rai was in just now, Alex. He said how much he enjoyed meeting you.'

I realised it wasn't Dickens, after all, but was Trollope who would have put her straight into a novel. Her manner assured me that arrangements in Castlemaine had been adjusted a significant step closer to her ideal. It wasn't long after this that Rai and I were shovelling gravel together at his country home, Shalvah, and walking in the rain over his old childhood country around Baringhup. He was telling me of his childhood and taking me to his sacred sites, showing me the implements his father had used, the beautiful wrought-iron gates he had made and the old shed on the farm where his father had worked and where as a boy Rai himself had turned the handle of the homemade tool for twisting the hot straps of iron. These were scenes that reminded me of my own early years as a farm labourer in England when I had become joyfully intimate with the skills and the hand tools of those days. I was very aware while shovelling gravel with him and visiting his father's old work sites with Rai (these events occurred on different days but were of the same feeling) that he and I both loved physical work and the peculiar quality of mental contentment and wellbeing that came with it. There was a connection between us in this that was deeply important to me and which I knew also to be deeply important to Rai. We might not agree on every social and moral question, but we would both delight in shovelling gravel and loading his ute with firewood for my Rayburn. I knew I could rely on that. I knew I could rely on him.

Our friendship has flourished since then in action and in talk, and we have done a great deal of both. Rai and his wife, Yael, have travelled with me to the Stone Country, in the Central Highlands of Queensland, where they met the dear friends on whom the characters in two of my novels were based. Rai was overcome with emotion and wept when he stood among the stone arrangements of the sacred playgrounds of the Old People, in that strange and mysterious opening in the bendee scrub at the heart of Jangga country, to which Col McLennan, elder of the Jangga, had invited him. And I was reminded that day of the depth of Rai's love of the country around Shalvah, a place as sacred to him as the stone arrangements in the wild bendee scrub are to Col and his people. Rai and Yael and I lived together, cooked and ate and travelled together in that sublime country for a week during which we came to know each other at an open level of trust and intimacy I have rarely experienced. Although ours is a young friendship in years, it is one of the most important and influential of my life. I quite often feel ambivalent and uncertain about my decision to live away from the city in the quiet country town of Castlemaine (Sophie's town), but whenever Rai and Yael are at Shalvah I feel reassured and less ambivalent and more aware of having been admitted generously into a special love of country—just as I did when I was first invited by Col McLennan to journey with him through his country in the hinterland of the north. When Stephanie and I moved back to Melbourne for our daughter's last two years of schooling a few years ago, Rai wrote to me from London, 'Don't get too fond of Carlton, mate. I want to grow old with you in the bush.' It is a thought I too cherish. Not growing old (I think I've already done that) but continuing to enjoy our friendship.

Rai's complex and deeply passionate attachment to the country of his childhood has its roots not only in his love and admiration for his father but also, and no less deeply, in his longing to reconnect the broken threads of his love for his mother. It is a longing that has been a powerful source of inspiration for him. Without that longing we would not have *Romulus, My Father* or his courageous and deeply moving essay about his mother, 'An Unassuageable Longing'.

During our journey around Rai's home country he took me to the cottage he rented in Maldon where he wrote *Romulus*. 'I wrote it in five weeks,' he said—he may even have said three. 'It was already written in my heart,' he explained. As we sat in the car looking at the cottage I was thinking of Rai's mother and remembering Colm Toibin's heartbreaking story 'A Long Winter', in which the father and the boy search for the mother who has run away from them, a story pervaded by that sense of guilty responsibility that all children endure for the failure of love in the family, and by a longing to recover the lost love of the mother. The mother is never found, of course, in such stories and we are left with her poignant absence as a powerful presence. Writers are often inspired to write by an irresistible urge to recover what has been lost. This urge may not be fully conscious at the time of writing; it is the process of writing itself that uncovers the poignant, the impossible, and the heartfelt necessity of responding to the longing and makes the longing more immediate, bringing the absence into the presence of the writer. It is Henry James at that pivotal moment in his life, returning to America after thirty years in England and anxious to know if he is going to be able to recover the America of his early years that is to be so important for him.

The separation of writers from their homelands (their mother country) and their mothers has often been the source of inspiration for masterpieces of literature—and by literature I mean all forms of writing. *Romulus* is one of the finest examples of this intense lucid masterpiece of family emotion, of love and the failure of love to be enough, in which the author writes above him or herself under the influence of what we once happily called inspiration, and what Rai called writing from the heart.

Romulus was surely an important part of the beginning of a new chapter, or perhaps more accurately a new stage, in Rai's return to his home country, in which the move to Shalvah was also an important act of recovery for him. The landscape around Shalvah is not only rich in sites of deeply cherished incident with Rai's father, but is also rich in sites of sacred significance for Rai's mother and her tragic history, places intimately associated with her suffering and her final despair. Reading Rai's essay on his mother it is impossible to believe that his unassuageable longing will not continue to be a powerful prompt of memory and imagination for him, a precious source of energy and inspiration for his writing. The story, I believe, is not over yet. When he began writing *Romulus*, Rai said to me, he did so wanting to write about his mother, but he was not able to do it at that time. His mother, of course, was to become the great absence of the story, the poignant presence of her despair and loss. Some of the greatest works of literature are about those very things the writer cannot say but which haunt the work with the poignancy of their absence. It was his mother's tragedy that had most deeply affected me in the book, and had left me with a longing for the resolution of her absence in her son's life.

We are only a few pages into *Romulus* when we encounter the young girl of sixteen, sensitive to the cultural values and educated in the ways of the German middle class. She enjoys Shakespeare and opera and is prone to melancholy and asthma. That she falls in love with the intensely romantic blacksmith six years her senior, his unsettling gaze and his hard muscles, the challenge to her values of his contempt for what he considers to be her snobbishness in loving such things as Shakespeare and opera, terrify her parents—they think of Romulus as a gypsy. From their cultural perspective this is just about the most damning thing they could say about him. In the recounting of their meeting the young girl's doom is foretold, almost in the tones of a classical tragedy. The portent of those few opening pages is as powerful as anything I know in literature. It is what first grips the reader, and it is what holds the reader until the end—or, I should say, which held this reader to the end. Christine dies in chapter eight, two-thirds of the way through the book, but the unresolved conflicts her life and death have left behind remain for me the source of the book's energy to the very end—the last two words of the book are 'my mother': a foreshadowing of the long essay that Rai has at last found himself able to write and an acknowledgment of the presence of the mother's absence as the guiding spirit of the book that was written in the author's heart before a word was set on paper.

What parent could remain unmoved by the scene in *Romulus* when the boy Rai tells the headmaster of St Patrick's that he does not wish to see his mother if she should ever again visit him at the school? The tragedy is that of an educated and refined European woman who loses everything in the move to the Australian bush in the 1950s, an environment for which she was totally unfitted and which left her no room or opportunity in which to even begin to change or to nurture her natural gifts. Unlike Hora and Romulus, there is nothing Christine can do. There is no place for her to turn to. There are many father-son books but there is none I know of that carries a greater tragic force than *Romulus*. It was the move to the Australian bush in the early fifties that drove Christine into the arms of madness and other men. The irony is that it was she herself who chose to come to Australia. As Virgil said, *We make our destinies by our choice of gods.* For the migrant, surely destiny is determined by the choice of destination. We, all of us, are capable of breaking—breaking emotionally and spiritually, I mean. The break, when it comes, will take a different form in each of us and will reveal where our weakness has lain all along. Given the right environment, I believe Christine would not have been pushed to the point where she displayed the symptoms of the defeat of her reason.

Trustingly, with an extraordinary generosity that I've learned to treasure in our friendship, Rai sent me an unedited draft of his essay on his mother in early April. It is written with great courage and honesty. It is written with a confessional honesty far beyond anything I would be capable of if I were ever to write about the private emotional wounds of my own family's history. I was greatly moved by the essay and wrote to Rai at once.

I have just finished reading your chapter. It is very beautiful and deeply moving. I was gripped by it and wanted it to go deeper and deeper into the elusive life of your mother—I wanted it to find her. And it was terrible in that she remains unsighted in the tragedy. It is a grand and wonderful piece of writing. I could never write of such intimate moments in the life of my parents and myself, but I am glad you have found the courage—or sufficient cause—to do it. It took me through the emotional and historical landscape of your life in Central Victoria once again—the landscape of *Romulus*—like a tour you needed to make, going back and revisiting *Romulus*, still haunted by what had remained implicit in that book—for all this, the tragedy of your mother that you render explicitly here was already in the book and was, more than anything, what moved me when I first read it. The presence of her absence was at the core of that book. I am very grateful to you for writing this, Rai, and I can understand your need to do it. To look again and know, once and for all, that you can never know her.

Alex with Rai Gaita, Castlemaine, 2013

People who write—or, for that matter, who attend sessions of psychoanalysis—are almost always surprised by how much of the seemingly irrecoverable we are able to recover once we begin to write. Memory opens up under the stimulus of our close attention. It takes courage to write memoir; more courage, I believe, than it does to write fiction, where one hides one's intimate sins behind the mask of make-believe. All art, I believe, is engaged in a search for truth. But for Rai truth is a sacred good and he is incapable of consciously falsifying for effect—as, say, a fiction writer or a painter will often do. It is, I believe, that for Rai truth itself is the work of art. While truth may be sacred to him, it is not a given but must be striven for. And for this courage is required, including the courage to fail, the courage to find that the truth may not be available to us. Rai's search for truth in his books—in all his books and in his daily life—is a conscious striving that is beautiful and good and which is often nearly impossible, is elusive and is sometimes difficult beyond words. The richness of his mind is exemplified for me in that we can never know in advance what he thinks but must hear from him. It is a great privilege for me to know myself his friend, and to know the friendship and love I feel for him is cherished by him in turn. I hope you'll forgive me, Rai, for this inconclusive personal meander. You can tackle me on some of my obscurities next time we're shovelling gravel from the back of your ute at Shalvah or collecting firewood for my Rayburn.

2014

The Mother of *Coal Creek*

My boss on Goathlands Station, Reg Wells, took me down to the yards on my first morning and asked me to choose a horse for myself from the mob milling around in the big yard. He had yarded up the horses the previous evening and they were restless and thirsty and bad-tempered with each other. He leaned on the rails and smoked a cigarette and watched me climb into the yard. I was carrying a bridle. The horses backed off, leaving a wide space around me, watching me and forcing up against each other, then making a sudden rush by me, the way a mob of sheep will make for an open gate. The yard was inches deep in fine bull dust and it was hard to see. I was being tested and I knew it. The Gympie office of the Australian Estates Company had sent me up to the Central Highlands of Queensland to fill Reg Wells's request for a young ringer to take the place of the man who'd left him a month earlier. Reg had asked for a man who knew horses. I'd spent the last two years riding second horse for a hunting farmer on

Exmoor in the west of England. I'd cared for that man's two hunters and helped the farrier shoe them every six weeks, so I knew what I was doing around horses.

The horses in this yard at Goathlands Station were not of the quality of those Exmoor hunters and looked pretty rough to me. The mare I chose was a dark blood bay, short in the body and muscular. When she saw I was wanting to cut her out of the mob she squared up to me and tossed her head, giving a snort and fixing her eyes on me. She did not object when I put the bridle on her. I led her out of the big yard into a smaller yard and Reg climbed in and came over. The mare was unshod and I told him I'd shoe her. He asked me if I didn't want to climb on her back first. I said there would be no need for that as I believed she was keen to work.

That mare's name was Mother. She was the most willing horse I have ever ridden and had some good ideas of her own for dealing with wild old cows that liked to break out of the mob and make for the scrub when we were bringing a mob down the valley. Mother was alert to these breakaways and was quick to get onto them. As we drew up alongside the heifer, going at a good pace by then, Mother propped and swung her backside around and let go with both hind feet. If the beast did not go down, as some did, it always made a beeline back into the thick of the mob. Mother and I worked Reg Wells's wild country together for two years. I was riding out on the night horse one foggy morning to fetch the horses into the yard and Mother was lying among the dark lime trees. She was all swelled up, her legs sticking straight out, her eye dead and cold. We assumed it was snake bite. She was still young and in fine condition. I had often thought of paying a tribute to her.

2015

EXCERPT FROM
Coal Creek

After we come up out of Coal Creek, Mother planted herself on the bank and she spread her legs and give herself such a mighty shake I thought the gear was coming off her. When she was finished shaking she straightened up and tossed her head, rattling the bit and letting me know she was ready to move off. I set her over towards the moonlit skyline of that saddle where the last of Long Ridge comes down off Mount Esson and peters out in a stretch of poison bendee. Mother knew where we was heading and eased into the long striding walk she had, which was the easiest ride I had ever had on any horse. Mother was not a horse to stumble and she could weave her way through the brigalow at a flat-strap gallop when we needed to head some beast, which was usually an old cock-horned cow making her run with the knowledge of what was waiting for her in the yards. Once they had read the story them wild cattle was slippery, but Mother could outpace them and turn the fastest of them. I do not wish to exaggerate the ability of that horse, but I cannot help myself paying a tribute to her in this account whenever I see the chance to do it.

2013

Teetering

We are sitting at a table by the window. The street is deserted except for a group of black men standing at the entrance to the park, as if they are on duty, or perhaps are charging a fee for admission. They say things to people who go past, but are mostly ignored. Every now and then someone, usually another black man, will stop and speak with them. They seem menacing to me and make me feel aware of being old and a stranger here and vulnerable without a word of the language. There is rubbish blowing about in the street and in the gutters. Paper and plastic and broken bottles. Large garbage collection bins are parked on the footpath next to the black men.

Me and my wife of thirty-seven years. So we don't have a lot to say to each other. It is small signs and a kind of telepathy these days. Our silence embarrasses me. Young people see in our silence the aura of old age. Sainthood. We wear it uneasily and would rather be at home where there is no need for us to talk to each other. When I look out the window again the black men are staring back at me. They speak to each other and laugh and look across at me sitting in the cafe window with my wife. It worries me that they might decide to come over and enter the cafe and say something to me. Issue a challenge of some kind. I will not be able to answer them. I will not know what they have said. I fear to be shamed by them. My wife and I look out the window frequently. We do it anxiously and together, like the Queen's guardsmen turning their heads to salute the passing of their monarch. But our daughter is not coming along this strange street in Berlin. The black drug dealers on base at the park gates opposite are at the same time idle and alert in the windy sunshine. I can't help looking at them. Lilac trees thrash about behind them. Theirs is a manner I could not hope to mimic. I think of the German Erich Auerbach's wonderful book, *Mimesis: The Representation of Reality in Western Literature*, and the great pleasure and consolation it has given me. In the park behind the group of black drug dealers, through a small green opening between the wall and the lilacs, I see girls and young men jogging. They are wearing little shorts and singlets. And there are dogs running after balls. And then, as I watch, a young man goes past pushing a pram. He is smoking a cigarette and talking on his mobile phone. This little window of normality reassures me. All the young people smoke. I too loved to smoke when I was young. Every wall surface is covered with graffiti tags, the language of a newly arrived alien civilisation. Doors too. Everything. Undiscriminating. Everything. I stare at it and understand nothing. In its presence I am illiterate. Like Australians looking helplessly at the intricate knowledge maps of Aborigines and claiming the Aborigines had no written language rather than admit their own illiteracy.

I say to my wife, 'What did she say the name of this suburb was?' My wife says something. I don't catch it. It sounds like, Half an hour. Then she adds, 'It's a bit much.'

I agree but I don't say anything. We finished our coffee a long time ago and I wonder if the young man behind the bar would like us to either order some lunch or vacate the table. I look at him but he is talking on his mobile phone and appears to be indifferent to our presence. When I was a young man. Oh, then!

I'm looking at the menu again. It is written in German. My wife watches me flicking through the pages. I feel her mounting irritation. After a minute she says, 'The English version is at the back.' As if I am not able to understand the simplest of things. But I don't want to see the English version. There are several other customers in the cafe. They are all in their twenties and they talk and they laugh, their voices loud and free and full with enthusiasms. I recognise the word *Berghain*, it stands out from my daughter's talk. Muscled-up, sweating, half-naked men being excessively polite in tricksy voices to half-naked young chicks. Like my daughter. Everyone enjoying themselves and dancing to the music until four or five in the morning. A scene from Fellini's *Satyricon*, is it? *The Degenerates*? Was I ever so free? Even then?

My wife says, 'Three quarters of an hour. It's not fair.'

We both look out the window. I am relieved to see the black men jumping around and engaged among themselves. My confidence returns.

'It's so thoughtless of her,' my wife says.

The menu is illustrated with photocopies of grainy black-and-greyish-white photographs from a hundred years ago. One is of a group of young men and women, the women in long dresses to the ground and broad hats and the men in dark suits and hats. They are standing very close to the edge of a sheer rocky precipice above a valley and have assumed various poses for the camera. One girl stands on the very lip of a jutting piece of the cliff that looks as if it might break off under her weight at any moment, her head thrown back as if she is defying someone who has told her to come away from the edge. A parent, I suppose. In her mind. In her memory of parents and home. The village in the valley is tiny and is several thousand feet below them. Have they climbed up from there by some circuitous path? Are they on a picnic? Out for the day? Are the men artists and the women their models? Will the women pose naked for the men on the rocks later, after they have drunk the wine and made love? They are not English, after all, and might be like the expressionist artist Kirchner and his group of soulful libertines.

My wife says irritably, 'What are you writing? You're always writing something.'

I say, 'It's some notes I'm making. An idea for a short story.'

She looks at her watch and then out the window.

'An old man waits for his daughter in a cafe in Berlin,' I say. 'The old man hasn't seen his daughter for more than a year. When his daughter doesn't turn up to greet him at the appointed time he becomes anxious and begins to lose the dream he has had of meeting her and of them both embracing joyfully, and to fear that something has happened to prevent her from keeping the appointment with him.'

My wife says something but I don't catch it.

'I'm afraid I have to leave you out of the story,' I say. 'A solitary old man waiting in the cafe is more inviting for the reader to engage with than an old couple. If I say you are with me in the cafe it becomes a story about the old man's relationship with his wife.'

My wife says, 'I'll bet she's forgotten and is still asleep. I bet you that's what's happened.'

I decide to repeat myself. 'If I put you in the story,' I say, 'it becomes a story about the relationship of these two old people. The way they have nothing left to say to each other and how when they get anxious about their daughter they begin taking out their anxiety on each other. Picking at each other irritably without seeing what they are doing.'

My wife is looking at her watch again. She was given the watch by her parents for her twenty-first birthday and she has to remember to wind it and often forgets to wind it and needs to check with me to find out if it is showing the correct time. She gave me my watch for my seventieth birthday. It is a Longines and keeps perfect time without ever needing any attention from me. She frowns at her watch now and winds it. The face of her watch, she has told me often, is crystal and does not show any wear or scratches after all these decades of use. She is proud of it and dreads to lose it one day. To leave it somewhere or not notice that the band has broken and it has slipped from her wrist. The insensitivity of skin as it ages. The peril of her watch. She clings to the past with it. I watch her winding it and frowning at it and I suppose there is another story in her fears for her watch that goes all the way back to her twenty-first birthday.

The next photo is of another group of young people, or perhaps it's the same group but they have moved on and rearranged themselves into a new tableau. They are balancing precariously on a huge boulder that is itself balancing on another enormous boulder which appears to be teetering on the brink of an abyss. The slightest shift of weight, it appears, will send them all hurtling to their deaths. I can see their skirts and hats flying through the empty air, the grey boulder keeping alongside them, dislodged from its perch after how many millions of years? Was it glacial activity that perched it there? Or is it the weathered core of something much vaster and more ancient even than that? Now, of course, they are all dead.

My wife says, 'You wait here. I'm going to call her and go and see if I can find her flat.'

I sit at the window in the cafe and watch my wife walking away along the strange road and I feel an immense longing and love for her and my throat tightens with fear for us all.

2012

Alex and Stephanie Miller, White Sands, New Mexico, 2013

Song of the Good Visa

I was on a train going somewhere,
Somewhere pleasant.
The sun was shining
The country we were passing through was beautiful.
The fields soft and green;
So deeply familiar.
And I always thought: the very simplest words
Must be enough.

You could say, I suppose, it was my country.
Not a fine country of my own
Where I was at home, but
The divided country of
My childhood
Seen from a passing train.
And I always thought: the very simplest words
Must be enough.

The train was comfortable, and
Not going too fast for me to enjoy the scenery,
So it must have been an old train,
Furnished with blue plush upholstery
And burnished timber,
Smelling of Erinmore pipe tobacco,
Or perhaps it was Digger Shag.
It was my father who smoked Digger Shag.
And I always thought: the very simplest words
Must be enough.

The window at which I sat,
Facing the direction of travel,
The best seat in the carriage,
Trembled, the tremor inside the boy inside me
When I closed my eyes
And touched the tips of my fingers to the glass.
And I always thought: the very simplest words
Must be enough.

I was content;
With my achievements in life
You could say.
It was there,
The sense of my accomplishments,
Knowing myself
To be among the privileged.
And I always thought: the very simplest words
Must be enough.

The train stopped at the station
And I got off.
It was the frontier.
I lined up and waited with the others.
I had no fear, knowing my good visa
Would admit me to any country on
This Earth.
And I always thought: the very simplest words
Must be enough.

And did I tell you
I was wearing my new jacket?
The black tweed; the weaver declaring himself
On the silk label in the lining: 'I have woven this tweed by hand
In Donegal Ireland
Exclusively for Kevin & Howlin
Of Nassau Street, Dublin.'
And signed it, he had: J.J. Campbell, Weaver.
And I always thought: the very simplest words
Must be enough.

I was proud to be wearing it.
Proud of myself, of who
I was with my good visa,
Safe in the inside pocket, right-hand,
Earned by the sweat and struggle
Of my own hard weaving days.
My wife bought a cap there

And looked great in it,
Smiling the way she did.
God bless her memory.
And I always thought: the very simplest words
Must be enough.

The frontier guards wore green,
Smart and efficient, they were,
Uniform, you could see that.
And not smiling.
The family of four ahead of me
Were quietly asked to stand to one side.
There was no banter in the exchange,
But a gesture of the gloved hand,
Directing them; the words murmured,
There! Stand over there, please.
And I always thought: the very simplest words
Must be enough.

I was asked for my visa.
Beyond the barrier other guards stood
Watching, hands clasped behind their backs.
The one on the left smoked
A thin black cigar. Which made me smile.
Senior officers, I supposed, keeping an eye
On the juniors.
I resisted a desire to flourish my
Good visa, and instead laid it modestly

In the open glove of the guard.
There, that is who I am.
And I always thought: the very simplest words
Must be enough.

He stamped my visa and,
Saluting me gravely,
Handed it back.
And that is how I crossed the frontier
Into the new country.
And I always thought: the very simplest words
Must be enough.

As I passed the family of four,
The mother holding the smallest child
In her arms, the other child holding
Its father's hand,
Their eyes begged me to intervene
And help them. Their despair
Struck a blow to my chest.
But what was I to do?
And I always thought: the very simplest words
Must be enough.

Beyond the town the road
Led the eye into the interior of the desert.
The prospect reminding me
Of the road from Tunis to El Djem,

Which I had travelled with my beloved wife,
And our companion, the archaeologist, Nejib,
From the Institut National d'Archéologie et d'Art,
Tunis. A man of learning,
He asked me not to speak so freely of
Politics to our driver, a man with
A large moustache who, at lunch, refused
My offer of wine with a disdainful,
'Alcohol has never passed my lips.'
'He reports you to Ben Ali's men,'
The archaeologist said. 'They wonder why
You are really here.'
And I always thought: the very simplest words
Must be enough.

As a young boy I wrote in my black book:
I wonder why I am really here?
For in that year I was suddenly unable
To believe in God.
And something needed to be done.
Something that now, in middle age,
I have yet to do.
How to put a name to it?
And I always thought: the very simplest words
Must be enough.

In the beginning . . .
In the end . . .
The new country to which my

Good visa had gained me admittance
Was a desert.
And I always thought: the very simplest words
Must be enough.

Ahead of me, barring the road,
Which was dusty and unmade,
Was a crude barrier, as if it marked
Another makeshift frontier,
An unofficial outpost.
And I always thought: the very simplest words
Must be enough.

I reached into the right-hand pocket
Of my tweed jacket, woven by J.J. exclusively
For Kevin & Howlin of Nassau Street, Dublin,
In the free Republic of Ireland,
The ancestral home of my mother,
The forlorn village of Ballyragget,
In the county of Kilkenny,
Where my old people lie
By the ruined stone church
Among the black yew trees.
And I always thought: the very simplest words
Must be enough.

And my fingers found
My good visa safely there.
A visa with which I might surmount

All barriers, with which I might
Go any road I chose.
So why was I afraid now?
The soldiers watched me approach.
They sat and leaned and smoked,
A slovenly bunch, they seemed to me.
Not like the others.
And I always thought: the very simplest words
Must be enough.

There was nothing to stop me
From going around their barrier,
The desert lying empty on either side.
But in my pride I wished to let them know
Who I was;
To see them straighten up
For a man with a good visa.
And I always thought: the very simplest words
Must be enough.

They observed me coming on along the road,
Their mocking laughter on the desert air now;
Those blood scavengers we have seen
At the remains of slaughtered beasts.
But I could no longer retrace my steps;
Return to the town, and to lost opportunities there.
As I drew close to the soldiers
Fear was in me.
And I always thought: the very simplest words
Must be enough.

the simplest words

They leaned against
Piles of truck tyres and forty-four-gallon drums,
Their attentions sinister, smoking
Cigarettes and spitting on the ground.
Unshaved, their sweat-stained tunics open,
Guns held loosely across their bellies.
I saw in them men who had been given pointless work,
Men demoralised by inaction,
Disheartened, bored and cruel
In the face of their meaningless lives.
And I always thought: the very simplest words
Must be enough.

An older one among them stepped towards me.
'Visa!' he said, thrusting out his hand.
And did not meet my eyes.
I laid my good visa in his naked palm.
He took it without a word,
Without a sign, without looking at it,
Failing to note its special features!
Then turned and went inside the guard post,
Built like an Australian country dunny,
It was, make-do of tin and wood,
Rattling in the desert wind.
And I always thought: the very simplest words
Must be enough.

I stood in the road and waited,
The heat like a glove over my mouth,
My heart struggling,

The soldiers watching me.
The desert sun on my back through J.J.'s
Black weave.
Their gaze was pitiless,
They were expectant of an entertainment,
Contempt for the solitary traveller.
Insolence and derision in their eyes.
The thought came to me; it
Is important to be philosophical about
One's death. But fear trumped philosophy.
For fear holds the ace of hearts.
And I always thought: the very simplest words
Must be enough.

The older guard at last came out
And with a nasty smirk said,
'Here's your visa.' And he smiled at
His comrades, who laughed
And spat and jigged about
Like children at a Christmas party
When Santa's arrival is announced.
I looked at the thing in my hand:
It was a filthy scrap of linen,
Torn from a woman's dress,
Or from a man's shirt.
The sweetish smell of rotting flesh
Rising to my mouth.
And I always thought: the very simplest words
Must be enough.

And I recalled the first time
I had encountered the smell of death:
I was a boy of eight or nine and walking with
My father in the Kentish woods,
Elms and oaks and a scuff of leaves
Under our boots. Then came the smell
That made me cover my mouth.
My wounded father held my hand;
'Something is dead nearby,'
he said to me. 'This smell was with us
Every day over there towards the end.'
And I always thought: the very simplest words
Must be enough.

Smeared in blood across the shred of cloth
In my hand, the letters V-I-S-A.
The soldiers rocked and slapped at each other
To witness my dismay.
And fear gripped my beating heart
Like the hand of a giant.
I was a crippled bird
At their mercy, and was never
Again to rise from this ground.
And I always thought: the very simplest words
Must be enough.

I looked up into the eyes
Of the old soldier;
'This is not the visa I gave you,'
I said. But my voice was small,

Dry in the hot desert wind.
'If you don't give me back my
Good visa, I shall report you
And you will be in big trouble.'
Words simple enough for
The very simplest of men.
And I always thought: the very simplest words
Must be enough.

The old soldier addressed his companions.
'He doesn't want his visa,' he said.
Sensing the trap, I clutched the bloody rag
And muttered my thanks.
They did not lift the barrier for me
But watched me duck
Under it, their laughter following me
As I went on; expecting a kick
Or a bullet from behind.
And I always thought: the very simplest words
Must be enough.

I was an old man,
Alone in the desert of time,
My good visa a delusion,
My past accomplishments
But scraps blown about.
And when I turned and looked back
The soldiers and their false
Border were gone.
And I always thought: the very simplest words
Must be enough.

Once I had thought it possible
For one world to end
And another to begin.
But it was only a dream.
The road I had come by
Was the road I was going.

2014

Note: The lines, 'And I always thought: the very simplest words/ Must be enough' are from Michael Hamburger's translation of the Bertolt Brecht poem *Und ich dachte immer* ('And I always thought').

Publication Details

'In the Blood', *The Age*, 9 August 2008.

'Ross and the Green Elfin', Summer Read Blog, State Library of Victoria, 2008.

'In My Mother's Kitchen', *The Age*, 12 May 2012.

'My First Love', in Reilly, G. (ed.), *My First Love and Turning Points*, Albert Park, Vic: Julie Morgan Marketing, 1995, 3.

'Travels with My Green Man', *Weekend Australian*, 31 May 2003, 4–5.

'Once Upon a Life', *The Observer Magazine*, 26 September 2010, 12–13.

'How to Kill Wild Horses', *Quadrant* XX, no. 2, February 1976, 58–62.

'Destiny's Child', *The Age*, 5 August 2002, 6.

'Living at Araluen', www.alexmiller.com.au/writing, 2009.

'In the End it was Teaching Writing', *Australian Literary Review*, 5 March 2008, 17.

'The Last Sister of Charity', *The Age*, 18 November 2000; in Corris, Peter and Wilding, Michael (eds), *Heart Matters: Personal stories about that Heart-Stopping Moment*, Camberwell, Vic.: Viking, 2010.

'On Writing *Landscape of Farewell*', www.alexmiller.com.au/writing, 2009.

'Australia Today', published as 'What Happened to Our Open, Welcoming Land?', *The Age*, 26 January 2014.

'The Writer's Secret', *The Age*, 30 October 1999.

'Speaking Terms', *Australian Literary Review* 3, no. 11, December 2008, 19.
'Impressions of China', paper delivered at the World Chinese Writers'
    Association Congress, Singapore, December 1995; in 'Impressions
    of China', *Meridian* 15, no. 1, May 1996, 85–9.
'Chasing My Tale, *Kunapipi* XV, no. 3, 1993, 1–6.
'The Wine Merchant of Aarhus', *Kunapipi* XV, no. 3, 1993, 7–45.
'The Mask of Fiction', in Dixon, Robert (ed.), *The Novels of Alex Miller:
    An Introduction*, Sydney: Allen & Unwin, 2012, 29–41.
'The Inspiration Behind *Lovesong*', www.alexmiller.com.au/writing, 2009.
'How I Came to Write *Autumn Laing*' in *Autumn Laing*, Sydney: Allen
    & Unwin, 2011, 446–52.
'Comrade Pawel', *Meanjin Quarterly* 34, no. 1, 1975, 74–85.
'The Story's Not Over Yet', Association for the Study of Australian
    Literature, Public Lecture, Docklands Library, Melbourne,
    23 August 2014. Unpublished.
'Prophets of the Imagination', Australia: Making Space Meaningful,
    9th Biennial Conference of the Association for Australian Studies,
    Hamburg, 3–10 October 2004; *The Age* and *The Sydney Morning
    Herald*, 29 May 2004; in Burke, John Muk Muk and Langford,
    Martin (eds), *Ngara: Living in this Place Now*, Wollongong, NSW:
    Five Islands Press, 2004, 76–82.
'Sweet Water: The Proposed Damming of the Urannah Valley', *The
    Bulletin*, 16 December 2004, 100–104.
'The Black Mirror', *Art & Australia* 43, no. 3, Autumn 2006, 446.
'A Circle of Kindred Spirits', the Hazel Rowley Memorial Lecture,
    Adelaide Festival, 6 March 2013; *Southerly* 73, no. 3, 2013, 13–23.
'Sophie's Choice', in Taylor, Craig with Graefe, Melinda (eds), *A Sense for
    Humanity: The Ethical Thought of Raimond Gaita*, Clayton, Vic.:
    Monash University Publishing, 2014, 28–36.
'Teetering', *Kenyon Review* XXXV, no. 4, Fall 2013, 58–61; published as
    'Görlitzer Strasse', *The Monthly*, December 2012–January 2013;
'Song of the Good Visa', *The Australian*, 25 January 2014.

Novels

Coal Creek, Sydney: Allen & Unwin, 2013.
Autumn Laing, Sydney: Allen & Unwin, 2011.

Lovesong, Sydney: Allen & Unwin, 2009.

Landscape of Farewell, Sydney: Allen & Unwin, 2007.

Prochownik's Dream, Sydney: Allen & Unwin, 2005.

Journey to the Stone Country, Sydney: Allen & Unwin, 2002.

Conditions of Faith, Sydney: Allen & Unwin, 2000.

The Sitters, Ringwood, Vic.: Viking, 1995; Sydney: Allen & Unwin, 2003.

The Ancestor Game, Ringwood, Vic: Penguin, 1992; Sydney: Allen & Unwin, 2000.

The Tivington Nott, London: Robert Hale, 1989; Ringwood, Vic: Penguin, 1993; Sydney: Allen & Unwin, 2005.

Watching the Climbers on the Mountain, Sydney: Pan, 1988; Sydney: Allen & Unwin, 2012.

Further Reading

Robert Dixon, *Alex Miller: The Ruin of Time*, Sydney: Sydney University Press, 2014.

Robert Dixon (ed.), *The Novels of Alex Miller: An Introduction*, Sydney: Allen & Unwin, 2012.

Images

All images are from the private collection of Alex and Stephanie Miller.

Acknowledgements

I wish to thank my editor and publisher, Annette Barlow, and my wife, Stephanie Miller, for selecting and arranging this collection over the past two years. I also wish to thank Siobhán Cantrill and the team at Allen & Unwin.